"Peter Penneyjons, do **that society will suffer** **waits until he finds a w** **him happy in marriage? One who makes his heart sing?"**

"The ladies awaiting my title might suffer. They have been waiting anxiously for me to do my duty."

"You make it sound as if you are a commodity and not a man."

"That is not so far from the truth, Anna Liese." He stepped closer. Their umbrella brims clicked. "You confuse me."

He confused her, too. "How do I confuse you?"

"You..." He touched her cheek with his rain-slicked fingers. "Well, you—you are—"

"Waiting for true love..." Was he going to kiss her this time? Would she allow it, knowing that love was not important to him?

Inch by slow inch, he dipped his head. She wanted this kiss more than she had ever wanted anything. She feared it even more.

A kiss would make her fall in love with him in a vastly different way than the way she always had been.

Until this moment she had loved her young childhood friend. In a blink, a touch, he would change everything.

If his lips touched hers, it would all be different. The boy would be forever replaced by the man.

Author Note

Thank you so much for reading *The Viscount's Christmas Proposal*. At this time of year life can keep us extra busy and I appreciate that you have chosen to spend a bit of your valuable time with Anna Liese and Peter.

This is a Christmas reunion story that, this year, is more fitting than ever. I hope the holiday finds you spending joyful time with friends and family.

You might remember Peter Penneyjons from *The Viscount's Yuletide Bride* and *To Wed a Wallflower*. Now the time has come for Peter to wed, but he really would rather not. Not if such a union involves giving his heart. Naturally that all comes into question when he reunites with his childhood friend Anna Liese, who will settle for nothing less than a true love match.

Peter wants a marriage of convenience. Anna Liese wants one of love. I hope you enjoy seeing how they bring it all together.

Wishing you every blessing of the season.

CAROL ARENS

—

The Viscount's Christmas Proposal

HARLEQUIN®
HISTORICAL™

ISBN-13: 978-1-335-40747-4

The Viscount's Christmas Proposal

Harlequin Enterprises ULC
22 Adelaide St. West, 40th Floor
Toronto, Ontario M5H 4E3, Canada
www.Harlequin.com

Printed in U.S.A.

Carol Arens delights in tossing fictional characters into hot water, watching them steam and then giving them a happily-ever-after. When she is not writing, she enjoys spending time with her family, beach camping or lounging about a mountain cabin. At home, she enjoys playing with her grandchildren and gardening. During rare spare moments, you will find her snuggled up with a good book. Carol enjoys hearing from readers at carolarens@yahoo.com or on Facebook.

Books by Carol Arens

Harlequin Historical

Visit the Author Profile page
at Harlequin.com for more titles.

Dedicated to Jeremy Iaccino,
my awesome and much-loved son-in-law.

Prologue

January 1873—Woodlore Glen, England

He was dying and he was only twelve years old.

Peter Penneyjons heard footsteps tapping across the floor. They paused at his bedside. Whoever was standing over him gave a great, sad sigh and pronounced, 'Poor lad. It is better this way with his family all gone in the night.'

Mother gone? And Father?

Someone was fibbing. Because they would not go away without him—not go anywhere with him lying abed and sick to death. They would wait for him to heal and then all go to London together just as they'd planned.

'If you please, speak your negative thoughts outside this room. He might hear you.'

'Not in his condition. He has only the slightest grip on life as it is. You may count on him not hearing anything.'

'Doctor Fillmore, you may wait in the hallway. I will summon you if you are needed.'

But he could hear! Voices seemed like scratches in his ears. He had to strain to listen. What he could not do was open his eyes or his mouth to tell them that he could.

More than anything, he was confused. If his family had gone to visit his uncle in London, why was his uncle here holding his hand?

He would have returned Uncle Robert's squeeze, but he could not flex his fingers. All he could do was feel too hot and too cold in turns—and thirsty. He was so thirsty.

'You must prepare yourself, Lord Cliverton, the boy is very ill and with his family dead—'

'I am his family and I am here.'

What did the doctor say? He thought he heard but—no…he could not have heard that!

'I feel duty bound to remind that you should not be in this room. This strain of influenza is more deadly than usual. It will do no one any good for you to perish along with the child.'

'The child will not perish, nor will I. I cannot say the same of you if you do not quit your blathering and leave this chamber.'

A door closed. Uncle Robert lifted Peter's hand, pressing it to his cheek which felt prickly, as if he had not shaved in some time.

An odd thought drifted through his mind—he would never grow old enough to have a beard. He felt sad about it, although in a rather detached way.

'If you can hear me, Peter, I promise I will not leave

you. You will recover and I will bring you to Cliverton where you will never be alone.'

There was no reason for his uncle to say this unless his parents really were dead.

Peter wished he could not hear. He wished he could not feel the beat of his heart or the rush of blood in his veins.

Mother and Father were gone for ever. It hurt too much to think—to feel. As if the fever were not awful enough, this revelation made him fear he would vomit and choke.

It did not matter if he did because being dead with his parents would be better than alive without them. If he died, they could be together again.

But what would become of baby Deborah? His sister was only two years old and she would need him to live and take care of her.

But had the doctor not said that his family had perished? Could he have meant Deborah along with them? His uncle had not said he was bringing Deborah to Cliverton.

With his sister gone there would be no reason for Peter to stay alive. All he needed to do was stop breathing and they would all be together for eternity.

Very well. He would simply stop—

'Peter!'

At Uncle Robert's bark, his lungs jerked, filled with air.

'You will not die, do you understand me?' Peter felt his shoulders being squeezed, firmly yet with utter tenderness. A tremor shook his uncle's strong fingers.

'Your Aunt Grace has forbidden me to come home without you.'

He did love his aunt. She would weep if he died and he did not wish to make her weep. Nor did he wish to make his three younger cousins sad. If he died, who would be their prince when they played castle and dragon?

Was it possible for a boy who only had 'a slight grip on life' to hold on tight and survive? The yes or no of it might not be up to him—or to Uncle Robert.

The click of his bedroom door opening sounded distant—everything did, even Uncle Robert's voice telling whoever had entered to come no closer.

'Please, Lord Cliverton, may I sing to Peter?'

Anna Liese! If only he could sit up and warn his friend to run from the wicked disease slithering about his room. His sweet neighbour was only ten years old, which was even younger to die than twelve was.

'The doctor says he cannot hear, my dear. You should not risk being here.'

'But we do not know for sure.' Her voice caught on a soft sob. 'Perhaps, sir, it might be a comfort to Peter—and to me.'

It would be. He had always thought his friend had the voice of an angel, there was not much he liked better than hearing her sing.

Still, if he could tell her to leave, he would.

Since he was unable open his mouth or summon his voice, he would cherish the sound of her voice, imagine she was singing him goodbye of an evening while they stood on the stone bridge over the stream which separated her grand manor from his family's humbler cottage.

Of all the songs, he liked the evening one best. Hopefully, she would sing that one.

Mostly he joined in, but since he was no good at tunes, they ended up aching with laughter while they sang. It was all the funnier because on its own the song was sentimental, but they changed the lyrics to silly ones which was great fun. On days when they were weary of climbing trees or the weather kept them indoors, making up silly song lyrics was what they liked doing best.

'By yon bonnie banks and by yon bonnie braes, Where the sun shines bright on Loch Lomond, Where me and my true love will never meet again, On the bonnie, bonnie banks of Loch Lomond.'

This was the right tune, but also different! She had never used the actual words to the song before—especially the 'true love' words. 'Where me and my true friend will always meet again' is what they sang, because they were only children with long lives ahead of them—and they were too young to be 'true loves'.

Trapped within his useless body, he was crying great loud sobs because he understood what she was doing. She was saying goodbye, perhaps singing of what might have been had he grown to be a man.

She sang a bit about the high road and the low road, but then she stopped. Her soft weeping crushed his heart. Uncle Robert whispered something to her, but Peter could not make out what it was.

Then Anna Liese began again, the sound pure and angelic. No one would know how desperately he wept inside since he could make no sound and the fever burned up his tears.

''Twas there that we parted, in yon shady glen, On the steep, steep side of Ben Lomond, Where in soft purple hue, the hieland hills we view, and the moon coming out of the gloaming...'

'I'm sorry, Lord Cliverton.' Anna Liese's voice caught on a sob. 'I cannot go on.'

Peter knew why. There was a bench on the hilltop overlooking their village. He and his sweet friend often sat on it, gazing down at folks hurrying about their business. They giggled over how good it was to be children, free to spend their days racing each other over meadows and wading in the stream which gurgled happily between their homes.

He heard the bedroom door click in closing.

It hurt to know it, but they would never share such moments again—never again stand on the stone bridge while bidding each other goodnight with a song.

How was it possible to sob so awfully on the inside without tears leaking from his eyes?

Because he was dying of a fever and was as dried out as an old bone.

'Take your rest, Peter, my boy.' Uncle Robert picked up his useless hand, held it between both of his. 'Rest and heal.'

He would, in one way or another. Either he would awake in heaven and be healed, or he would rise from this bed and be healed.

Until either of those things happened, he would hold on to his uncle's hand and keep Anna Liese's song in his heart.

'The wee birdies sing and the wildflowers spring,' he imagined the rest of the words. In his imagination they were as clear as if he and Anna Liese were standing on the bridge with the sun slipping behind the trees. 'And in sunshine the waters are sleeping. But the broken heart kens, nae second spring again, Though the woeful may cease from their grieving.'

Grieving felt very wicked. He would not put his aunt and uncle through more of it if he could prevent it.

No, he would live if he could.

Feeling his uncle stroke back the hair from his hot, dry forehead, Peter decided he would not stop breathing again. At least, not on purpose.

He would try to heal and perhaps one day he would meet his friend again.

Chapter One

December 1891—Cliverton

It was too quiet in the garden, but not as quiet as in the manor house.

Quiet was not something Peter Penneyjons was accustomed to. Who would have guessed how much he would miss the hum of feminine activity that used to buzz about the premises at all hours, both indoors and out?

Standing alone among the hedges, watching the last golden leaf of the autumn garden drifting down from a sycamore, he found himself listening for the rustle of skirts.

He ought to be used to silence by now since the last of his cousins to marry had left home months ago.

Ginny, the youngest of his cousins, had surprised everyone by overcoming her shyness and reuniting with a childhood friend. She had wed him quite hastily in Gretna Green. Had Peter been there at the time, he would have tried to dissuade her. Just because her husband had been her perfect match as a child did not mean he would be as a man. Time would tell, he imagined. For now they did seem did seem devoted to one another.

Felicia had been no wiser. Before Ginny got married, his middle cousin, had wed a surly stranger. Peter knew he was surly because he had met the man when he'd delivered Felicia to him in a marriage arranged by their late mothers. Frankly, he was surprised and relieved to know his cousin was blissfully happy.

Of his cousins, Cornelia was the only one to make a match involving a properly long engagement, observing her vows with appropriate pomp and circumstance.

Becoming guardian to his former playmates had not been easy. When he had made the transition from carefree young heir to Viscount Cliverton, the shift in his relationship with them was the most difficult of all the changes he had been required to make.

It was one thing to act their prince and slay their dragons in play and quite another to enforce rules the girls were to live by.

Or try to enforce them, at any rate. Until he had taken on their care, he had never fully understood how lively a trio they were. No doubt it was because he had been lively right along with them.

In the end he had done his duty by them and seen them safely married—not that it was really any of his doing. One and all they had been set on their marriages. His opinion on any of it made not a whit of difference.

But married they were and here he stood, listening for echoes.

Loneliness was not an emotion he cared for. After

his parents and baby sister had died, he had lived with the weight of a crushed spirit. Were it not for the love showered upon him by his aunt, uncle and cousins, he was not sure he would have managed to dig himself out from under it.

A bird chirruped overhead but received no answering twitter. Did the poor creature feel as companionless as he did?

Were it not for the company of his friends in the Anerley Bicycle Club, he would be bereft of any sort of interesting company.

As a gentleman of society he attended the obligatory social engagements, but they were dull affairs compared to pedaling about with other bicycling enthusiasts.

Indeed, only last evening he had attended a soirée and been speaking to a young lady on the fascinating subject of the 'safety bicycle', but the woman had looked uninterested. By the time he had mentioned the invention of pneumatic tyres, she was glancing about for a more interesting companion to speak to.

Perhaps he ought to invite Aunt Adelia to visit. His late aunt's sister was a vibrant lady who scattered good cheer as naturally as trees scattered autumn leaves.

With her quick mind and keen sense of adventure, Aunt Adelia would probably enjoy talk of the growing bicycle craze. It was his firm opinion that within a few years everyone would be pedaling merrily about.

But of course, he could not impose on his aunt to visit again. She had spent a week here last month, planning the ball to be held at Cliverton during the week before Christmas.

It was said that 'time is a healer' and he supposed it must be so. Here at Cliverton, he had learned to put the past away, to be happy and love without fear of loss.

No. If he were to be truthful, he did fear loss. It would be more correct to say that he had learned to go about his day-to-day life in spite of the fear.

Losing his mother at such a young age had crippled his heart until Aunt Grace stepped in to fill it. But then, he had lost her, too.

The passing years did help with grief, but not with the fear of experiencing it again.

Glancing about the familiar garden, seeing long shadows of evening creep across the stones, he felt as at home as if he had been born here.

While he might not have been born within these walls, he had been born for them.

After his uncle produced three girls it was understood that Peter would become Cliverton. Sadly, he had not expected to fill the role when he was twenty.

A carriage accident, an uncontrolled skid on ice had left the family bereft of both his uncle and his aunt.

He thanked the good Lord daily for Aunt Adelia. She, in large part, had pulled them through the tragedy. It was that dear lady who had helped him deal with the responsibility suddenly pressed upon his shoulders.

Evening shadows crept longer, grew darker and chased the lingering light from the garden.

He had always enjoyed this time of day—but at this moment he felt rather alone.

There were staff aplenty, but still, they were not family.

The rustle of dry shrubbery caught his attention. A

kitten dashed out of a bush to bat Peter's trouser leg. He picked it up.

'What do you think, little chap?' There were always cats in the garden, not tame exactly, but not wild either. 'What this place needs is a family. I imagine you would enjoy having children to romp with.'

Yes, children to dash about the house—to play dragon and princess. For that to happen Cliverton needed a viscountess, which meant it was time to fulfil his obligations and wed an acceptable lady.

Which was the reason he was hosting the Christmas ball.

Setting the kitten down, he smiled, watching while it scampered after leaves blowing on the path.

He was not certain he wished to wed as his cousins had, for love and nothing less. An acceptable match would suit him better. He would be quite content with it, in fact.

The thought of losing another woman he loved was too much to bear. First his mother and then his aunt. There was only so much grief a soul could bear. He was not convinced that love was worth the price.

In a sense he had lost his cousins, too, albeit not to sadness and he would see them again soon. Until then house was far too quiet.

Sitting down on a garden bench, he watched the full moon rise above the treetops and thought about society's eligible ladies, both the debutantes and those in their second and third Seasons. There were a few who would suit nicely. Happily, none of them made him view marriage as anything but the fulfilment of duty.

A duty he had neglected for too long. It was beyond time he got married.

While he watched the moon creep slowly higher into the sky, a voice came to him from the other side of the garden wall. Faint at first, the sound grew louder as the woman passed by. She had a clear, lovely voice, but it was her song more than her voice which touched him unexpectedly.

It is not as if he had not heard 'Loch Lomond' performed over the years—but he had not heard it in the quiet of early evening. Not heard it sung with the same light, sweet quality that his long-ago friend had possessed.

The singer beyond the wall was not a child, but still she brought to mind Anna Liese. How long had it been since he had thought of his young friend?

So long that he could not remember it. There had been a time when spending all day with her was all he had thought of.

Eighteen years had passed since he had last heard her voice. Eighteen years spent making a new life at Cliverton—a good and happy life.

Looking back at the past, to the blissful times he had spent with Anna Liese—with his parents and sister—was not something he often did because in the end, happy thoughts turned to grieving ones.

He had even heard whispers that Anna Liese had fallen ill with the flu. Of course, no one had spoken to him of it for fear he would never come out of the sorrow consuming him. One more loss would have been more than he could have borne. It was better not to know.

But, for a time, his childhood had been idyllic.

His father had disliked London and society. He had often made a point of saying how glad he was to be a younger son to the Viscount and not the one burdened with the title. The family had lived in a sweet cottage beside a stream. It was larger than most cottages. In fact, what they had called home had long ago been an inn.

Papa had always said he had the best brother there could be because, knowing how Papa was uncomfortable in London, he had purchased the large cottage which, at the time, was a part of the Barlow estate. Uncle had also settled a large sum of money on Papa so they had never wanted for anything.

While they lived simply, Papa had been wealthy—although Peter had not been aware of it. Those had been the best of times, and they had ended in the blink of an eye.

Over the years he had not allowed himself to look back. If he did, his good memories might be tainted with shadows of tragedy. Even though he had later discovered his friend had survived, he refused his uncle's offer to take him to visit. The past hurt too much to be revisited, so he had put the cottage, Anna Liese and their lost friendship, behind him.

Ah, but this evening the woman's song shot him back to Woodlore Glen, to the bridge where he used to say goodnight to sweet and pretty Anna Liese.

What had become of her?

Being the daughter of a baron, she would naturally have married long ago. It was highly likely that she was mother to several children every bit as lovely as he recalled her being.

Full dark was now settled over the garden. Inhaling a breath of fresh evening air, he watched stars begin to take their ancient places in the sky while he thought of his first home.

It was not easy with so much time and shadowed memory between then and now. He had only vague memories of the place. After offering to take him back that one time, Uncle Robert had not pressed the matter again. No doubt it would have been as painful a visit for Uncle Robert as it would have been for Peter.

Over the years his uncle had rented the house to various tenants. After becoming Viscount and in charge of the property, Peter continued to do so through a property manager. For all that he had avoided visiting the place, he had no wish to sell his first home.

Perhaps the time had come to pay a visit. The house had now been vacant for a more than a year. In all the hustle and bustle of weddings, he had given the place little thought, but now that he had, he realised it was irresponsible to let it go unoccupied any longer. With his cousins settled he now had time to devote his attention to the cottage—personally—without the buffer of a property manager. There would be plenty of time to visit, see to its care, and still get back in time for the ball.

'There you are, my lord!' Mrs Boyle, his housekeeper, exclaimed. 'Why are you sitting in the dark while dinner is growing cold in the dining room?'

Growing cold in the dining room where he would sit at the long table with only a footman keeping him silent company.

He could not imagine why the housekeeper seemed

surprised to find him here since it was where she found him most evenings. Well, perhaps he could imagine after all. She had clucked about him like a mother hen since the day he first came to Cliverton. Now that he was the only Penneyjons in residence she was even more devoted to his care and keeping.

'Mrs Boyle,' he said as he kept pace behind her rustling skirts—was it silly to find the swish of fabric comforting? It was what came of being raised with girls, he supposed. 'I will be taking a trip to Woodlore Glen next week.'

Mrs Boyle stopped, spun about to stare at him, surprise arching her brows nearly to her hairline.

'It has been many years—are you certain, my lord?'

'Quite.' Perhaps he was certain—but perhaps not.

'When shall I inform the staff to be ready to travel?'

'I won't need staff. It is only a cottage, after all.' He would much prefer to spend a day or two alone. He could not say if the home was even fit to live in having been neglected all these months. More than that, though, he had ghosts to visit and he would prefer to greet them on his own.

'You will need me, sir! I would rather not see you starve.'

'I can manage my meals in the village for a time. I'll send for you and some of the others after I have seen the condition of the house.'

'Very well,' she answered with a sniff. 'Between now and then I shall be sure cook puts a few pounds on you—just to tide you over.'

'Thank you, Mrs Boyle. I do appreciate it.'

Following Mrs Boyle, her lantern swinging golden

beams across the stone path, he decided he was excited to go to Woodlore Glen. Before he turned his attention fully to the duty of finding a bride, he would attend to his first home.

Duty was duty and he would not shirk it, but a visit to the past was in order.

Chapter Two

Anna Liese stood at the drawing room window watching her pet goose, Fannie, waddle across the stone bridge, her tail feathers flicking while she squawked at a bristle-backed cat.

She refused to shiver over the tingle creeping up her neck and smoothed her hands over the chill prickling her forearms.

The uneasy sensation had nothing to do with the goose or the cat. Nor did it have to do with the temperature in the drawing room. No, indeed, a bright fire snapped cheerily in the hearth and spread warmth to every extravagantly decorated corner.

More than likely the unwelcome sensation had to do with her stepmother. The crawly feeling was familiar enough that she knew better than to ignore it.

Over the years Anna Liese had developed something of a sixth sense—an intuition—when the Baroness was hatching a scheme. A scheme directed against her.

Without moving her head, Anna Liese shifted her gaze towards her stepsister. Mildred was frowning at her mother, her bottom lip curled in an unattractive pout.

Mildred swung her disgruntled expression at Anna Liese, then grunted in an unbecoming way.

What, she wondered, was Stepmama up to this time?

There was little doubt she was concocting some trickery which might land Anna Liese in a compromising situation with a man—someone she would thereby be forced to wed. Her stepmother did not care how it happened or what unscrupulous person she became saddled with, only that Anna Liese was no longer a stumbling block to Mildred's prospects.

Ever since Anna Liese had come of age and gentlemen began to show her favour, Stepmama had made it her goal to get her out of Mildred's way.

Would the woman never tire of it? If gentlemen callers were not attracted to Mildred, it was not because of Anna Liese, it was because Mildred was not the most congenial of ladies.

Which was understandable, in her opinion. How else could Mildred have turned out given that, for all the sixteen years they had lived together, Stepmama had compared her to Anna Liese and found her own child lacking?

It was hard not to feel some pity for Mildred. How would anyone have an ounce of respect for themselves growing up and hearing things such as, 'Mildred, do you see Anna Liese having a second helping of tart?' or, 'Watch and learn how your stepsister smiles at a gentlemen, otherwise you have no chance at surpassing her.'

Then there was the worst comment, which Anna

Liese had overheard shortly after her father had married Lady Hooper. 'You shall try harder to be pleasant to your stepfather, Mildred. The Baron must see you as his favourite daughter. Anna Liese is prettier than you are which means you must be more charming than she is.'

It was a horrid thing to say to Mildred. To this day, she recalled her younger stepsister's sobs as she ran out of library.

The saddest part was, that, in the beginning she and Mildred had begun a sisterly relationship. Had it not been for Stepmama putting them at odds, perhaps they still would have been friends.

And yet Anna Liese did have some pity—almost—for Stepmama.

What kind of joy could there be in a life consumed with seeing one's daughter wed to a title? As far as a life goal went, what happiness could it really bring her in the end?

And honestly, at twenty-six years old, Mildred was not the most sought-after lady in society. It was unlikely that Stepmama would ever see her dream satisfied.

Besides the issues with Mildred's age and disposition, there was the difficulty of residing in Woodlore Glen. It was a quaint and lovely village, but, being a few hours from London, they were isolated from society. It was a rare day when a gentleman paid a call.

Sadly, there was truly little which Anna Liese and her stepsister had in common.

But there was one thing.

They were pawns of the Baroness's ambition. The

woman would do anything to get what she wanted which was to see both girls married.

While most mothers wished for the same, they also had a care for whom their daughters wed. Stepmama did not.

It was not their happiness she sought, but only that Anna Liese be out of Mildred's way, and that Mildred should have a title. And that said title would be above the rank of Baroness.

While love and romance meant nothing to Stepmama, it meant everything to Anna Liese. If she decided to spend her life with a man it would be because she adored him—because if she did not marry him, life would be colourless. If her life was to be colourless, she might just as well remain here in the home she loved.

Honestly, she had made up her mind long ago that without love there was no point in marriage. Memories of her parents' marriage was her guiding light. She would settle for nothing less than the love she recalled shining from her father's eyes for her mother.

'Anna Liese, my dear.' There it was—further proof that Stepmama was scheming. She never used an endearment towards Anna Liese unless she was up to something. 'I fear I have left my shawl in the carriage and my old bones are feeling chilled. Do be a dear and fetch it from the stable.'

Where, Anna Liese suspected, she would find some brash overzealous gentleman hiding. She would not find Stepmama's cloak. The woman had come in earlier wearing it.

How much had Stepmama offered him? Quite a lot, she imagined. Lady Barlow was an extravagant spender. Her late father's fortune had to be nearly gone. Mildred would need to wed a wealthy peer in order to see them through.

She wondered why her stepmother continued to see her as such a threat to Mildred. There had been a time when Anna Liese was sought after. While a suitor might still see her as a better choice than Mildred, she had no interest in a marriage—would refuse one outright if it were not based upon love.

With each passing year, spinsterhood seemed the likely outcome for both her and Mildred, yet Stepmama did not stop her attempts to compromise Anna Liese into matrimony. And it mattered little who the man was, as long as he was not titled and someone who might offer for Mildred.

As it had been when she was younger, her choice was love or spinsterhood. Since she loved Maplewood, she did not mind so much. Surely in time, watching couples walk arm in arm, laughing and clearly in love, would not make her heart ache. Indeed, she had only cried into her pillow over it twice this year.

If she was going to cry into her pillow, she did not want it to be because she had a husband who considered her an obligation fulfilled—one who did not really see her at all.

Stepmama was looking far too congenial, her smile bright and friendly. Anna Liese knew she must be on guard. On one occasion after such a smile, she had found her evening stroll interrupted by a stranger stepping out from behind a tree. He had tried to embrace her, which had not worked out best for him. Another time the third son of a baronet had attempted to secrete her away and keep her in a shed. He, too, had lamented that action.

The most daring, and most recent, of Stepmama's schemes had involved a gentleman who had looked for all the world like a pirate. His narrow chin had sported a black pointed beard and his small eyes had glittered as he peered over the windowsill of her bedroom. Truly he had been the most menacing of the gentlemen that Stepmama had sent her way.

She had managed to blacken both of his eyes before he had gained entry to her room. The cad had not seemed nearly so threatening as he scrambled back down the heavy trellis, sobbing like an injured child.

Anna Liese might be small of stature, but years spent hiking the woods and walking beside the stream had made her strong.

If they lived in London, her stepmother's schemes would be easier to accomplish. All she would need to do would be to get Anna Liese alone with a man at a ball, in the garden or an alcove.

But then, no. There were titled gentleman at balls whom Mildred might steal away with into a garden or an alcove. More often it was scoundrels of lower social status who Anna Liese had to fend off.

'I would be happy to do it, Stepmama, but I would not wish to offend Thorpe.' Whom she suspected would be hiding behind a haystack waiting to witness her fall from respectability. 'He does dote upon you and might be hurt if you do not ask him to see to it.'

'The footman is under the weather.'

'Very well, then,' she answered, making sure she sounded as unsuspecting as a newborn lamb. 'Would you like to walk with me, Mildred? It is not quite dark and the air is crisp and lovely.'

'I would enjoy a walk.'

Would she? That was not the answer Anna Liese expected. Mildred disliked venturing out of doors especially with evening settling in. Her willingness to do so now must mean she knew of the scheme and wished, for some undreamed-of reason, to quash it.

Perhaps Anna Liese's surprise 'suitor' was Woodlore Glen's banker, or someone acting on his behalf. Mildred did her best to disguise her interest in the man, but, sadly for her, she was not adept at hiding her emotions.

It would be a great coup for her stepmother to force Anna Liese to wed Mr Grant. In doing so she would have Anna Liese out of the way while at the same time ensuring the man's false admiration would go no further.

And false it was, most sincerely false. Mr Grant had an expression in his eyes that was easy enough to see if one looked behind his deceitfully handsome face. That expression was greed, for both money and social status. While Mr Grant would like to elevate that status by wedding the daughter of a baron, Stepmama would never allow Mildred to bear a title lower than viscountess.

Yes, it made sense that it was the banker awaiting her since Anna Liese was also the daughter of a baron. Mr Grant might be quite willing to settle for Anna Liese.

Poor Mildred. It was no wonder she had grown to be

bitter and petty, having been little more to her mother than a means to achieve her own ambitious ends.

'It is too cold for you to venture out. You will remain here with me.'

'I shall wear a coat, Mother.'

Oh, good for Mildred for speaking up for herself! It was a rare thing when she did.

Stepmama's mouth thinned, the tip of her nose beginning to pulse the same red colour as a beetroot when sliced open.

Anna Liese and Mildred both knew it would be risky to push the woman further.

'Hurry along, Anna Liese, before he—' In her rising ire, the Baroness nearly blurted out the secret which they all knew anyway. 'Before I catch a chill.'

'It might take me a while to find it, Stepmama. You should sit close the hearth.'

Where she might swelter.

Perhaps it was not charitable to wish the woman to roast, but neither was it charitable to try to trap one's own family.

Slowly, Anna Liese strolled out of the drawing room, then mounted the steps to her bedroom.

'I'll need my coat, Martha,' she said to her maid who was drawing the curtains closed against the night.

'Surely you are not going out, miss. It is time to dress for dinner.'

'I will not be needing you until morning. You may enjoy the rest of the night off.'

'You are hiding away from that old besom again! If you will forgive me saying such a thing about your— your relative. Although I hate to call her such. I remember how it used to be when your mother was alive. Oh, your father adored her so—and you. Then that woman came and Maplewood Manor has not been the same since, believe you me.'

Nor would it ever be. Until the deadly influenza robbed them of Mama, life had been so lovely—a bit of paradise fallen to earth.

Anna Liese, too, remembered how it used to be.

'You will be in your secure place? Wherever it might be.' Martha settled Anna Liese's cloak about her shoulders, then buttoned it under her chin. 'You always come home in the morning so I suppose you must be safe enough.'

'You need not worry. I'll be close by and far safer there than here.'

Ever since the 'pirate' in the window she had been extremely cautious.

'Sit by the fire for a moment, my dear, and I will bring you a basket of food.'

Moments later Martha returned, setting the basket on Anna Liese's lap. The scent of warm bread wafted from under the napkin.

'You are too kind, Martha. I thank you.'

'It is not my place to say so, miss, but I do have an opinion on all of this.'

Having cared for Anna Liese all her life, Martha rarely withheld that opinion.

The bread smelled delicious and she was hungry. She broke off a piece of crust and nibbled it.

'It just seems to me you would save yourself some trouble by marrying one of the better gentlemen the Baroness sets in your path. You could move away from here. Surely there is one among them who can offer more than what you have now.'

'It is the banker this time.'

'Oh, my. Well, not Mr Grant. But perhaps the next gentleman.'

'I have no wish to leave my home.'

Martha shook her head, several wisps of grey hair shimmering in the brown. 'I fear it has not been the home we knew for a good long time now.'

'It is where I—where we all—knew love. At least here I have my memories of that time.'

It was where she had been crushed with grief. But it was also where the memories of love wrapped her up, then healed her. Grief was strong, but love was stronger.

'You might learn to love a husband. Many women do.'

Annaliese looped the basket handle over her arm, then stood up.

'And many do not. I will be in love with my husband first and he with me. Otherwise, I shall remain here just as I am.'

'But are you happy, my girl?'

Well, no. She could not claim she was, but at least she was not happy in the home where, for a time in her life, she had been.

Ordinarily, Anna Liese enjoyed moonlight. But not tonight when it shone so brightly on the bridge that anyone looking out a window might see her crossing.

Although such a thing was unlikely. If her step-mother did happen to look out of a window it would be on the east side of the house where she could spot Anna Liese walking 'unawares' to the stable. No doubt she was even now wringing her hands in anticipation of her scheme working this time.

Quickening her pace, she wondered how long the banker and his witness would wait.

They would become good and cold while they did.

Since the scoundrels lay in wait by their own choice, she did not feel an ounce of pity for them.

With the temperature dropping as quickly as a stone in a wishing well, she shrugged deeper into her cloak and hurried along the path towards her sanctuary—the abandoned Penneyjons cottage. She had spent many happy hours there as a child and still felt the welcome within those walls.

Naturally, she did not enter by the front door, but by a window in back. Luckily for her, the previous tenants had failed to properly shut up the cottage when they left. She used this back window as her secret entrance.

As always, it screeched when she shoved it open, then again after she climbed over the sill and closed it behind her. Securing the latch then testing it, she sighed. The night was shut out along with the mischief lurking in it.

Taking a deep, grateful breath, she removed her cloak and lay it across the back of a chair. She had always loved this cottage, but never more than she had over this last year when its vacant rooms had been at her disposal. Crouching beside the hearth, she put in enough wood to start a cosy little fire.

There now, this was lovely. It was unlikely that anyone from the manor would notice a tiny smoke swirl coming from the chimney. Until morning, time was her own. There would be no one to demand she fetch a shawl or comb their hair before bed. If Mildred misplaced a bed slipper, she would have to find it on her own. Or as often happened, if Stepmama required a cup of midnight tea, she could fetch it from the kitchen herself.

The reason she was treated as more of servant than a daughter was clear. Her stepmother must believe that if living at Maplewood was difficult, Anna Liese would be willing to marry anyone just to be free.

Stepmama was quite wrong in that. Unless her one true love came striding through the doorway, she would reside at Maplewood longer than they would. The home was hers, legally given to her by her father. Nothing Stepmama did could force her away.

She opened the dresser drawer where she kept a few things and withdrew a jar of salve. Sitting upon the bed, she smothered her chapped hands with it.

Perhaps next she would read, or sing.

Or sleep. Ever since the incident with the 'pirate', his beady little eyes peeking at her over the sill of her bedroom window, a peaceful night's sleep was rare and found only when she escaped within the cosy walls of this room.

Peter's room.

Taking off her shoes, she lay down on her side, plumping the pillow under her cheek. From time to time, she dreamed of her old friend. She had loved him. Quite adored him as only a girl with her first crush could. Although, she would have told anyone that what she felt for her neighbour was more than a passing infatuation. He had been her only friend and she, his. During those wonderful days, they had spent every day together doing what children do.

Those had been the best days of her life. She and Peter had raced each other across meadows, waded in the stream and climbed the hill which overlooked Woodlore Glen. They had spent hours watching busy villagers go about their business. Sometimes, back when life was still safe and innocent, they had crept away into the night to sit on the hilltop bench, trying to identify the constellations moving across the sky.

Precious days and treasured nights that came to an end when death had slithered through the streets of Woodlore Glen.

The last she had seen Peter was in this room. He'd lain in his bed, closer to death than life with only his uncle to hold him back from it—and perhaps she had in some way as well with her song.

She had not known for sure if he had heard her singing. Halfway through, she had fled home, her heart caught in intolerable grief. She could not lose her friend, she simply could not.

But of course, she had lost him. Not to death, as she had her mother, but to his uncle who had taken him away to live in London.

'Peter,' she whispered. 'I still miss you still and our friendship. Whatever became of you?'

She had thought of writing to him, back then—but life had been in such upheaval with Mama dying and Papa remarrying. And she had not known what to say to him. How many times had she set her pen to the paper, only to stare at it, then push it away, her eyes too damp with tears to see what she was writing?

Sitting up, she decided she was hungry and not yet ready to sleep. Opening the basket of food, she asked God's blessing upon Martha for thinking to send it.

Nibbling a square of cheese, she tried to remember what Peter looked like. For some reason it was easier to recall how she felt about him than what he looked like. Eighteen years could create quite a blur.

'Let's see…' She closed her eyes, chewing a bite of bread while attempting to conjure his image out of time and space. 'You had freckles on your nose—oh, and your hair! It was something between red and blond, I think. You had the best smile and the worst singing voice—I remember that quite well. And you did know how to make me laugh.'

Indeed, she had never had a better friend—or another friend, truth to tell. While he had lived here, they had had too much fun together to want to include any of the village children. Afterwards, Stepmama had not liked other children visiting the manor.

There was a brief time when Mildred might have become a friend, but then, after Papa remarried, love had not been the reigning banner at Maplewood.

This cottage, though—it seemed that everyone who lived here over the years had been happy within its walls. How many times had she gazed across the bridge in envy?

She had learned from its example. If she ever married, she would live in a joyful home which took its spirit from a couple in love with each other. Nothing less would do. Her longing for true love was not some fairy-tale idea of romance and happily ever after. Not the fluffy sort that every little girl fantasised about.

No, it was bone-deep love she craved. The kind which saw people through trials and lasted over years. Love which rejoiced in good times and grew stronger even when hair turned grey and wrinkles etched smiles.

True, abiding love.

Setting aside the basket, she lay down again, closed her eyes and drifted towards sleep. In the instant balanced between reality and dream, she saw a funny, freckled face laughing at her.

Chapter Three

The train arrived in the village of Woodlore Glen behind schedule.

All in all, Peter did not mind disembarking near midnight. The village was peaceful in these wee hours.

He instructed the porter to have his luggage delivered to Myrtle Stone Cottage—to home—in the morning. There was no point in dragging anyone from their beds at this hour to do it.

He also refused the ticket-master's offer to give him a ride home. The man had already worked late, waiting for the train to arrive.

The walk from the village to the cottage was just over a hill, no more than half an hour's walk. He welcomed the exercise, even though the chilly air forced him to draw his coat collar up and his hat low.

Memories popped out at him from every street corner of the village, events long forgotten drew fuzzy pictures in his mind.

He stopped in front of the village's bakery, surprised to find Victoria's Sweet Shop was still in business. The establishment was closed at this hour, but that did not prevent him from seeing himself and Anna Liese as children.

Yes! Just there they rushed out of the shop grinning, each of them gripping a bag of gingerbread squares.

He could nearly feel the children they had been brush past his trouser legs in their haste to rush to the top of the hill where they would sit on a bench and gobble them down before an adult could tell them not to.

Was the bench still there? He could not imagine it would be, but why not walk to the cottage that way and find out? Going over the hill would take more effort than walking the easier but longer path around, but would be worth it.

Coming to the crest, he found there was a bench. Not the same bench, but one remarkably like it.

Since no one was expecting him, why not sit here for a moment? The sky was bright, twinkly and worthy of admiration.

Since he was sitting here, why not imagine he was holding that bag of gingerbread, laughing through a mouth full of crumbs with his long-ago friend?

It would be easier to do if he recalled exactly what she looked like. So much time had passed, he could not expect he would, but he did remember thinking she resembled a princess. Smaller than other girls her age, she was delicate looking. But strong, he recalled that clearly. And her hair…it was blonde and it sparkled in sunshine and in moonlight. She liked running, singing and twirling while her skirt flared around her.

Perhaps he would pay a call at Maplewood tomorrow. It might be that whoever resided there now would know what had become of Anna Liese.

He sat a few moments longer and then a few more. Were his toes not beginning to ache from the cold, damp ground, he might have carried on sitting.

While he was indeed enjoying the night and the memories, there was more to him spending time on the bench than that.

If he were to be honest with himself—and what was the point of not being so?—he was afraid of seeing his old home.

He was bound to be overwhelmed with emotions, good and bad. It had not been for no reason that he and his uncle had never paid a visit over the years.

This was where his family had laughed and loved— it was where they had died.

None of which would change by him continuing to sit here. What had happened had happened. Could not be changed. What could be changed was what would happen from here on.

Rather than leasing the abandoned cottage to new tenants he intended to make his former home a place where his family could gather. Only Cornelia still lived in London and it would be good to have a quiet retreat for his cousins and their families to spend time together. Beginning this Christmas after the ball, he hoped.

Such a happy outcome would not occur unless he faced the place, assigning good and bad emotions— which were bound to pummel him—to the past as was reasonable.

Rising, he walked down the back side of the hill which would bring him to the rear door of the cottage.

He would think about Anna Liese, draw her memory out of cobwebs if he could. Recalling his time with his childhood friend would give him the smile he needed to face the rest.

Coming closer, he decided he would not sleep in the master bedroom tonight, rather he would take his old room. Perhaps he would find peace in it, the same as he had when he was a child. Until that awful day when—

Never mind. It would be better not to dwell on that, but allot it a place in the past as he had resolved to do. He would think of the time before when life had been as wonderful as a boy could wish for.

But—wait! What was that?

He almost stumbled over his boot toes, squinting hard through the darkness at the cottage. Pale light leaked from around a curtain in a window. If he recalled correctly, it was his childhood bedroom. An intruder, a vagrant it seemed, had taken up residence. Well, that is what came of neglecting his property for nearly a year.

He drew the key to the back door out of his pocket, glancing about for some sort of weapon in case the intruder resisted being evicted.

Ah, just there to the right of the door was a stick. Something of one at least—it was more of a thick twig. He curled his fingers around it. Having never chased off an intruder, he could not imagine what to expect. But he could scarcely let whoever it was remain.

Entering the dark kitchen, he caught not a scent, but the memory of one. Gingerbread. He'd forgotten how often his mother used to bake it. He nearly called out 'Mama'.

Noiselessly, he took off his boots, setting them beside the door. It would be important to get the upper hand on the vagrant, not allow him time to become the aggressor.

Tiptoeing down the hallway, he twirled the flimsy stick in his fingers. Perhaps the man would leave willingly and he would not have to poke him with it and be humiliated when it snapped. He paused outside the door, trying to determine if the interloper was sleeping.

No snoring, but he did hear light breathing, soft and regular. The doorknob clicked sharply when he turned it. He might as well have fired a warning shot! His breath caught and held in his lungs as he quickly shoved the door open.

What the blazes? Not a man, but a woman!

Or an angel.

Dim light from the fireplace softly illuminated her face. Dammit, if the lady did not look more ethereal than flesh and bone.

All at once her eyes snapped open. 'Pirate!' she screeched, springing from the bed. She fired a pillow at him. The twig snapped in half.

'Pirate!' Anna Liese screeched.

'Miss?' The man looked as stunned as she felt.

How had he discovered her? And how had he got in?

Of course, he'd broken in! What else would a cold-blooded predator do?

'Fiend! Get back!' Her fingers trembled. Her heart trembled more. Who was this? It wasn't the banker!

He obeyed—but took only one step. She wondered briefly if he was as surprised to see her as she was to see him.

But that could not be since the only people who would come looking for her were the one, or two, who had been waiting to trap her in the stable.

'You wicked, vile cad!' She had not a second to spare for cloak or shoes. She opened the window and escaped into the night, casting glances over her shoulder all the way across the bridge.

Oh, but those stones were cold!

At least it did not appear that he was chasing her. Gradually her heart slowed enough that she felt confident it would remain within her ribs. But where was she to go now? The manor house would be locked for the night and she did not dare knock to be let in. Oh, dash it! Her wonderful hideaway was now lost to her. The hired villain was bound to report where he had found her.

The stable was really her only choice to flee. It was risky. What if one of the men remained? And she did believe there were two of them, one to do the deed and one to witness.

But she must find shelter. Given a choice between freezing to death or fighting, she would face fisticuffs. Years ago, Peter had taught her a thing or two about it—but all she recalled was to ball up her fist and aim for a nose.

The stable door was ajar. She slipped inside without sliding it closed behind her. The less noise she made, the better. Towards the back of the stable was a tall heap of straw. Shivering, she burrowed inside it, clearing a small hole to peep out of.

With the door left open it was exceedingly cold inside. She could only hope the chickens and their only horse were not shivering the way she was. Still, all in all, things were not as bad as they could be. She was hidden. If not in her lovely, secret room, she was at least grateful not to be cowering among reeds growing near the stream.

Nor, apparently, was Fannie cowering among them. Not one to cower anyway, she must have been roused by the pirate fellow. Even from here Anna Liese could hear the goose honking an alarm.

Oh, drat! The squawking was coming closer. Her pursuer, probably realising she had no place to go but to the stable, was returning. Through her peephole she saw the door slide open. The miscreant strode inside, the loyal goose attached to his trouser leg.

'Miss?' he called while swatting at the bird and missing. 'Are you in here?'

By the heavens, she was not likely to answer that!

'Do not think you must remain here and freeze.'

What was that he was holding? Her cloak!

This man was not as ugly as the pirate who had peered over her chamber sill, but he was more cunning, attempting to lure her with the promise of warmth.

'You may return to the cottage. We will discuss this in the morning.'

Discuss it? Was the man mad? She would punch him in the nose before she discussed how he might compromise her.

'Very well, have it your way.'

How congenial of the rogue. But if she truly had her way, she would kick him in the rump. Although Fannie was doing a rather splendid job of accosting that area of his anatomy as it was. There would be an extra treat at breakfast for the good goose.

The man stood for a moment, frowning. His gaze passed over the haystack. As rogues went, this one was rather amiable looking. In other circumstances she might consider him handsome. And he had not wrung Fannie's neck as he might have. Still, she supposed his air of congeniality made him even more dangerous.

He shrugged, then draped her cloak over a barrel.

She watched it cover the oak, wishing it covered her. It was not as if she could venture out to retrieve it. Mr Handsome Pirate would no doubt pick that instant to pounce upon her, whereupon she would be hauled before a minister and wed within a week.

No, thank you very much.

She would freeze in the haystack before she would spend her life with anyone who did not share at least a few qualities in common with her first true love. Suddenly, she missed Peter Penneyjons more than she had in a long time.

One dull-sounding thud hit the floor, followed by another. Having dropped her shoes, the handsome, wicked man pivoted sharply, then left the stable, sliding the door closed behind him.

The woman had not returned to the cottage overnight and he felt sorry for it. She must have been awfully frightened of him, coming upon her in the dead of night as he had.

Returning to his room last night, he discovered that she must have been staying there for some time. There was a brush and comb in the bureau drawer, a small mirror—and a blue ribbon twined about the bedpost.

In her flight the woman had left behind a basket with half a loaf of bread in it along with a wedge of nibbled cheese. Also, she had run away without her cloak and shoes. He dearly hoped that she'd had the sense to pick them up off the stable floor after he left. The haystack she had been hiding in could only provide scant warmth.

There was nothing he could do about it now, except wonder about her. Who was she? Why had she felt it necessary to seek shelter in his cottage?

He had not slept last night, but rather spent the hours wandering the rooms and revisiting his ghosts. To his surprise he found the good ones more comforting than the bad ones grievous. Glancing about, feeling memories fall into place, he had smiled more than he wept, although he had done both.

In all, the cottage was in fair condition. It needed cobwebs swept off ceilings and walls. Fresh paint, perhaps cheery new wallpaper and new curtains. Certainly, a good airing out and vigorous scrubbing. Every corner of the cottage needed attention, except for his boyhood bedroom. That space was clean, well kept.

It smelled good, too. Even though the lady was not here, a fresh, delicate scent lingered—lavender, wasn't it? It was unlikely he would see her again, so he tried to put her out of his mind.

Today brought a bright new morning with much to look forward to. First, he would walk to the village and have breakfast, over which he would come up with a strategy to renovate the cottage and get it done before Christmas. It needed to be done quickly in order for the family to gather and celebrate.

After breakfast he would pay a call on the manor across the bridge. The current resident of Maplewood might know what had become of Anna Liese. He had no hope that she lived there still. Certainly, she would be married and be mistress of her own home. His childhood friend had been on his mind a great deal since arriving at Woodlore Glen.

And, despite his best efforts for her not to be, so had the angel from last night. While he had every right to be resentful of her intrusion, he was not. No, what he felt was guilty for having turned her out, although, that had not been his intention. She had fled before he could reassure her and he felt sorry for it. Frightening women was not something he normally did.

No doubt, in her eyes, he was the interloper.

As interlopers went, she was lovely—he could hardly deny what he had seen. A sleeping beauty, her bosom rising and falling in peaceful slumber, her fair hair splayed across the pillow. And when her eyes snapped open, he had discovered them to be an exquisite shade of blue. Even in the dim light cast by the hearth he could see how pretty they were.

More than her beauty, which was quite stunning, he had been taken with her voice. What she had shouted at him had been odd. Pirate?

Then by the time she had called him 'cad', his heart had taken the oddest tumble. There was something about the quality of her voice that had caught his heart.

Made him want to smile and weep all at once. He had never had that disconcerting reaction to a stranger before.

Perhaps it had to do with the fact that she seemed so vulnerable. Until recently, he had been guardian to his cousins so that might have something to do with it. Relinquishing his role as protector might take some time to accomplish.

Anna Liese stood in the hallway outside the dining room, trying to decide if eating breakfast was worth joining her stepmother and stepsister at the table. She was hungry, but was she hungry enough to face Stepmama's ire?

No doubt she was steaming because Anna Liese had not gone to the stable as instructed to do and once again her stepdaughter had not fallen into a scheme to get her married off and out of Mildred's way.

The only sound coming from the dining room was the irregular click of utensils on china. Then, 'You ought to have done more with your hair this morning, Mildred. What if we have a gentleman caller?'

'A gentleman caller?' There was a clack, as if a fork had been intentionally dropped on a plate. 'That is quite unlikely, Mother.'

'But you must be prepared, in the event.'

'When was the last time such a miracle happened? Two months, three? But it was not a gentleman who called last, was it? As I recall it was the banker trying to sell a loan and you sent him away before I could have one word with him.'

'My, my… Your mouth is impertinent this morning, Mildred. Do remember that you are not meant to be the wife a common banker. Both your father and your stepfather were barons. I will not settle you upon anyone less than a viscount.'

'I shall dry on the vine waiting, then.'

'No doubt you will if you fail to take care of your appearance. As I said, your hair needs attention.' Suddenly Anna Liese heard a quick, sharp slap. 'Are you certain you wish to eat a fourth slice of bacon?'

'You need not strike my hand.' Mildred sniffed. 'Besides, Martha dislikes my hair. She never puts it in the pretty curls she does Anna Liese's.'

'And do you know where your dear sister is?' The word 'dear' was clearly uttered with a sneer.

'I imagine you would know better than I do. Did she not return from fetching your shawl last night?'

The shawl which was never in the stable to begin with? The one which had been a ruse to get her out there and was probably hanging neatly in her wardrobe?

Yes, she had returned, but only after shivering in the haystack for two hours. It had taken that long for her to be certain the man was good and gone. Half-frozen, she had climbed the sturdy trellis to her second-storey window. Once inside she collapsed in a heap on the rug in front of her hearth, more grateful for warmth than she could ever recall being.

Bless Martha for having the forethought to keep the fire going. Not only in case she returned, but because anyone looking for her would assume she was within and search no further.

But, by the heavens, what was she to do now that her sweet hiding place at the cottage had been revealed?

'Would that she had not returned. Mark my words, Mildred, gentleman callers will not give you a second glance, not if they see Anna Liese first.'

Anna Liese flinched as if she were the one to have been cut by Stepmama's words. With comments like that it was no wonder she and Mildred did not get on. One could only wonder what might have been had Stepmama had a different attitude towards her only child.

'Honestly, did you think I would allow you to dally with a banker?'

A sniff. Silence. And then, 'I would not lower myself to the likes of him. As you say, I will have a viscount.'

How belittled must Mildred feel.

It was no wonder her stepsister had a misguided attraction to the banker. The society climber often smiled at her in a less than wholesome way. Being desperate for attention, her stepsister mistook it for admiration.

While Anna Liese did not often agree with Stepmama, she did in this instance. The banker, preening peacock that he was, would make an awful husband to any woman.

Anna Liese hoped Mildred did manage to wed well. It was the only way she would be free of her mother's hurtful comments. On occasion Anna Liese dreamed of being free of them, too. She wondered if she ought to run away and, despite her position in society as a baron's daughter, seek employment.

But, no, she would not—could not.

Her heart was as much a part of this home as the

walls and gardens were. It was where she had grown up, been a part of a loving family for a time. She was not about to lose the home her father had given her, where at every turn she still saw his smile and heard Mama's laugh.

If she went away, she feared the Baroness would find a way to steal Maplewood. As long as she remained in residence, it was not as likely to happen.

'Put the toast down. It will go straight to your waist.'

'My sister eats toast and look at her waist.'

Mildred's sister wished she had a slice of toast with jam and a cup of hot chocolate to go with it. But she did not wish it badly enough to join their company.

Instead, she decided to go to the kitchen and see what was to be found. Last night she had promised Fannie a treat. Given what a beautiful December morning it was, going outdoors in the crisp air would be a delight.

She was a dozen steps down the hallway when she heard a knock at the front door. Being the closest to the door it would make sense for her to answer it, but Stepmama had forbidden her from doing so, insisting it was the job for the butler and not a lady.

Rubbish and more rubbish. Stepmama never considered any of the other chores she assigned her to do to be beneath a 'lady'.

The knock came again. Hurried footsteps hastened from the back of the house. The elderly butler who had served the family ever since Mama and Papa wed rushed into the hall, winded.

If Stepmama did not spend so frivolously on things

of no real value, they might be able to afford to give him his retirement and hire someone younger.

The knock sounded a third time. Who could it be possibly be?

She slid behind a curtain. This was not the first time she had made use of this rather perfect hidey-hole which made her privy to what was said in the drawing room. Even better, there was a rip in the curtain just the size for a curious eyeball to peer through.

A man's voice ushered from the hall. She could not make out his words, but he spoke like a gentleman. Given the rarity of such a visit, Anna Liese could imagine the stir going on in the dining room. She did not need to see Stepmama's face in order to know her eyes would be glittering, her mouth set in a thin, calculating smile. By the time she greeted her guest in the drawing room a mask of charm and congeniality would be settled over her features.

Poor man. Whoever the butler was leading to the drawing room had no idea what was coming down upon him, that while he waited to be introduced, a wedding was being planned. Perhaps the man was not titled and would be safe from them.

'If you will wait here in the drawing room, sir, I will announce you.'

The visitor walked past the rip in the curtain. No! It could not be! But it was! Bold as day, the less than dastardly-looking pirate strode past her hiding place. This was an outrage! How dared he look so—so—pleasant?

Anna Liese clamped her hand over her mouth to keep from gasping aloud. She backed up against the wall with a hard thud which made him stop and glance about. Oh, how brazen he was, acting the part of a welcome guest and not a knave come to collect his ill-gained due. Not that Stepmama was likely to hand it over since he had failed to malign Anna Liese's virtue.

Standing utterly still, she listened to footsteps approaching the drawing room from the dining room.

'Lift your chin and for pity's sake smile like—' she heard Stepmama say when she and Mildred passed by.

Stepmother's greeting carried out of the drawing room. Could she gush any harder over the man?

But wait. Why would she do that? Surely once she recognised who he was, she would chastise him rather than welcome him. The fact alone that he was not the gentlemen visitor she had hoped for ought to turn her stepmother's mood sour.

It was imperative for Anna Liese to listen to what they were saying in case they concocted another plan to waylay her, especially as she no longer had a secure hiding place to flee to.

'I hope I have not called at an inopportune time,' the man said.

Truly? She nearly snorted aloud. He excelled in doing so, she would point out if she dared speak up.

'Not at all, sir. Guests are always welcome at Maplewood.'

Sir? All right, she did have to confess the stranger had looked handsomely dressed when he passed by her peephole. But it did seem strange that Stepmama did not seem to recognise him.

Perhaps she had made her negotiations with the footman only and that is why she was acting so politely towards him. Once he stated why he had come, the fur would fly. She could not help but smile at the thought of him getting his due—or a small portion of it—at least.

'I arrived in Woodlore Glen late last night.'

Indeed he had! No one knew it better than Anna Liese did. Why, the worm did not sound at all ashamed of it.

'Since we are to be neighbours for a time, I thought I would come by and make your acquaintance.'

What? Neighbours!

'Are you the new tenant of Myrtle Stone Cottage, then?' Stepmama asked.

'No, I own the cottage. I grew up there for a time.'

Oh, what a bald lie. She did not recall anyone but Peter growing up there, not boys, at least.

This man was up to something. If she were not in hiding, she would charge into the drawing room and accuse him of—whatever it was he was about.

'What a delight!' Anna Liese could all but see Stepmama rubbing her hands together in anticipation. 'I am Baroness Barlow and this is my lovely daughter, Mildred Hooper.'

Anna Liese's hands grew damp with the sinking feeling in her stomach that something shocking was about to be revealed. Nothing about this conversation made sense.

She knew who the true owner of the cottage was. Only last night she had slept in his childhood bed.

'I am Viscount Cliverton and I am quite pleased to meet you both.'

Her stomach took a dive straight to her toes, which knocked her off balance. Why could the earth not open and swallow her? Her one true love—of a sort—had come home at last. Of a sort indeed. This man was not her Peter! Not the boy she'd held fast in her heart over the years. Viscount Cliverton did not have freckles on his nose or a mop of windblown hair. He certainly was not gangly. And his voice was deep!

For some reason he had never aged in her mind. How could he have imagined him older, when he might have grown to be tall or short, slim or muscular? Some people's hair darkened as they aged. Had she aged him in her mind, she would not have come up with the handsome man on the other side of the curtain.

Mildred was surely casting cow eyes at him while Anna Liese hid behind the drapery!

Oh, drat and curse it! Yes, curse it that she was wearing a serviceable gown and not one fit for a happy reunion involving an embrace and happy tears.

For most of her life she'd dreamed of being reunited with Peter. Somehow, she had never imagined it would be as a trespasser in his house! Who could ever imagine such a thing? What would he think of her once he made the discovery?

Nothing could be worse. How long did he intend to stay in Woodlore Glen? She pressed her fingers to her flaming cheeks, blinking back the moisture gathering in her eyes. It was out of the question to be reunited with him now.

Peter Penneyjons had known her as a cherished daughter, a beloved friend. Not as a squatter in his home! Clearly, she must avoid him. No matter what, she was determined to remain a memory to him.

Unless…

Perhaps he did not remember her? That possibility left her feeling rather ill at heart. But truly, it had been such a long time since his uncle took him to live in London. Eighteen years was an awfully long time. It was possible he did not remember her. His life in London would have been full elegant people and grand events.

Thinking reasonably about it, it was likely that he did not recall his childhood friend from the quiet countryside. Which broke her heart, made her want to let loose of her tears and sob into the curtain.

'May I ask you something, Lady Barlow?'

'Of course, my lord!' There was a rustle of fabric, as if perhaps Mildred had been thrust forward. 'But perhaps you would like to take a walk with Mildred. I'm sure she will have the answers to anything you would like to know.'

'It's one question only. I am looking for someone. I wonder, do you know what became of the Baron's daughter?'

'Why, she has grown to be a well-tempered and beautiful woman, as you can see.'

'Indeed, yes. I can see that. However, it is Anna Liese I am enquiring about.'

She pressed her palms against her chest to keep her wild heartbeat from giving her presence away—it did seem that loud to her own ears.

This development was wonderful and horrible all at once. How on earth was she to hide away when she wanted to speak with him more than she wanted her next breath?

'Oh. I see. My stepdaughter is away from home.' Stepmama might have found a career onstage, her voice sounding as warm as sunshine on a summer morning as it did.

'We were close as children and I was hoping to see her again.'

'Why, naturally. But, if I might say so, old friendships are rarely as wonderful as we remember them. People do change. But Mildred would be delighted to reacquaint you with the village. What could be lovelier than a new friendship, I always say.'

Wouldn't sugar melt in Stepmama's mouth? It was acting such as this which had captured her father years ago. The last thing Anna Liese intended was for Peter to fall prey to it, although, she was not sure how to prevent it since she was going to avoid encountering him.

With goodbye greetings exchanged, she peeked at Peter who, accompanied by the butler, walked towards the front door. Seconds later she heard Stepmama and Mildred chattering excitedly as they went back to the dining room.

Dashing from behind the curtain, she ran for the drawing room window. Now that she knew the man to be Peter, she needed to see more of him than the slice she'd had through the drapery.

Of course, she had seen him last night, but only briefly and she had believed him to be a scoundrel and a knave. A very well-knit-together knave. Even in her fear she had recognised his handsome bearing.

Hopefully, he would not turn to look back. If he did, he might spot her watching him through the glass with great admiration. Not that he would recognise her as the girl he had gambolled about the estate with, any more than she recognised him.

Suddenly he halted, taking off his hat and scratching the top of his head. The gesture went straight to her heart. This man was very much her Peter, after all. Oh, dear. He spun about, caught her staring at him. In the instant it took for her to stumble out of view, she noticed his brows draw together in confusion.

She pressed her chest to settle her heart. That frown was remarkably familiar and completely endearing. It did not matter how long it had been since she had seen it on his boyish face, it seemed as if it had only been yesterday. What a horrid and wonderful turn the day had taken. She could not decide whether to rejoice or lament.

Cry. She would do exactly that when she got the chance. Happy tears and sad ones came from the same eyes, after all.

Chapter Four

Peter walked beside the stream listening to the rush and gurgle of water, to the chirrup of birds seeking a meal before sunset. Given the afternoon he had spent, he needed this soothing peace.

What he had intended was to spend the day in the cottage, taking note of what needed to be done and making lists. He instead found himself in the company of the Maplewood Manor ladies.

All the live-long afternoon.

No matter how many times he courteously suggested they part company for the day, he found himself more deeply sucked into their company.

There had been lunch in the village, then a stroll about the grounds of Maplewood, which were as beautiful as he recalled them being.

For a time, he thought himself free of the ladies' company. He had been whistling while crossing the stone bridge leading to his cottage when Mildred scurried after him, insisting he remain for tea.

Since he had no ready excuse not to and the lady did seem exceptionally needy of company, he agreed.

Unfortunately, tea dragged on interminably.

One would think he was Prince Charming the way the women seemed rapt on each word he uttered. Of course, he was not fool enough to think it was he they were so enamoured of, but that a viscount had come to call.

This sort of attention, the kind that bordered on unhealthy adoration, was something he was not used to. In London he associated with people of equal or better rank. Among his peers no one was impressed overmuch with his status.

Being isolated in the country, he imagined the ladies did not have much opportunity to entertain. He supposed it was understandable they would enjoy company. It was also understandable how relieved he was to be free of it for the moment.

But only for the moment. He had been invited for dinner and once again could find no polite way to turn the invitation down. Besides, he might see the lady he had spotted in the drawing room window at Maplewood.

No doubt the pretty woman was a servant in the employ of Lady Barlow. Which did nothing to explain why she had been sleeping in his cottage.

The day might not have been such a loss had he been able to get an answer to his first question of the day: What had become of Anna Liese?

Each time he turned the conversation towards his old friend, Lady Barlow redirected it towards her own daughter. He still knew nothing more of Anna Liese than that she was not at home. After all this time he doubted he would even recognise the child she had been in the woman she would have become, if he happened upon her.

Free for the moment to be with his thoughts and not having to supply clever conversation, he let his mind relax, wander where it would.

While Anna Liese was greatly on his mind, so was the servant he had chased from his childhood bedroom. Why had she been there?

Rather than spending the day with the ladies, he ought to have been trying to find her. Clearly, she was in some sort of dire circumstance otherwise she would not have broken into his house. Hopefully, she would not seek refuge in the stable again. A haystack was no place for a woman to sleep.

Perhaps on his way home from dinner, he would search there for her just on the chance she had returned.

There must be something he could do to aid the lady. In a sense, he owed her a safe place to sleep. It seemed his bedroom had been her sanctuary for some time until he burst in upon her.

It was hard to forget the way she had looked at that moment—so beautiful and peaceful. How she had seemed part-angel and, at the same time, quite a desirable woman.

Over the course of the day he'd found himself smiling at the picture she'd made. Which he wished he had not done because he suspected Mildred construed the expression on his face as having to do with her. He did not wish her to misunderstand. He was not here to find a wife, but to restore the cottage.

Once he returned to London, he would hold his Christmas ball, face that next step in his life and seek a bride. For now, he had but two desires regarding women: first, to discover what had become of little Anna Liese and, second, to find the angel woman.

A bird settled upon a low-hanging branch, fluttering its feathers. Peter stood still, closed his eyes and listened while it sang the day into evening. He had nearly forgotten how much he enjoyed simply standing quietly and listening to birdsong. There were birds in his London garden, but here in the country they were easier to hear.

But wait—what was that? Not a bird but a woman singing, her voice far lovelier than a twitter. From here he could not identify what it was she was singing, but it was beautiful beyond words. There was a quality to the woman's voice that shook him.

It was hard to know if he felt like weeping or humming along.

Peter Penneyjons was coming for dinner which meant Anna Liese was not. Just where she would be at eight o'clock, she could not imagine. While it would not be possible to avoid him for ever, she simply was not ready yet. Nor would she be ready by dinnertime.

Maybe she would remain here, sitting on the stream bank watching Fannie paddle about in the water. What an awful prospect that was. This was December, not July, and the tips of her toes had only now warmed from last night's misadventure.

Neither did she wish to be inside where the temptation to leap upon Peter and enfold him in a great, teary hug of reunion would be difficult to resist. Better to avoid the temptation for the time being. Wherever she spent the evening, it would not be in the Viscount's company.

Some things were too humiliating to be borne. To be revealed as his intruder would be mortifying beyond the pale. Why, she did not know what his reaction to discovering her intrusion would be. He would be within his rights to hand her over to the village constable. Young Peter would never do such an unkind thing, but he was no longer young Peter. London and society might have changed him so she had no idea what he might do.

And would it not be a dream come true for Stepmama to get her out of the manor, shamed and incarcerated?

Well, shamed at least. Being incarcerated might reflect badly on the family.

Afternoon sunshine faded, giving place to early twilight. Fannie waddled out of the water, shook her tail, then settled into the tall grass for the night.

Not ready to go back to the manor house, Anna Liese decided she might as well sit for a bit and sing.

Singing always calmed her soul.

Did Peter know that she had sung to him the last time she saw him? Perhaps not. The doctor hadn't thought so but, thankfully, Peter's uncle had allowed it.

How awful it had been, believing he was dying and singing a bit of peace to him. She remembered the song well, although she had not found the heart to sing it since. Sitting with her knees drawn up to her chest, she now felt it rising in her lungs.

Peter was home. The sun was setting and the urge to sing their goodnight song overwhelmed her. Closing her eyes, she let it out.

'By yon bonnie banks and by yon bonnie braes, Where the sun shines bright on Loch Lomond...' Words springing from her lips were born of her heart rather than her lungs. *''Twas there that we parted, in yon shady glen...'*

She did not realise she was crying until salty tears dripped into the corners of her mouth. Words and melody welled from her soul, the past becoming as present as the cool, damp ground beneath her. She had not been able to finish the song that wicked awful day, but now...

'O ye'll take the high road and I'll take the low road and I'll be to dinner before you, where me and my true friend will always meet again, On the bonnie, bonnie banks of Loch Lomond.'

She sniffed, wiping her eyes with her sleeve. Her true friend was here and yet a thousand miles away. It was unlikely they would meet again since she intended to avoid him.

'Is it really you?' A man's voice yanked her completely into the present time. 'Anna Liese?'

Gasping, she opened her eyes and leapt to her feet. Oh, no! No, no, no! She spun about, set her feet to flee and would have had she not glanced over her shoulder.

Peter, her Peter, stood mere feet away, a hesitant smile on his face. It was as if a veil was lifted from her eyes, from her memory. Knowing now who he was, she could only wonder that she had not recognised him from the first.

'It is you!' he said, his grin breaking wide.

'No, it isn't.' She backed away. This was not a fib. She was not the child he knew any more than he was the boy she knew. What they were…were strangers.

'Who else would sing our lyrics?' He stepped closer. She did not run as she ought to have. 'But why are you crying? Are you not happy to see me?'

'All right, I confess it. I am she. And why would I not be crying? Last I saw you I thought you were dying and now here you are.'

For a moment he simply stared at her, silent and his grin gone flat. But then—

Then he opened his arms. It was as if time and distance vanished and he expected her to run into them, exchanging hugs as they used to do. But there had been time and distance. He was a man and she was a woman.

'Why didn't you write to me, Peter?' she said, uttering the first protest to come to her aid. She could not simply go back to the way they had been as children. Neither of them was that carefree person any more. 'Would no one bring you to visit?'

He shrugged one shoulder, tilted his head to the side. His smile slipped and a frown creased his brow.

'I imagine I meant to. As soon as I recovered.'

'And yet you did not.' Perhaps it was not right to feel offended that he had not thought of her over the years. But she had thought of him so often, wondered about him, prayed he was well and happy.

'Life dealt me a wicked turn, Anna Liese.'

As it had done to her, but that had not kept her from thinking of him.

'If I'd looked back, I think I never would have moved forward again. It took a while before I even wanted to live. Longer than that to be able to smile. I was afraid of coming back here, even for you.'

'My mother died, too. Did you know that?'

'Your father sent word of her passing and I'm deeply sorry for it. I remember how loving she was. So much loss, Anna Liese. It is a wonder we made it through. Won't you forgive me for not writing or visiting?'

She must, of course, since she never had been able to write to him either, although she had tried.

'Yes.' She had never truly held it against him, anyway. The only reason she brought it up now was because she needed to distance her emotions from this man who was, by now, a stranger.

Except for the way he shrugged his shoulder and tilted his head. That gesture was quite familiar. So was the curve of his smile and the brackets that lifted each corner of his mouth. Oh, have mercy, but a hint of playful mischief shone out of his eyes now, the same as it had in years past. Perhaps he was not such a stranger.

Regardless, he was bound to recognise her any second now as the one who had been trespassing in his cottage. Light in the bedroom had been dim, but not completely dark. If she did not wish to face her crime, she must hurry away.

'It is growing late and I must go home. But it was pleasant to see you again, Peter.'

As goodbyes went this one was formal, meant to let him know—well, she was not sure what, but...

Giving him a nod, she turned.

'One of the things I remember best about you is your singing. I forgot a lot over the years, but not that.'

Oh, well, for some reason hearing him say so made her go soft inside. Shot her back to who they used to be. The Anna Liese and Peter who roamed green hills and splashed in the stream without a thought of their world ever changing.

To the children who loved each other in complete innocence.

'I'd hoped you did, but—well—goodnight.'

She would have made it safely away but then he opened his arms once again, nodded, asking for the hug they had always shared before going to their own homes in the evening.

Well, then, what could it hurt? A quick embrace to complete the circle of their friendship. To put a period to the years that had passed rather than a question mark.

Stepping forward, she raised herself up on her toes to give his neck a quick hug, same as she had done a thousand times. But unlike the thousand times, Peter did not laugh and instantly let go of her. His embrace drew her to his chest, which was no longer all ribs and gangly adolescent angles, but well muscled, manly and—oh, my word.

Oh, my word, indeed! Grown-up Peter made her aware of herself as a woman and not a flat-chested child. Her heart racing madly in confusion, she pressed her palms on his chest, pushing back out of his arms.

This man might be called Peter Penneyjons, but that was all he had in common with the boy she had known. All right, there was the grin, but it was hardly enough to erase years of being apart.

If, like they had done as children, they stole away in the night to sit on the hilltop bench, it would not be to point out constellations. She had better not let her mind wander to the bench because she was growing rather warm…flushed.

Spinning away from him, she was too aware that it was not a boy's scent lingering in her senses while she crossed the bridge and ran for home.

Peter stood in front of the bedroom mirror, tugging his necktie into place. It was not as easy a task as his valet made it appear to be, but then nothing was as easy as anticipated, he decided while shooting his mirror image a grimace.

In the beginning this visit had seemed simple enough. Come to Woodlore Glen, repair the family cottage and deal with the ghosts of his past. Then, while he was about it, enquire about Anna Liese.

That was all he had wanted: knowledge. To discover what had become of her and then put her away with the rest of his ghosts.

It ought to have been a simple thing.

But, no, as startling as it had been to find a woman in his bed last night, it had been even more of a shock when he realised his angelic-looking intruder to be Anna Liese.

More shocking, he had hugged her.

The scent of her hair lingered in his mind. He could not forget her quick intake of breath when she had pushed herself out of his arms. Even now he could scarcely believe he had done such an impulsive thing. What had prompted him to do it?

Enchantment brought on by December twilight and her song, no doubt. Hearing her voice had nearly brought him to his knees, his heart quivering in his chest. Even so, the last thing he had intended to do was hug her, certainly not to linger over it as he had. In his defence he had been astonished to discover his playmate had turned into a woman more appealing than he could have imagined—far more enchanting than any woman he had ever held in his arms.

Anna Liese had intriguing curves and smelled like lavender. Coming back from the stable last night he had stood over his bed, the fragrance drifting up from the pillow. In case he had any doubt as to who his intruder had been, the scent put the question to rest.

Another thing he had not anticipated was her reaction to seeing him. He had thought she was not best pleased by the surprise. Perhaps she really had been harbouring ill feelings towards him all these years because he had not written.

While dressing for the coming dinner at Maplewood, he had many questions and not many answers. The only answer he did have was that he knew where Anna Liese was. Not what had become of her, only where she was.

His childhood friend presented a mystery. Why had she been sleeping in his bedroom when she resided in the manor across the bridge? While it made no sense, he intended to make sense of it soon.

For the moment he would struggle with this cravat, grateful to know she was, if perhaps not doing well, at least whole and sound. And he would think of her voice—her song—which was even more beautiful than he recalled. All of her was more beautiful than he recalled.

'Why, there you are, Anna Lise!' She had only stepped on the bottom stair when Stepmama's voice brought her up short. 'Where have you been? Your sister and I have been beside ourselves with worry.'

'I cannot imagine what dire thing could happen to me here at Maplewood, can you? We must have missed each other in passing, that's all.' She started up the steps, but paused, looking down. 'I trust you had a pleasant day in spite of the worry, Stepmama?'

A pleasant day trying to trap Peter. She'd heard the servants whispering about it. They had spent much of the day together and he was coming to dinner tonight.

'It was mostly uneventful, as our days tend to be. But, my dear, something has come up and I fear I must ask for your help.'

The staff was all abuzz about Viscount Cliverton coming for dinner tonight. It was unlikely that she wished for Anna Liese's help in keeping him entertained.

'It seems there is a fox prowling about the stable and the hens are nervous about it. Would you mind spending a few hours with them tonight? If they do not calm down, I fear it will be days before we have eggs again.'

'Is there not a lad you might send to do it?'

There was certainly no fox. Even if there were one, the door would be shut against the animal.

'Oh, but you have such a way with animals. The

hens will settle at once when they know you are with them.'

Another scheme! Anna Liese was becoming weary of them. The only fox close by was the one speaking to her. In any case, it would suit Anna Liese very well to be absent for the evening. If Peter had not yet recognised her as the woman sleeping in his bedroom, he soon would. It would be beyond humiliating for it to be revealed in front of Mildred and Stepmama. It simply would not do.

Hurrying up the stairs, she entered her bedroom and closed the door, leaning against it with a relieved sigh. After the events of last night, she was content to remain here, snuggle into the chair beside the hearth and read a book. She would become so engrossed in the story that she would forget altogether that Peter was downstairs, that he was likely to be under assault from Mildred and Stepmama.

Poor man, but there was nothing she could do about it unless she was willing to join them for dinner, which she was not. Even if there was not the issue of her being exposed, she would not go down.

Life with those women would be miserable if she intruded. Stepmama clearly did not want her there. Anna Liese's mere presence at dinner would cause the Baroness to redouble her efforts to trap Anna Liese into marrying the next cad who wandered by the gate, or perhaps the banker.

Yet, despite the wisdom of remaining here, she could not help but imagine how nice it would be to spend the evening with her old friend. She did want to know about him—about how his life had been since they parted.

Hmm, what would she wear if she did join them for dinner? It could not hurt at all to wonder. She did not have many gowns, not compared to the number Mildred had, but the few she did have were quite pretty.

Walking across the bedroom to the wardrobe, she drew open the doors. What on earth...? Her pretty gowns were gone! All that hung inside were the serviceable dresses she wore every day.

How clever of Stepmama to have them removed in order to ensure she remained in her room. She would have realised that Anna Liese would recognise the story of the marauding fox to be a ruse and so taken this step to ensure she would not come down.

She need not have gone to the effort of making it up. Anna Liese plonked down in her chair which was positioned to give her a view of the fireplace and the window. This was where she would spend the evening. It was where she would remain until she spotted Peter crossing the bridge going home to his cottage.

Apparently, he would be walking back in the rain. Big fat drops began to hit the window. They rolled down, making the glass look as if it were weeping. Which is not what she would be doing sitting here. It did not matter that Peter was downstairs being entertained by Mildred.

He really was no more than a childhood friend. It was none of her business whom he found attractive— although she could not imagine he would be attracted to Mildred. Then again, she did not know him well enough to judge the kind of woman he was drawn to.

The bedroom door opened. Martha bustled inside, carrying Anna Liese's favourite gown over her arm.

'I thought Miss Mildred would never be satisfied with her hair. But here now, there is just enough time to arrange yours before dinner.'

'You needn't bother, Martha. I'm not going down tonight.'

'There is not time to play at refusing. Our young man is already here—and look, I retrieved your gown from the laundry. Miss Mollie, bless her soul, set it aside in case you might need it.'

Playing, indeed. She was not playing at anything. She was not going downstairs. She simply was not.

Chapter Five

'Will your stepdaughter be joining us for dinner?' Peter asked, glancing at the empty chair at the far end of the long dining table. It was oddly placed since the chairs they sat in were close together at the opposite end.

His hostess appeared to suck in a breath, then release it in a slow, barely concealed hiss. In an instant, her expression transformed, the corners of her mouth perking up in a smile. Even her cheeks blushed a congenial pink shade.

'I do hope so, but I fear she will not even though she has returned.'

'Is she ill?' Anna Liese had not seemed to be a few hours ago, but the question bore asking.

'Healthy as can be—however, she is a bit of a shrinking violet. Mercy knows I have tried to draw her out of it. As old as she is, she still rejects the suitors I introduce to her. Perhaps she simply distrusts men. Some ladies do.'

'You cannot blame her, I suppose,' Mildred said,

her fork halfway to her mouth. 'Poor Anna Liese withdrew into herself after dear Papa married my mother. It must have been a sad thing to discover her own father preferred my company to hers. I tried to tell her it was not so. Still, discovering such a thing is bound to influence a young girl.'

He could not imagine this was true. Anna Liese and her father had shared a close and loving bond. The man he remembered had always been devoted to his child. But years had passed, people did change, so perhaps it was true.

It hurt to think that his sweet friend had grown to be a recluse. If she had, it might go some way to explaining why she had been sleeping in his deserted cottage. Perhaps she was avoiding visitors.

Mildred chewed her food, her expression elated. It was odd, but she gave the impression of savouring the bite as if it might be her last. The woman was not terribly attractive, with narrow eyes set in a round, cheeky face. She was saved from being homely by a pretty smile, though.

How sincere was that smile? he wondered. He had no way of knowing whether she would give Peter Penneyjons the same coy attention she gave Viscount Cliverton. Both Mildred and her mother were attempting to win him over, of that he had no doubt. He did not judge them for it, naturally. It was a lady's role in society to marry as high as she might.

He had a role as well when it came to marriage, which made him no different than Mildred and her mother were. But since he had no intention of considering marriage until after his business here was completed, the Baroness and her daughter were wasting their efforts.

'I fear we will simply have to carry on without Anna Liese,' Lady Barlow said cheerily.

'Good evening, everyone.'

Pivoting in his chair at the sound of the voice, Peter saw the most beautiful woman imaginable standing in the doorway. Truly, she had to be. Dressed in a gown that looked like pink froth floating about her shoulders and feet, with a white rose tucked into her hair at her temple, she was ethereal.

Earlier, when he'd come upon her by the stream, she had stolen his breath. In this instant she did it again, only this time he was certain he would not get it back.

'Good evening, Anna Liese.' He stood to greet her.

The footman pulled out the chair at the far end of the table as if it was where she was to sit. Did Peter imagine the brief, but smug glance the fellow shot the Baroness? And her even briefer nod?

'If you please, bring the chair to this end of the table,' Peter instructed.

'Yes, my lord,' the footman answered, then carried the chair and set it down next to Mildred.

'How lovely that you could attend dinner, Anna Liese.' Lady Barlow maintained her smile and her happy blush—however, the welcome was oddly absent from her eyes.

'Lovely, as always,' Mildred muttered, casting a sidelong frown at her stepsister.

'Please accept my apologies for being late.' Anna Liese melted his heart with her smile before she turned her attention to Lady Barlow.

'It was reported that there was a fox disturbing the hens. It turned out not to be true.' Anna Liese cast the Baroness an odd, speculative glance. 'Whoever reported the warning was mistaken. But rest assured, the hens are content and we will have eggs for breakfast.'

As much as he would like to devote his attention solely to Anna Liese it would not be appropriate, so he turned the conversation to one of his favourite subjects: bicycle racing. Surely speaking of his visit to George Singer and Son's establishment, where the newest in bicycles were made and distributed, would distract everyone from Anna Liese's late arrival. Her family was clearly annoyed with her and he supposed her tardiness was the reason why.

While he told them about the Anerley Bicycle Club, he kept part of his attention on the sisters. Watching them, he found it difficult to imagine that Baron Barlow had shown a preference for Mildred over Anna Liese. It simply did not fit with the man he remembered.

Apparently bored with talk of bicycles, Mildred said, 'Your hair looks especially pretty tonight, Sister. Martha must have spent a good deal of time seeing it so nicely styled. And a rose to go with it.'

'Your hair looks lovely, too, Mildred.' Looking at Anna Liese's smile, Peter was certain she meant it.

'Oh, yes. Martha did not spend nearly the time on mine as she did on yours. But of course, she would not need to. Isn't that right, Mother?'

'Oh, my dear. You have the loveliest hair of anyone in Woodlore Glen. It has been remarked upon over and over again.'

Love was blind, people liked to say. It must be especially true when it came to one's daughter.

Anyone with eyes could see that Anna Liese's hair looked like sunshine even with only lamplight to illuminate it. Not that there was anything wrong with Mildred's hair, but since she had brought it to the fore of conversation, he could not help but notice the difference.

The meal passed in pleasant conversation. At least he thought so, but that might have to do with how pleasant he felt inside himself. Being in Anna Liese's company again after all these years made him want to grin. It was going to be a delight over the next few weeks getting to know her again.

'Would you care to join us for breakfast, Lord Cliverton?' Lady Barlow asked with a bright smile—and a wink? Yes, that is exactly what it had been, a wink. 'Apparently we will have eggs.'

'As lovely as that would be, I fear I have burdened your staff far too much already.'

'I'm certain they do not find their jobs to be a burden,' Mildred stated.

'Nevertheless, I will take breakfast in the village.'

Now that it was time to return to the cottage, he found he did not wish to. Not because he would be drenched before he dashed halfway across the bridge, but because he did not wish to lose Anna Liese's company.

Looking at her, watching her smile and hearing her voice, he was beginning to remember how life had been for him as a carefree child…how innocent and happy he had been in the time before death altered their lives.

'Anna Liese,' he said when Mildred and her mother seemed to be involved in a discussion about the rain. 'We have much to catch up on. Would it be appropriate for me to ask you to join me for breakfast at the inn in the village?'

For all that being alone with her was not quite acceptable, it did feel the most natural thing in the world. Feeling the other ladies' attention shift to him, he added, 'All of you ladies, I mean.'

'What a grand idea!' Lady Barlow declared, clapping her thin fingers. 'We shall be happy to join you.'

He was not certain Anna Liese thought so. She smiled at him, but he read hesitation in her eyes.

'I would like that,' she said.

'Good, then.' He stood to take his leave, greatly regretting that he had been required to extend his invitation to them all. At some point he would find time to be alone with his friend. There was so much to talk about without the other ladies to divide his attention.

'I was all but forced to go downstairs to dinner, Fannie.' Swimming, the goose kept pace with Anna Liese while she walked on the stream's bank. 'After Martha went to the trouble of going out in the rain and picking a rose to put in my hair, it would have appeared ungrateful had I not. Not to mention what a waste of a lovely flower it would have been. What a wonder it was to find one this late in the year.'

Fannie dipped her head underwater, came up with a waterweed, then gobbled it down. She shook the water off her beak, giving a loud, strident honk.

'It was picked from an old bush Mama planted so you see what sort of a situation I was in.'

Fannie waddled out of the stream, honking again. Anna Liese stooped down, swiping water from the bird's feathers with a flick of her fingers.

Those were excuses, not reasons. She wanted to go down and so she had. There was no point in pretending there was any reason for it but that she wanted to see Peter again. So down she had gone to dinner, feeling something of a princess thanks to Martha's effort.

She had been all but chilled by the frigid reception she got from Stepmama, although the woman had done her best to hide it from her exalted guest. It was hard to think of Peter as exalted, but she imagined many people did.

Standing, she walked on, the goose waddling beside her. 'Honestly, I was not all that sorry for sending Stepmama into a mood. But, why am I explaining this to a goose when I ought to be explaining it to Peter? It is time I owned up to sleeping in his bed. If I do, perhaps we will find a way to strike up our friendship again. That would be…' She stopped walking, gazing at blue sky broken by a single white cloud drifting west. What a pretty backdrop to imagine ways a renewed friendship would be wonderful…ways it would be different.

Leaving the goose at the water's edge, Anna Liese proceeded to cross the stone bridge spanning the water between Maplewood and Peter's cottage.

If she did try to rekindle a friendship, she must accept that it would not be the same as it had been years ago. She was not who she had been and neither was he. Oh, indeed he was not. All night long she had been restless, comparing the differences between the boy and the man.

Pausing to stand on a point exactly halfway across the bridge, she listened to the wind playfully whistling through bare branches. A single yellow leaf blew off and tumbled across the surface of the water where it was caught, then floated away.

Standing where she was, she knew she must make a decision: keep her distance from Peter as best she could or continue across the bridge and knock on his front door. She did not know if renewing their friendship was for the best or not. Things might not be the same between them as they had been. And if they were not, the memory of what had been between them could be tainted.

Nonetheless, she needed to know. The affection they shared might remain and, given time, it might become even better. The seeds of a lifelong friendship had been planted when they were children. Had they never been separated, what would their lives be like now?

Taking a long, slow breath, she shook her head. The past could not be changed and the future had yet to happen. All she had was this moment and what was she going to do in it? Over the years she had crossed this bridge hundreds of times—why was it so difficult this time?

She could tell herself that it was because she was about to become hugely embarrassed when she admitted it was she who had trespassed in his house. While true, it was not the reason she remained standing on the halfway point of the bridge.

Was she willing to risk the memories of the past for

what might be in the future? That was what her hesitation came down to. Could she replace her laughing, freckle-faced friend with a stranger who made her feel fluttery when he smiled?

If she chose to knock on that door, things would never be the same. But perhaps they would not be anyway. The fact alone that Peter had come home changed things. Nothing could go back to how it had been. Well then, off she went over the bridge, relieved to have the decision made. What she had set in motion could not be gone back from now.

She raised her hand to rap on the door, but it swung open before her knuckles touched wood.

'You cannot imagine how relieved I am to see you, Anna Liese.'

'You are?'

Even after years of separation her smile felt familiar. It was as if a forgotten flicker of sunshine radiated from his heart.

'How wonderful,' she said.

Indeed, it was wonderful and he was awfully glad to see her.

It had been a disappointment when she had not joined them for breakfast in dining room of the village inn. The meal had become an ordeal with Mildred consuming his attention.

Whenever someone approached to make his acquaintance, she put herself to the fore, giving the impression that she was his close friend and anyone who came between was intruding. It had been beyond troublesome since he did wish to make the acquaintance of people in Woodlore Glen.

'I missed you at breakfast.' He swept his arm in a gesture, indicating she should come inside.

He wondered if she would be offended by the invitation given that they would be unchaperoned in the house. But neither of them was a blushing youth. Besides, since they had spent so much time together as children, to his mind this was not unfitting. Also, with the village over a mile away, strangers did not wander this way so no one would know.

'My cook is still in London so I cannot offer refreshment.' This said, she now knew they would be alone and could gracefully decline if she wished to.

With a nod, she stepped inside.

'Stepmama decided my time this morning would be better spent taking inventory of the pantry, or I would have come.' Her smile brightened the hall far better than the vase of green foliage he had placed on a table beside the front door.

Filling vases was not something he normally did, but his mother had always placed a display of seasonal colour in the hall. Just seeing it gave him the strangest feeling. Longing for her was all he could think it was. He had never got over missing his mother.

'What a lovely way to honour your mother,' Anna Liese said, pausing to touch a sprig of red berries.

His heart took a leap. It was as if in touching the berries, she touched his heart.

'I can scarcely believe you remember.'

'Berries and holly in the winter, daffodils in the

spring, roses in the summer, leaves in the autumn. How could I forget?'

'Filling the vase was my way of telling her I remember.'

Seeming at ease, Anna Liese walked ahead of him into the drawing room. It made sense that she would be comfortable in the cottage. Since she had been staying here, she was probably more familiar with it than he was.

'I have always loved this room, Peter.' She sat down on the sofa, spreading her cheerful-looking yellow skirt while glancing about with a smile.

Good, then.

He sat beside her, relieved that her casual attitude set the stage for their renewed friendship to develop naturally and not be stifled by societal rules. Rules such as having a chaperon in attendance at all times. As children, they had tended to ignore rules in favour of fun. Deep in his gut he felt they were still those children, that something remained of who they had been.

'Anna Liese, I must ask you something.' For some reason, she glanced away from him, staring at the rug as if the vined pattern were suddenly mesmerising. 'It has to do with why you were not at breakfast. One would think taking inventory of the pantry would be a job for the cook, not the daughter of the house.'

He could not imagine why, but his question restored her smile.

'You have no idea how offended Mrs Graham would have been had I tried. We passed the time speaking about her grandchildren. Did you know they are the brightest and most handsome children ever born?'

She laughed. The sound soothed the stress of the morning. Even as a small girl she had a way of settling him. How often had he been anxious about something, only to have the very look she was giving him now make the day better?

'I missed you, Anna Liese.' Until this moment he had not understood how deeply he had. Years had gone by without him thinking about her, and now? Now he regretted the years they missed. He ought to have asked his aunt and uncle if she might visit Cliverton.

'Would it have caused a great problem for you to ignore your stepmother and come to breakfast?'

He caught her hand, in a simple, friendly squeeze, but then had to release it. The touch of her warm, smooth fingers cupped in his palms was not all that simple. Indeed, the kick to his heart left him confused.

'It would, of course. My stepmother can become quite cross when her will is thwarted. I imagine Stepmama has rather grand plans for you and Mildred, so be forewarned.' She twirled a strand of hair around one, slim finger. He could not help but stare. It resembled silk around a maypole. How lovely that she did not wear it bound in some frivolous hairstyle. 'It wasn't because of her that I did not come, though. It was because of me. I chose not to join you.'

That statement was a dagger to the heart. He placed his hand flat on his chest in an exaggerated gesture of deflecting pain. Which he did truly feel.

'Oh, but I wanted to. Do not think I was not miserable all morning, imagining what you were suffering in the company of my family.'

'I must admit to being confused.'

'After I have made my confession and offered an apology, it will be clear.'

'I'm sure you have no need to—'

'Peter.' She touched his arm, looking him steadily in the eye. His heart kicked against his ribs.

Suddenly she blinked, sucking in a breath, as if touching him had been—well, he could not guess what she thought of the touch. To him it had felt comforting and exciting at the same time. And still confusing.

He might have also sucked in a sharp but discreet breath.

'Surely you recognise me as being the intruder in your bedroom?'

'I didn't at first, only later. How was I to know it was you? But why did you run away?'

'Because I did not recognise you, either. I thought you were—' Her voice faltered. Her cheeks flared bright pink.

'A pirate?'

'Something of the such.'

'We are a bit inland to be troubled by the likes of them.'

She waved her hand as if to dismiss that last odd bit.

'In the event, thank you for bringing my shoes and my cloak.'

'Why were you hiding in the haystack, Anna Liese? If you were afraid of me, why not simply go home?'

'I did go home eventually, once I was certain you were not coming back.'

'Surely you did not think I meant you harm?'

'Not harm in the usual sense of the word. Had I known who you were, it would have made a difference. I must say, my friend, you have changed a bit over the years.'

'So have you. Had I recognised you, I would have made sure you did not mistake me for a pirate.'

'Neither of us look a bit like we did then.'

For what seemed a long time, they stared silently at each other, no doubt each taking a moment to observe the differences brought by the years.

He admitted he liked the differences he was seeing. While she had grown to be an exquisitely beautiful woman, what did she think of him? He could not help but wonder. Outwardly they had changed—but inside? Pray there was enough of the friendship they used to share to begin again.

Now that he remembered how it had been between them—how she had been as dear to him as his own family—he wanted that again. It would be good to have a friend in Woodlore Glen, a place where he knew no one. There was the Baroness and her daughter, but—

'I don't mind that you were using my house,' he said. 'But I would like to know why you felt a need to.'

For as flattering as it would be to think she had been in his bedroom because she missed him, he doubted that was the case.

'Sometimes a lady has private reasons.' She glanced away when she said it, which made him wonder if she intended to reveal them.

Private was private—he would respect that and not press the matter. Her reasons were her own. Perhaps in time she would confide in him.

'Now that I have confessed my sin, you understand

why I could not join you for breakfast. I simply could not face you until there was only truth between us.'

'Think no more of it.' He would because he was intensely curious about her rather vague, private reasons. 'With that out of the way, I could use your help with something.'

Now that he thought about it, she might be a great help to him if she wished to be. Her eyebrows arched in what he hoped was interest. Her eyes flashed brighter blue and her smile—it was exactly the smile he remembered from when they used to find mischief to get into. Young Anna Liese had always enjoyed a bit of fun. It made him happy to know she had not lost that quality.

Although it was not mischief he had in mind, but work. She might not consider helping him renovate the cottage to be of interest.

'I want to revive this place.' He took in the drawing room with a sweep of his hand. 'The whole cottage needs renovating. I could use your advice.'

'Please say you are not renovating it in order to sell it, Peter. If you are, I must say no, I would rather not.'

'Why?'

She shrugged, looking thoughtful. 'I suppose it would feel as if you were selling a part of my past—giving it to strangers.'

'The tenants who lived here in the past were strangers.'

Even though the last thing he wanted was to sell the cottage, he did want to know what she was thinking.

'Only until I made their acquaintance. Over the years I felt that as long as you owned the property, you might return one day. And look, here you are.'

Now he felt like a cad. All this time, she been hoping for him to return, while he had assigned Woodlore Glen a place in the back of his mind. The idea that she had been thinking of him over the years—perhaps trying to keep his memory vivid by living in his house—made him feel something of a worm.

'I have no intention of selling. My past is here, too.' He stood up and walked to the wall. He tapped a finger on the image of a faded flower in the wallpaper. This was only one place the house looked dingy and sad, if a wall could look sad. 'What I plan is to bring my family here for holidays.'

'What a lovely idea.' Once again, the vine on the rug captured her attention. 'I did not hear that you had married. Have you children, too?'

'Not that sort of family. I realise I am late fulfilling my obligation to the marriage market, but I have been occupied with seeing my cousins settled first. Do you recall them? Cornelia, Felicia and Ginny?'

'They visited from time to time. I do remember them, of course. I enjoyed it when they came.'

'Now that I think about it, I remember wishing they would go home so that you and I might resume our romping.'

Anna Liese laughed, which made him feel odd—in a dizzy but pleasant way.

'I recall how I disliked it when you went to visit London. Romping on one's own is not nearly as much fun.'

'What I intend will not be as fun as a romp, but I hope you will help me turn the cottage into a holiday home, a getaway from London.'

'As much as I would enjoy helping you, I do have a concern.'

'I promise I will not occupy all of your time.'

'What I mean is that it must appear as if you are not occupying any of my time. If Stepmama and Mildred discover we spend time together, I cannot tell you the misery that will follow.'

'Because we will be unchaperoned... I do understand. The last thing I wish is to cause you trouble.'

'Chaperoned? Truly, I am not all that concerned about it. I am hardly a blushing, susceptible debutante. It is not me I am concerned about, Peter. It is you. They will make your life unbearable if they know. Believe me, they must never know we are meeting.'

'That adds some adventure to the prospect,' he noted, following her out of the drawing room. 'Clandestine meetings and secret plans.'

He opened the front door, feeling years younger. More carefree than he had been since—well, he could not remember when, but before his uncle died and left him as the new Viscount.

'Are you still an early riser, Peter?'

Knowing she remembered that about him made him warm and fuzzy. Many were the mornings he used to get to the bridge first, watching the sun crest the hilltops while waiting for Anna Liese to emerge from the manor.

'I still do my best work early in the morning.'

'It could work. My stepmother and Mildred sleep late so we will have time.'

He watched her walking away through a last drizzle of late autumn leaves. She had grown graceful over the years. He was certain in the old days that her hips had not swayed in such a manner.

All at once she turned, waved and grinned. For half a second he felt thrown back in time to the boy he had been, but in the next second, he realised her grin was not at all the same. Her lips were rounder, pinker and quite desirable.

Looking back was all very well, but, all things considered, the present was going to be more interesting.

Chapter Six

For as much as Anna Liese would prefer keeping out of the way of her relatives, at some point she would need to go inside the house. The wind was rising, sweeping in a mass of dark, stormy clouds.

Coming in the back door, then through the kitchen, she heard feminine voices issuing from the library. She could not determine what they were saying since the voices seemed to be trying to speak over one another.

Curious, she paused in front of the library door. Bolts of fabric in every imaginable hue and texture were strewn across sofas, chairs and half of the floor.

Anna Liese watched while Woodlore Glen's modiste, Mrs Creamer, held a bolt of fabric underneath Mildred's round chin.

'That colour makes you look ill,' Stepmama announced, dashing the other ladies' comments of approval.

Mildred frowned. Alice, Mrs Creamer's assistant, dropped the bolt on the floor with a thud while the modiste bit her lip.

Anna Liese did not envy the two women having to do business with Stepmama.

'What we need is a hue to bring a blush to Mildred's bosom. Chartreuse, I think.'

Stepmama never did have an eye for colour, nor was she able to discern the difference between what was becoming and what was ostentatious.

'If I may point out, my lady,' Mrs Creamer put in, 'the bosom should be hidden enough so that one does not know it is blushing. By raising the bodice, one raises the mystery of what is behind the bodice. If there is a blush, it is more properly displayed in the cheeks. Fabric colour can help with that. It can also enhance the eyes which are on display no matter the cut of the gown. Hold up the ivory, Alice.'

'I have chosen chartreuse, and chartreuse I shall have.' Next thing, Stepmama was going to stamp her foot and pout.

'As you wish, naturally, but I assure you that some skin tones call for bright shades and some for subtle.'

'Are you suggesting that Mildred is not attractive in both? Surely you must agree that wearing such a pale shade as ivory will cause my daughter to fade into the wallpaper. Our gentleman will not fail to notice her in the bright one.'

Oh, dear, poor Mildred would be seen, just not in the way the Baroness intended. Clearly it was what the dressmaker wished to point out, but did not dare. Speaking one's mind to Stepmama was rarely worth the ill temper sure to follow so the woman usually got her way.

Taking pity on them, Anna Liese entered the library, stepping carefully over rejected bolts of fabric. Hopefully, a new presence would change the mood in the room.

'Good afternoon,' she said, giving each woman a smile. 'New gowns? Are we having a grand event, Stepmama?'

'A small event, to welcome Viscount Cliverton to Woodlore Glen.'

'How thoughtful.' How calculating. 'When will it be?'

'Soon. Our Viscount returns to London before Christmas.'

'And I have not had a new gown since, oh, I cannot recall when,' Mildred said, casting a frown at Anna Liese as if, somehow, her presence interfered with it.

'Three weeks ago,' Anna Liese supplied helpfully.

'Yes!' Alice exclaimed. 'It was a lovely thing. Rose with ivory stripes. I remember because I spent until the wee hours sewing the hem.'

'It's an adequate gown,' Mildred admitted, pushing the another bolt away from her face. 'But now that we will be frequently entertaining Lord Cliverton, I will require something more elegant.'

Frequently? Peter was here only for a short time. Did they mean to commandeer every moment of it?

'Something chartreuse,' Stepmama persisted.

Anna Liese wondered if she had failed to notice the grimace which shot between Mrs Creamer and Alice.

The women had vast experience at dressing ladies and, in Anna Liese's opinion, they were wise to advise a colour other than bright, glaring green.

'I've a solution, perhaps. Stepmama, you are right

about the colour being beautiful and that Mildred will shine wearing it. However, taken all at once it is intense.' Anna Liese stooped to snatch up a bolt of fabric near her foot. 'What if we use this lovely cream lace for the body of the gown and accent it with a chartreuse border and sash?'

She swirled a swathe of lace in the lamplight to show off its sheen.

'That way Lord Cliverton will remark on how pretty Mildred is rather than how pretty the gown is,' she said, noticing a flash of hope cross Mildred's expression.

'Hmm…yes, then. I suppose that might do. Just be sure that you add chartreuse to the bodice. The pink of Mildred's maidenly blush will look outstanding with green.'

Oh, dear, poor Mildred and her blushing maidenly bosom. For all that she and her stepsister were not close—not even allies most of the time—she did feel sorry for her.

'And what colour gown shall we make for you, Anna Liese?' Mrs Creamer declared. 'It has been ever so long since we have designed one for you and you have the prettiest figure—I quite enjoy sewing your gowns.'

Glancing about with a smile, the dressmaker clearly did not notice Stepmama's scowl.

'Here we are!' Alice picked up a bolt of blue satin the shade of the sky on a summer afternoon. She draped it across Anna Liese's shoulder.

'Why, it does look stunning with your hair,' the designer pointed out.

'That one is for Mildred.' Even if Stepmama had

dismissed the fabric a moment ago, it was not to go to her stepsister.

'I look pitiful in blue, Mother—you know I do.'

'If you insist on having a new gown, Anna Liese, you may have the grey silk on that bolt in the corner.'

While the rest of them turned their attention to the creation of yet one more gown, Anna Liese quietly left the library. She was only steps down the hallway when Alice came after her.

'It is not a horrible shade of grey,' she whispered. 'And once I adorn it with what is left of the blue, you will hardly notice the grey at all.'

Anna Liese suspected Peter would not know the difference between a new gown and an old one, let alone which colour combinations worked. He was not the sort to entertain fashion as uppermost in his mind.

Since it was uppermost in Alice's mind, Anna Liese said, 'Thank you, Alice. I have no doubt it will be the most beautiful gown I own and a great credit to your skill.'

'It is my pleasure, Miss Barlow. I will make sure you are the loveliest lady at the Christmas ball.'

'Christmas ball? Are we to host a ball? I thought it was a welcome dinner.'

Alice must have realised she had revealed something she ought not to have because she blushed.

'Your stepmother discovered that Lord Cliverton is holding a Christmas ball in London. She is ordering gowns in anticipation of being invited. I fear I have said too much.'

'The Baroness will not hear it from me.'

With a nod, which seemed quite relieved, Alice returned to her duties in the library.

Anna Liese dashed upstairs to her bedroom where she intended to remain for the rest of the afternoon and evening. A Christmas ball in London? Peter should not have let that be known. He would not have a moment's peace until he added both Stepmama and Mildred to the guest list. As for Anna Liese? She was content not to attend a grand ball. She imagined London would be interesting, but Woodlore Glen was where she preferred to be.

Spending a rainy evening in her room, going over this idea and that for the cottage, seemed delightful to her. She was anxious to jot them down and picture the result in her mind. Also, to imagine Peter's smile when she offered her suggestions. A smile which was different from the one she recalled from their childhood years. While she had always been delighted in his boyish grin, she was now delighted and fascinated.

A flash of white light blazed beyond Anna Liese's eyelids. Lightning brought her from deep sleep to awareness.

Awareness of someone touching her hair!

Feeling the slight tug, hearing the bare whisper of the strands shifting between someone's fingers, she kept her eyes closed, feigning sleep. If this was an intruder bent on impugning her virtue, he smelled intensely of rosewater.

Mildred's preferred scent.

Thunder rolled over the roof, barely covering the

sound of a metallic click. Snip, snip, snip, she heard inches away from her ear.

Lurching out of bed, she saw her stepsister's face illuminated in another flare of lightning. Mildred's jaw fell open, her narrow eyes blinking as if she were confused to be standing in Anna Liese's chamber.

Anna Liese snatched the scissors from her hand. 'Were you going to cut my hair?'

'I suppose…' she stammered, an odd, startled look on her face. 'Yes, I did mean to. But…then you woke up.'

'Truly, Mildred?' Handing back the scissors, then gathering her hair into a hank, she extended it, calling her sister's bluff—hopefully calling her bluff. 'Here it is if you want it so badly.'

Mildred looked at the scissors, then glanced at the offering.

'What do you want it for?'

She let out a long sigh which sputtered her lips. 'I don't want it. But I don't want you to have it either.'

Mildred sat down hard on the bed, setting the scissors beside her on the mattress. Anna Liese sat down next to her.

'I realise we are not close, Mildred—but this? Did Stepmama tell you to do it?'

Mildred shook her head, silently denying it. 'Had I gone through with it, she would have had a raging fit. How would she explain such a scandal?'

'Do you think we might find some common ground? Trying to keep from being bullied by your mother, I mean?'

'It is true, Mama is a bully. But if she did not bully

you, I would be hidden in your pretty shadow. If she did not bully me, I would probably remain there. So, I will do what I can to marry to her wishes, in part to be away from her. What a wonder that the Viscount seems to have fallen neatly into my lap.' Mildred tapped her cheek in thought. 'But I wonder why you do not do the same—not with Lord Cliverton—but what is so awful about Mr Grant? The banker would have you.'

'I have no wish to marry him, but I thought you might.'

'Would it matter if I did? The man is smitten with me, of course, but he has no social position. Surely you see that our neighbour is a far better choice.'

'What about love?'

'What about it? Love can fade, but being Viscountess, that will last.'

This was by far the longest and most heartfelt conversation they'd had since they were small. Not friendly, but they were speaking of their feelings honestly.

Mildred started to stand, but Anna Liese caught her hand.

'Your mother is right, you know. You do have very pretty hair.'

'Mouse brown. It wants to go every which way regardless of how it is styled.' Mildred snorted. 'It is your hair everyone comments on. Light and sparkly as sunshine—it is enough to make one ill to be compared to you.'

Sadly, what she said was true. Thoughtless comparisons had been made over the years.

'Tell me something, Mildred. Do you think Isabella Haverton is beautiful?'

'Everyone says so. Yes, I think she is.'

'And yet she has no suitors. But look at Olivia Green—she is modest in beauty and yet has half a dozen men seeking her hand.'

'Please, do not preach to me that "beauty is only skin deep". Men are rather aware of beautiful skin.'

'It is true, some are shallow that way. What I was pointing out is that Olivia smiles and Isabella does not. Everyone responds to a smile.'

Mildred stood, grabbed the scissors and gripped them in her fist. 'I may not have your winning smile, but you, my dear sister, are every bit the spinster that I am.'

Evidently Mildred missed her point, or ignored it.

'You do have a winning smile! You simply need to use it.'

'Simply? Really, Anna Liese, what do I have to smile about with you sucking up all the attention?'

With that, Mildred stamped towards the bedroom door. Yanking it open, she stood for a moment. Thunder rolled over the roof and rain beat down hard. Her stepsister gave her a look, one which Anna Liese had never seen before.

'I apologise for nearly cutting your hair.' That said, she clicked the door closed behind her.

Stunned, Anna Liese sat on the bed blinking, her jaw in danger of an unladylike drop. While she could not pretend there was anything resembling friendship between them, they had spoken from their hearts. And this was the first time Mildred had ever apologised to her—or perhaps to anyone.

Although last night's rain continued to fall, Peter stood on the bridge, sheltering under a large black umbrella. He supposed it would have been more sensible to wait for Anna Liese inside, but for some reason he wanted to do it here, on the spot they used to meet as children, and at the time they used to meet.

Somewhere beyond these storm clouds the sun was rising. While he and Anna Liese had not assigned a precise time to meet, he hoped she would remember their schedule of old and come dancing out of the manor as she used to do.

Ah, just there! The door opened. Out she came, not dancing and twirling as in the past, but huddled under an umbrella and carrying a basket. Bless her if she had thought to bring breakfast. Once the rain stopped, he would need go to the village and buy a few things, then hope he could work out how to combine them into some sort of edible state.

Perhaps he would send a telegram, asking his cook to come and bring one or two of the maids. The cottage was large, having been an inn before his father purchased it, but not nearly big enough to summon more than those few. He was not sure that even those few could be spared with all the bustle of getting ready for the ball.

For all that he would like to have his cook here, he did not mind it being only him and Anna Liese this morning, especially if she was going to feed him.

Breathless from the dash over, she handed him the

basket. 'Good morning, Peter! I am bursting with ideas for your cottage. I can hardly wait to tell you of them.'

'Over breakfast.' Judging by the aroma lifting from the cloth over the basket, he was in for a treat. 'We can eat and talk if you don't mind.'

Her cheeks being nipped with cold looked pink and fresh. Excitement made her eyes bluer than he had ever seen them. 'I don't mind, but let's get out of the rain.' She was laughing when she said so. Some people complained about foul weather. As he recalled, young Anna Liese had never been a complainer. He was glad to find she still was not.

As anxious as he was to get a start on restoring the cottage, he was more anxious to get reacquainted with his neighbour.

By the time they reached the front door, Anna Liese's face was dotted with raindrops. She blinked dampness off her eyelashes. Suddenly breakfast was not as urgent as it had been. If he could, he would simply stand in the hall and watch her sparkle in the glow of the lamp he had left burning against the dimness of the morning.

Ah, but it was not to be because she folded her umbrella, then wiped her hand across her face.

'There is a fire in the drawing room hearth. Shall we have breakfast in there?'

She nodded, so he hurried to the drawing room, dragged over a small table and placed it in front of the fireplace. Then he carried over a couple of chairs.

He could not recall a time when the drawing room had looked cosier. The vision he had had of his old home was of it being homely and warm. This was just how he remembered it. Beginning with Christmas, this would be a happy spot for the family to gather, play games and laugh.

He was anxious to discover what Anna Liese's thoughts on it were. He hoped her taste did not run to the formal. Cliverton was formal in its common areas. He did not wish the same for the cottage since it was not meant to entertain the public.

Coming back to the hall, he slipped her coat from her shoulders, hanging it on a rack to drip and dry.

Anna Liese walked into the drawing room ahead of him which gave him a moment to simply look at her, watch how she moved with such grace and confidence.

As a child she had been confident, but her grace had been more of a gangly sort. Perfect for a child, but now she was—

'This is lovely, Peter, so warm and inviting. It's this area which has been on my mind all night.' She withdrew a sheet of paper from a pocket of her skirt. 'I have made notes on my thoughts.'

She'd made notes? Part of the reason he had asked for her help—a great part—was because he wanted an excuse to spend time with her, to get to know her again.

'Are you certain you do not feel awkward being here without a chaperon? Society would frown on this meeting.'

'Society is in London. The only ones who will care about it here are asleep and will not know.'

'If you are certain.'

'I would not be here if I were not. Let us speak no more about it.'

That would suit him since he was finding it difficult to recognise that their relationship should change from what it had been.

Sitting across from her, he could not help watching her hands while she unwrapped their breakfast from the napkins, such slim, graceful hands, lyrical in their movement. He nearly chuckled aloud at himself. He was not usually as poetic as to make up mental odes to long, lovely fingers, or to anything else. What he must keep in mind was that her reason for being here was practical, to be a helpful neighbour.

Nothing more.

If he forgot that, began to wonder about the way her lips had grown fuller and her slim little figure was no longer so slim, he ran the risk of feeling things he refused to feel. Risk a sort of grief he refused to feel again.

While it could not be denied that Anna Liese had grown to be an exquisitely beautiful woman, she was and would continue to be his neighbour, his pretty and ever-helpful neighbour.

'I appreciate your help. And breakfast. It was kind of you to think of bringing it.'

She smiled while spreading jam on toast. 'That is to Mrs Graham's credit. She rose in the wee hours to prepare it—all I did was put it into this basket.'

'Wasn't Mrs Graham here when we were children? As I recall, she used to pack us bags of biscuits for our daily romps.'

'She was. A few of the staff you knew are still here.'

'It was good back then, wasn't it?' He thought about it for a moment, during which he forgot about the clotted cream piled on his spoon. 'Your family and mine got along so well. We were lucky, I think. Not everyone is as blessed as we were with our families.'

'It is because we had parents who loved one another. It makes all the difference in a child's life. I have lived it both ways, Peter, so I know of what I speak.'

Recalling the clotted cream ready to plop from his spoon, he spread it on a scone.

'I'm sorry that your father did not find joy in his second marriage. I think, perhaps, you did not find joy in it either.'

'Papa married because he was lonely and Stepmama gave every appearance of being the answer to his sadness. He did not recognise that she only married him because he was titled.'

'It's not uncommon to wed for social position.' He would be doing it soon, after all. 'Such a thing does not exclude a satisfactory marriage.'

Indeed not. He reaffirmed his stance that it was better to wed for satisfaction rather than to invest one's heart in a wife who could be ripped from him in death.

'That is all well and good if one wishes to settle for satisfactory. But, Peter, you and I have seen what a happy marriage is. We have experienced the affection when a family is founded upon it.'

'One does not always have a choice.' Or might wish to choose a safer way.

'Of course one does and I have made it. I refuse to marry for any reason but love.'

'I cannot imagine that there have not been dozens of men in love with you over the years, Anna Liese.'

'Not as many as you might think—besides, there was never one whom I was in love with.'

'You've never been in love?'

She blinked, then glanced away.

'Perhaps once.' She shooed her fingers as if she did not wish to discuss a former swain. 'What about you? Have you been in love? I would think dozens of ladies would be infatuated with you.'

'With my title only. As I said, I haven't pursued marriage because I felt it best to see my cousins wed first.'

'I hope you did not force them into anything. A woman ought to be able to choose her course.'

'As if I could force them into anything. Of them only Cornelia wed at a proper pace. Felicity rushed headlong into a marriage arranged for her when she was a child. You will be happy to know I did not force her into it, but rather advised caution. She and her husband are in love. Then Ginny! Do you happen to recall how shy she was?'

'She did cling to your mother's skirts rather than play with us.'

'She eloped with her childhood sweetheart, a fellow she had not seen in years. I missed the wedding.'

She tapped her lovely, slender finger on the table for a moment, then said, 'I am happy for them all. Perhaps you will be as lucky one day and find a wonderful stranger to love.'

He would guard against it. Better to find an acceptable stranger to admire—to respect. For all that his cousins had married for love, he most fervently prayed they did not live to regret the risk to their hearts.

'More than likely it will be a proper marriage to a proper lady. As Viscount, I do not see myself indulging in a grand passion in my search for a wife.'

Rain beat on the windows while they ate in silence. Clearly their expectations for marital bliss were not the same. If his cousins were here in the room, they would tell him, *Peter, you must not close off your heart to love.* That was exactly what they would say. He nearly glanced about to see if they were here.

'If you wish to fill this home with the joy it used to have, you will need happy children which come from a happy marriage.'

'I didn't say I would not have a happy marriage, only that it was not likely to begin with a mad passion.' For a second, he looked at her lips where she licked a smear of jam from her finger, wondering if he should say what was truly on his mind. Since she was comfortable enough to do so, he said, 'I hope you do not live a lonely life because you refuse to settle for anything less than a mad passion.'

'I hope for exactly that, Peter.' And then she grinned at him. 'Now, how many people do you anticipate gathering in this room? With the way your cousins are so happily wed, I expect there will be plenty of children. It seems to me you will need more sofas.'

Sharing a modest breakfast in front of the drawing room fireplace with Peter had been better than a feast. They had shared more than mere food. To simply sit with him in quiet conversation, to discuss ideas for the redecoration of his cottage, was simply bliss.

Beginning the day knowing that tomorrow they would go the village to hire a painter, and visit the carpenter to make some furniture, made the day bright.

Even the weather seemed to be reacting to her mood.

Walking over the bridge, she watched rainclouds scatter, revealing bright blue patches of sky. Still, it was chilly and the breeze stiff.

Hurrying in the front door, she came face to face with Stepmama, who was scowling at her.

'And where have you been, miss?'

'Visiting my friend.'

Stepmama's face flushed and the tip of her nose pulsed the bright red shade it took when she was angry.

'You must under no circumstances visit Lord Cliverton!'

'The Viscount? I was spending time with my goose.' It was partly the truth. Fannie had been there waiting for her when she stepped out of the cottage. 'We took a short walk together. It was brisk and lovely.'

'I'm sure it was, although I do not understand how one can form a friendship with something which is not even human.'

'We should get a dog, Stepmama. A pup will teach you how it is entirely possible.'

The Baroness snorted. 'Absolutely not. I have no wish to make friends with the fleas and ticks which come with a dog.'

Mildred had wanted a dog desperately when she was a child, but had been refused repeatedly.

'I require your help with something, my dear.' Oh, no. What was the woman up to now? 'You have such lovely penmanship and I need you to write out the invitations to our modest dinner to honour Lord Cliverton. Come to the library.'

She sat down at the secretary, quickly jotting down the details of the invitations as Stepmama recited them.

Then she made note of the names to go on the invitations.

To her surprise, it really was a smallish gathering with only about twenty people invited. How interesting to note that there were no young ladies among the guests. When she thought about it further, she realised it was not surprising after all. Stepmama would not want any young lady to compete for Peter's attention except Mildred.

'The guest list seems unbalanced, Stepmama.' It was bound to be embarrassingly apparent why. 'Perhaps you should add Lord Hampton and his family.'

'Lord Hampton has two eligible daughters, both of them quite lovely.'

She heard the quiet rustle of fabric coming from the hallway. Glancing up, Anna Liese spotted the hem of her stepsister's gown barely visible where it peeped out from behind the frame.

'But you have no need to worry. They are not as pretty as Mildred is,' she said because her stepsister had to be feeling cut by her mother's words. 'Their presence will only serve to show her off.'

She would like to point out that in the event Stepmama managed to secure invitations to Peter's Christmas ball, there would be many lovely ladies in attendance and every one of them with matrimony on her mind.

Not that she could point such a thing out, since she was not supposed to know about the ball. Peter had not even mentioned it to her. Perhaps the reason he had not was because Woodlore Glen seemed a thousand miles away from London and his mind was not on the matters of Cliverton.

But for all that London seemed so distant, in truth it was an easy train ride which took less than half a day. The distance she was thinking of had more to do with the way life was lived. The peace of Woodlore Glen must be vastly different than the bustle of a London street. Although she could not say for certain, having never been to London.

'I'm looking forward to our little gathering,' Anna Liese said even though she assumed, when the time came, she would not be in attendance. Her stepmother would find a way to make sure she was not. 'What a nice way for the Viscount to become acquainted with our neighbours.'

Having said that, she knew that between now and then she would need to be wary. Just because Mr Grant had not succeeded in trapping her the other night did not mean he would stop trying. Although he was as handsome as the day was long, she did not believe him to be patient, let alone honest. He was a shifty-eyed fellow of low moral character, in her opinion.

Now that she had lost her hiding place, she must be more cautious than ever.

'Have them ready by morning.' Stepmama started to go out of the library, but stopped just outside the doorway. Apparently Mildred was no longer standing in the hallway. 'I would have Mildred help you, but we are dining at the inn tonight with Lord Cliverton.'

'How lovely. Please give Peter my regards.'

'Really, Anna Liese! You must not call him Peter, Lord Cliverton is the appropriate address.'

'But we have known each other since we were quite small,' she answered without looking up. 'He will think it odd if I call him that.'

'Nevertheless, you will address him by his title.'

When they met in the morning, she was going to call him Peter and it would feel the most natural thing in the world.

'You are correct, of course,' she answered.

It was unlikely that Stepmama was pacified by her apparent acquiescence. Indeed, no more than Anna Liese was fooled into believing that when her stepmother used the words 'my dear' it was a term of endearment.

The woman was cunning and, no doubt about it, Annaliese's freedom from matrimony depended upon which of the two of them, was more cunning.

Chapter Seven

A gust of wind whistled past the window of the village tearoom, making the table beside it seem snug. Peter was grateful that the place opened so early for tea and light breakfast.

He and Anna Liese would be finished before the layabeds at Maplewood roused themselves. The last thing he wished was to cause Anna Liese trouble for helping him.

'Christmas is coming,' Peter remarked. 'One can nearly smell it in the air.'

'Only three more weeks.' Anna Liese's smile made him feel as cheerful as the morning sunshine streaming through the lace curtain. 'Soon the shops will be putting holly and berries in the windows. Do you remember that?'

He did! It came back to him how cheerful everything had felt at this time of year. There had always been the anticipation of a visit from Father Christmas which made everything sparkle.

'Holly and mistletoe?' Joy and carols. 'I do remember now. I kissed your hand under the mistletoe once.'

'I remember it, too! Our parents were looking on, laughing at how sweet we were.'

'Sweet? I felt mischievous.'

'For us back then, mischief was sweet.'

The waitress carried a tray to their table, setting down two cups of hot chocolate along with a vase of holly and berries.

'It's as if you summoned Christmas cheer, Anna Liese.'

She tapped a red berry nestled in the greenery with the tip of one finger. 'Abracadabra.'

Her quiet laugh sounded like Christmas bells. There he went being poetic again, which was not like him in the least. Next thing, he was going to pluck that sprig of holly and place it in the buttonhole of his coat.

He had not anticipated feeling particularly festive this year. Not with the obligation of finding a viscountess pressing upon him. Especially not with his cousins off and married, leaving Cliverton absent of family. Yet here he sat, feeling light-hearted. It could only have to do with the woman sitting across from him.

'May I tell you something, Anna Liese?' He did not wait for her answer. 'I've missed our friendship more than I ever realised.'

He caught her hand, giving it a friendly squeeze. His heart rolled over at the feel of her hand squeezing back. He should not touch her. It never turned out to feel as casual as he meant it to be. If she had not been blushing when she lifted her cup of chocolate, he might have been able to breathe.

'To lost friendship being rekindled,' she said, lifting her mug in salute.

He picked up his cup in answering salute, took a sip of warm, rich sweetness, unable to deny that it was how she made him feel. Warm and sweet.

'Who could have imagined that choosing wallpaper and paint would be amusing?' he said, steering the conversation to the practical.

'We shall see about that. We might yet come to blows over whether the drawing room wallpaper should be green or yellow.'

'Blue.' Because that would remind him of her eyes. He suspected blue was becoming his favourite colour.

'Blue might be—'

A movement caught his eye. A gentleman pedalled industriously past the window on a bicycle.

'Come, Anna Liese!' He stood up, reached across the table and snatched her hand.

'Sit down, Peter. I see the waitress coming with our food.'

'I'll ask her to pack it up in a basket.'

'But—'

'Look!' He pointed across the street at the village shop. 'It is opening up.'

'As it usually does this time of morning.'

'But do you see what is in the window? Come, we are going cycling.'

Half an hour later, Anna Liese was the proud owner of a bicycle which she had no idea what to do with.

'You expect me to sit on this?' Not likely. 'I'll tip over.'

'Trust me, I won't let you fall.'

That remained to be seen, but at least they were on the little-travelled path which meandered around the outside of the village so if she did fall no one was likely to witness it. Still, she would rather remain upright.

'Ha! Like the time I was carrying a basket of eggs and you said you would not let me fall off the skinny plank crossing the stream? You said "trust me" then, too.'

'Did I?' He looked puzzled while he seemed to be searching for the memory. He shrugged, apparently not recalling the mess the basket of broken eggs had made. 'This time you can trust me. Watch this.'

With a great grin he mounted his new bicycle, then rode about in front of her, manoeuvring expertly in large circles, then small ones, cutting a figure-of-eight shape, and how proud of himself he seemed while riding backwards.

'It's easy.' He grinned.

Responding to his enthusiasm was easy, but getting on that risky, wheeled vehicle, that did not appear easy.

'For you. You're a member of a bicycle club and are clearly accomplished at dashing about. I am more confident of getting from here to there on my feet.'

He set his bike against a tree.

'Here, I'm going to help you.'

He held the bike steady. She could hardly refuse to try it even though she was certain to fail.

'No need to look so frightened. This is not one of those old-fashioned vehicles. It has pneumatic tyres. They are filled with air. It's a Rover bicycle with a chain drive.'

'I'm sure that is impressive, and I am grateful for the gift, but, Peter—' Suddenly the bike rolled.

She screeched, then grabbed his arms where they firmly steadied the contraption. It was on her tongue to demand he let her off, but then that would mean she would no longer feel his arms braced about her. They felt too strong and reliable to be let go of. Oh, but they were more than that. The strength made her feel excited as much as—no, more than—safe. She wanted nothing more than to lean into them and sigh.

'I won't let go until you have the hang of it.'

For all that she feared it, she thought perhaps she would not rush to learn the skill.

Being so close, she felt his breath near her cheek, heard air rushing in and out of his lungs as he trotted alongside her. She took a deep, discreet sniff. Beside her was a man, one who was not a thing like the boy she remembered. She knew the boy quite well, but who was this man he had grown into?

In truth, he was a stranger, one who at the moment held her life in his hands and was laughing over the fact. After years of waiting and watching for his return, she could scarce believe it had happened, that he actually here. Perhaps this was a dream and when she fell off the bicycle she would wake up, startled and alone.

'Are you beginning to feel your balance?'

Quite the opposite. What she felt was off balance. A woman would need to be made of marble to not react to the heat pulsing from his body.

Balance, indeed!

'I'm not meant for this,' she gasped in the instant he let go.

'You've got it!' he shouted while chasing after her.

She imagined he was waving his arms madly and whooping, but she did not dare to turn her head and look. Being on a downhill slope, she could not stop even had she wanted to, which she quite desperately, did.

But then—

Suddenly, amazingly, she did feel her balance. Oh, what a grand sensation! It was as if she were flying. She had never moved so fast in her life. She was like a bird winging joyfully along.

Until something jerked. Oh, no! The safety bike with its air-filled tyres hit a stone. The handlebars wobbled madly. The next she knew she was sitting on top of a pile of leaves and twigs, her arms and legs every which way, her skirt tangled about her knees and her petticoat exposed.

Peter was bent over at the waist, hands on his knees while laughing his noble head off.

'You did splendidly, Anna Liese.'

'I am lying in a bramble patch, in case you have not noticed.' In truth, it was not a bramble patch, merely a shrub. However, something sharp was poking her rump.

Rather than helping her up, Peter sat down next to her. 'I can't tell you how many times I've ended up just like this.'

'You could not have! Otherwise, you would not choose to get on that thing again.'

'Tell me the truth, Anna Liese. You felt liberated, like you were flying.'

She turned her face away, silent because he was correct and she did not wish for him to know he was.

His fingers touched her chin, turned it so that she could do nothing but look into his eyes.

'Admit it, my friend. You had fun.'

What she would admit was that she was happy he had not lost his playful nature over the years.

'Many things are fun which do not involve breaking one's neck in a fall.'

'Hmm, broken, is it?'

Boldly, he reached under her tangle of hair, touching the back of her neck, making slow, gentle circles with his fingers.

'It does not feel broken to me.'

Emotions crowded her throat, making it swell to the point she felt she might weep. Peter, her Peter, not a lofty viscount, sat beside her in the shrub, teasing her, laughing at her. Life, as it used to be before their parents died and her father remarried, clicked neatly into place. Nothing was different than it had been back then. The realisation brought her close to tears.

And yet, everything was different.

He was a man, she was a woman. Years ago, young Anna Liese would have flopped back on the ground, giggling and laughing at the sky.

Right this moment, she wondered what she would do if she did flop back. Would she grab Peter's shirt front, drag him down, so that she gazed into his eyes instead of the sky?

She might.

His fingers stilled, then moved around to her throat, his thumb rested on the spot where her pulse raced. If, in the weeks to come, they happened to pause under a sprig of mistletoe, she feared she would not settle for a mischievous kiss to her hand.

'Are you nervous, Anna Liese? You really must get back on the bicycle. It is the golden rule of cycling.'

The actual golden rule was of a 'do unto others' nature.

What she would have him 'do unto her' right now was kiss her. It was bold, but true, none the less. Did it now follow that she ought to kiss him?

She leaned forward, into the press of his fingers on her neck. Would he be stunned? Or would he—?

Oh, he would. Heat from his mouth skimmed hers. She could almost feel his lips, although they hovered just beyond a kiss.

'My dear Miss Barlow,' said a snide, unwelcome voice. 'I trust you are not being assaulted by this gentleman?'

Of all the wicked timing. The fellow must have come upon them while on his way to open the bank.

'If I were being assaulted, you would be aware of it, Mr Grant. I would not be sitting here involved in a pleasant conversation. I would screech and defend myself against any unsavoury and any unwise person to attempt such a thing.'

'Conversation, was it?'

Peter stood, helped her to her feet.

'This gentleman is my dear friend. He is teaching me to ride a bicycle.'

'An odd way to do it if you ask me.' Mr Grant's dark skinny brow inched up in his forehead. 'You must realise that many people consider bicycling an unladylike pursuit. Perhaps you need a proper friend who will not lead you to behave in questionable behaviour.' How anyone could put such a sneer on the word 'friend' was beyond her. 'One who will instruct you in respectable behaviour. Come now, I shall escort you home.'

He reached for her. Peter clamped his hand around the banker's wrist.

Hmm, what appeared to be a handshake hid a warning. At least Anna Liese suspected it did.

'You seem to admire respectable behaviour, sir, and yet you have failed to introduce yourself.' Peter sounded every bit the Viscount and not at all the boy she remembered. 'Allow me to introduce myself. I am Viscount Cliverton. And you are?'

A change came over Hyrum Grant's face. A mask of civility fell deceitfully into place.

Peter's answering smile was equally pleasant. No doubt he had been trained in false civility when he came to his title.

'Lord Cliverton! What a pleasure it is to make your acquaintance. I have been anxious to ever since I heard of your arrival. I do hope you will consider my bank for your financial needs.'

With a curt nod, Peter dismissed Hyrum Grant, took her hand and helped her to stand.

'I am certain you will find my establishment on a par with the best in London.'

'Come, Anna Liese, let us resume your lessons.'

They were silent while walking the path away from the village. There was one thing on her mind and it was not the banker or bicycling.

It was Peter and the kiss he had nearly given her, or

she had given him. She was not sure whose idea it had been, but was certain that had they not been interrupted they would both have been quite involved in it. At that point it would not have mattered whose idea it was.

Was he thinking of what might have been? She could not tell, and the silence was stretching uncomfortably.

'If I were you, I would not trust that man with a penny of my money, Peter,' she said because someone must say something.

'It is you I do not trust him with.'

He nodded at her bike, indicating she should mount.

She sighed. It truly had been great fun before she had spilled into the bushes and Hyrum Grant had made his intrusive appearance to ruin it all.

The bike began to move slowly along, she pushed her feet on the pedals, but not so quickly as to outpace Peter gripping the back of her seat.

'I would have a care about that man, Anna Liese. I have a bad feeling about him.'

'He is not one you would wish to encounter alone at night.'

'Did you think I was him that first night when I burst in upon you?'

'Him, or someone like him.'

'I'm sorry. I had no idea who you were that night or why you were there. If I had, I would have made sure you stayed.'

'Peter! Really, you could not have. Woodlore Glen might not be London, but it would have been a great scandal if it came to light that we spent the night alone in the same house. It is one thing to travel about without a chaperon, but that would be something else! Your reputation would be tarnished.' She cast him a sidelong smile. 'You may let me go now.'

He held on a moment longer. She thought he wished to say more on the subject. She did not.

Then he let go. Off she went, peddling down the path, Hyrum Grant forgotten, near-kiss remembered and her happy mood restored.

In order to return to the cottage by a ridable path, they were forced to pedal past Maplewood. Hopefully, no one was peering out a window. Still, it was early and they were likely to be safe.

Crossing the bridge, the stones were uneven and she nearly toppled. She did not, though, and felt emboldened by her newfound skill. Upon rising this morning, she would never have imagined she would learn such a thing.

'Thank you so much for this, Peter. I cannot recall when I have had more fun. Do you mind if keep my bicycle at the cottage?'

'Naturally not, but is there some reason you cannot take it with you?'

'It is for the best that Stepmama does not know.'

'Why? What would happen if she did know?'

She would rather not reveal how her stepmother treated her. Becoming submissive in order to avoid a temper tantrum was not much of a character quality. Along with it she had become an interesting mix of clever and wary. What she was not was who she used to be. Before she had come to dread her stepmother's bad moods, she had been brave. Brave enough to face down grief and come out smiling.

In her heart she felt this man was the Peter she remembered, her best friend and companion and that his opinion of her would not change if he knew. But he was also Viscount Cliverton and she knew nothing of him in that role. He had been gone from her life far longer than he had been in it, after all.

In dealing with Hyrum Grant, Peter's rank had been clearly on display. At that moment she had wondered if she knew him at all. Who was this man she did not completely know? Surely there were things about him she did not know just the same as there were things he did not know about her.

But then, just as quickly, the years fell away again, the Peter and Anna Liese of old as fast friends as they had ever been.

'She might feel that Mildred has been slighted and fall into a mood. If that happens, we will all be miserable.'

Should she let him know how badly Stepmama meant to have him for Mildred? That behind the friendly smiles and invitations it was all trickery? Or reveal that if Stepmama knew they were spending time together she would redouble her efforts to get Anna Liese out of the way?

She had hinted at what they wanted, warned him to be wary, but he could not know who those women were at heart. What they would stoop to in order to get what they wanted.

'There is more to it than you are telling me.' Peter leaned his bicycle against a tree trunk, then took hers, putting it next to his. 'How can I help?'

How good it would be to lean into his arms, to unburden her heart by revealing to him how her life at

Maplewood really was. She knew that her young friend would not judge her, but a viscount? How could she know for certain what his opinion would be?

Her secrets were humiliating. Any woman with a backbone would stand up to Stepmama, not run and hide the way she had been doing ever since she was thirteen years old.

'When my stepmother gets into one of her moods, no one can help.' She shrugged. 'But if you wish to wed my stepsister that would cure her of it.'

She found she was holding her breath, wondering what his reaction to that would be.

'While I will have to marry someone soon, I do not—'

Discussing his potential marriage made her feel rather sick at heart. Now that she was looking back, she recalled how she believed it would be the two of them getting married and living happily ever after. She had been as certain of it as sunrise, as the coming of Father Christmas and of ending each day in song.

Those carefree days had been so innocent. She would never have dreamed then that life could rip the joy out of one's heart.

'I will see you in the morning, my friend. We will make a decision on the wallpaper.'

With that she dashed across the bridge. It really was for the best that he did not know to what villainy Stepmama would sink. He did not need to know how desperately the Baroness wished to be rid of her.

It would be humiliating if he knew that she, the Baron's true daughter, was treated so disrespectfully and in her own home. A home which she intended to keep no matter what.

The girl he had known would never stand for such effrontery. Of course, the girl he had known had been adored by her family. For all that she wondered if he was the boy he had been, she thought he might not find her to be the girl she had been.

Halfway home, she nearly stopped to weep. She had thought herself clever by outwitting Stepmama. What she ought to have been doing was standing her ground and Maplewood was her ground! All at once, she missed the Anna Liese of old. That girl had disappeared so gradually she had failed to notice the change.

If only she could always feel as free as she had a short time ago, whizzing along the path on her gleaming new bicycle. She had not felt so carefree since she was a small girl, basking in Mama and Papa's love.

It was decided. Blue wallpaper for the drawing room.

He and Anna Liese had bicycled to the village tearoom, had breakfast while arguing between yellow and blue decor, then had gone to the village shop and placed the order for what they needed.

Peter supposed it was time to send a wire asking for his cook and one of the housemaids to come to Woodlore Glen. If his cook was in residence, he would have no reason to have breakfast in the village with Anna Liese each morning. This was a routine he had grown fond of.

He could honestly say he enjoyed her company as much now as he had when he was a child. Clearly, she kept secrets. Something was going on beyond her stepmother's ill temper, but unless she wished to speak of it there was little he could do to help her.

This afternoon he would concentrate on what he could do: make a trip to the village and hire a crew to clean the cottage. Before he could move ahead with new paint and wallpaper, everything needed a good scrubbing. He wished Anna Liese would join him, although she never did at this time of day. He could not help but wonder what she did in the afternoon.

Plucking his coat from the hall tree, he shrugged into it. The days were getting colder and the nights frigid. Opening the front door, he found himself looking into Mildred's face. Her blank expression bloomed suddenly into a smile. With a lift of her elbow, she brought his attention to the basket draped over her arm.

'Good afternoon, Lord Cliverton.' Quite boldly she took a step forward as if she would enter his house uninvited.

He blocked her way, which she might interpret as being rude, but he did not intend to be alone with her inside his cottage. He would hope to have a bit more choice in a marriage partner than being forced by scandal. Indeed, he had a couple of weeks until he needed to direct his attention to marriage and he intended to enjoy them. Enjoy them in the company of Anna Liese, not her stepsister, insofar as he could avoid it.

'Good afternoon, Mildred.'

'Oh, it is sunny and lovely, my lord.'

Sunny, yes, but it was more cold than lovely. He hoped to make it to the village and back before it turned bitter.

'I just stopped by to see if you would care to share a

pie with me. We have had so little time to get to know one another without being interrupted by this and that. The manor is a beehive now with all the preparation going on for your welcome dinner.'

He was rather stuck with sharing the pie, he supposed. Although he was not going to allow her to put one foot across his threshold.

'Shall we take a walk along the stream?' he asked, offering a polite smile while inwardly grimacing.

'How lovely, perhaps we shall find a nice quiet place to sit.'

It would need to be got out of the way quickly since it was the worst weather for sitting outside.

They had not walked far before Mildred spotted a place near the bank which was more secluded than he would have liked. Since she sat down, he did not know what else to do but sit beside her. Unfortunately, this spot gave a clear view of the cottage's back porch where the bicycles were stored. Since she seemed to be engrossed by the contents of the basket, she might not wonder why there were two of them.

He found he did not need to worry about keeping up his side of the conversation since she flitted from subject to subject with him only needing to nod occasionally while huddling in his coat.

Apparently having run out of topics, she sat in silence, shivering.

'Silly me,' she murmured while sidling closer to him. 'Rushing outdoors and forgetting to bring a coat.'

Silly or calculated, he had to wonder.

'I will escort you home.'

He began to rise, but she lunged for him. He leaned out of the way. Unable to stop her momentum, she landed face first on the grass. Rolling onto her back, she covered her eyes with her forearm, then reached her other hand towards him to be helped up.

The last thing he was going to do was touch this woman, if only she had not started to whimper. What was he to do now? He was nearly certain she intended to entrap him, but he could hardly walk away and leave her like this.

Staring at her, he was surprised when someone tapped his elbow. Jerking his gaze sideways, he sighed with relief.

Anna Liese. Thank goodness!

She pressed one finger to her lips, indicating for him to remain silent. He nodded. Anna Liese grasped her stepsister's hand and began to draw her up.

'Oh, my lord, you must not touch me,' she wailed, eyes pinched closed. 'I will be compromised for certain.'

'Do not fear, Mildred. Your virtue remains,' Anna Liese declared, shooting Peter a wink. Her playful expression made him want to laugh, though he thought it was best to refrain.

Mildred gasped and yanked her hand out of Anna Liese's. Scrambling up, she glowered at her 'rescuer'. Snapping her skirts into place, she settled her gaze upon him.

'Well, I must say it is a lucky thing she came along—from wherever it was she came from—who can say what might have happened. We must be more cautious in the future, my lord.' With a sniff, she snatched up the basket and hurried away.

'I cannot say how grateful I am that you happened along.'

'The truth is, I didn't happen along. I saw Mildred coming over and predicted you would be in peril. Good friend that I am, I followed.'

'You are a good friend, the best I ever had.'

All at once, he had the strongest urge to kiss her, this time really do it, not hover close to her mouth in delightful hesitation. Her smile, the humour shining in her eyes and the way the breeze caught her hair and blew it softly across her mouth…

His racing heart was engaged in battle with his mind which was urging him, quite strongly, not to act on the delicious impulse. He should not, not if he wished to avoid the risk of ruining the friendship growing between them. Their bond was renewing, but it was still fragile. He did not wish to make a great blunder.

Yesterday he had acted rashly in nearly kissing her. All things considered it was a lucky thing that that Preston chap had interrupted. Anna Liese was important to him. He did not want to lose her again.

It had nearly done for him years ago. So much loss—his fear of losing her again so great that he had refused to come and visit. He had shut her out without realising it, built a wall against future loss. Now here it was, tumbling down all about him.

What kind of cad would he be to kiss Anna Liese, knowing he would soon be proposing to someone else, whoever that someone might be?

A whisper tiptoed through his mind so quickly he nearly missed it. *Why not marry Anna Liese?* it suggested. They did get along well and had since they were children. Perhaps it would not be a love match, but he had not expected one—not wanted one. Not at the risk of exposing his heart to pain.

The question was, what did she expect of marriage? Love? A grand passion? Is that what she was waiting for and so had yet to wed?

He had never considered such a thing for himself. Having never experienced anything more than affection for the women he had been attracted to, he did not believe he was destined for grand passion. Was afraid of it, even.

As he looked at Anna Liese, feeling a distinct softening of his heart, it was getting harder to remember that it was better to wed a stranger whose affection did not matter greatly.

'Let this be a warning, Peter. You must be wary. I have reason to know that my stepmother and stepsister will do whatever they feel they need to in order to win you.'

'How do you know it?' he asked, even though after what had just occurred, he had a good idea.

Were they doing something to Anna Liese was the question on his mind? Perhaps the Baroness's moods were not at the heart of what troubled his friend.

He took her hand, cupped it in both of his. Far from the kiss he wanted, the feel of her soft warm fingers went straight to his heart.

'Good afternoon, Peter,' she whispered softly, backing away from him. 'I will see you tomorrow.'

He watched her go home over the bridge. Was his presence here putting her in some sort of danger? If so, he would discover what it was. The last thing he was going to allow was for her to suffer for being his friend.

Chapter Eight

Three days had passed without a visit from Anna Liese.

Peering out of the window this morning, he hoped today would not make day four. While he understood it was unreasonable to expect to take up her time every morning, breakfast without her was lonely. Beginning the day seeing her smile, hearing her laugh, set a positive mood for the rest of it.

Without Anna Liese the past few days had dragged by.

The cleaning team had been here and the cottage smelled as fresh as it looked. The past few days had also served to remind him how much he disliked living alone. Home was meant to be filled with bustle and noise. One could only revisit ghosts of the past for so long before one longed for actual company.

The company of one friend, in particular.

With Christmas getting closer—was it really little more than a fortnight away?—he longed for company more than ever. Yesterday the village had looked festive with fir boughs and garlands made of shiny red beads decking every window. And there had been carollers singing on a street corner. Anna Liese would have loved listening to them.

With the weather cold and uncomfortable, he had listened to only one song before he hurried home. Had his friend been singing, he would have lingered for an hour despite the chill settling in.

At least once his staff of two arrived, it would be more acceptable for Anna Liese to visit him here, indoors where it was warm. She had yet to see the cottage freshly scrubbed. Given that she had been involved in the renovation from the beginning, he thought she would be pleased to see it shine.

He ought not to spend too long staring across the bridge at the mansion's front door. What he needed to do was send another telegram home. Also, he had got word that the paint and wallpaper he had ordered were ready to be picked up from the village shop.

Surely Anna Liese would not wish to be left out of seeing their plan for the cottage come to fruition. But where was she? It was unlike her to miss their mornings together. By the looks of the weather, it would soon be raining so he ought to be on his way.

As he stepped outside, it occurred to him that she might be ill and that was the reason he had not seen her. He ought to pay a visit and find out.

Then again, after what she'd had to say about the ladies' aspirations, he hesitated. It would do Anna Liese no good to have them believe he was singling her out for attention, which is what he would be doing because, when it came down to it, Anna Liese's needs were foremost in his mind.

Ah, just then the door opened and she stepped outside. Crossing the bridge, she looked as healthy as a sunray. He was certain she was singing but could not determine what the tune was. She stopped when the goose waddled towards her, then bent to pet it.

After she crossed the bridge, she turned aside, walked down a path, then out of his view. When she reappeared, she was clutching a bunch of greenery to her heart. She walked the path to his front door with the goose waddling behind, honking off-time to the tune she hummed.

He felt like humming along, too. If a goose could do it, why couldn't he? He met her halfway down the walk.

'Good morning,' he said. 'I've missed you.'

'I've missed you, too. But it is all hands needed at the manor getting ready for your welcome dinner. Even Mildred swept a floor.'

'I do not know whether to be flattered or embarrassed.'

'You will need to decide that on your own. But I will say, I've never seen Mildred near a broom.'

Peter closed the door on the goose.

Anna Liese placed holly in the vase, arranged the branches to her liking, then plucked a red and green plaid ribbon out of her pocket. She tied it in a festive-looking bow around the vase.

'My mother used to do that,' he said.

'I remember. She always made things pretty.'

It hit him then, rather like a hug to his soul, how grateful he was that he was not the only person to have memories of his past, of the people he'd loved and lost. This reminder of his mother was a small one, but so incredibly poignant it made his heart swell and his throat along with it. It would be a wonder if he was not reduced to unmanly tears.

How many other things did Anna Liese remember from their childhood? All he wanted was to sit and talk, rediscover buried memories—look at them again and walk among them in his mind—along with his oldest friend. They could pick one as if it were a ripe peach, savour it and then pluck another.

'I'm on my way to the village to pick up the paint and wallpaper we ordered. Would you like to come along? We can have breakfast first. I've missed starting my day with you.'

'As much as I would like to, I don't dare be gone that long. I am needed at home to pull everything together for your visit.'

'I'm looking forward to it, to being able to spend an evening with you for a change.'

'It will be grand, for certain. I hope you are not expecting a casual affair. My stepmother is taking advantage of the chance to entertain a genuine viscount. It might be the most elegant affair ever to be held in Woodlore Glen.'

'As long as you are present it will be delightful.'

'What a sweet thing to say. Have a nice day, Peter.' She turned for the door.

'You only came to bring the holly?'

'That and the ribbon for the vase, and to say good morning.'

'May I see you again later today?'

If not, it was going to be another long, rather dreary day.

'I will not have a free second until it is quite late.'

'Meet me at ten on the bridge. Is it too late for you? We shall sit upon the bench on the hill and look at stars the way we used to.'

'By the looks of the sky, all we shall see are clouds.'

'Very well, bring your umbrella in case it rains.'

He opened the door for her to go outside. The goose, having settled on the porch, stood up. It gazed up at Anna Liese. Even though it was a bird, Peter could tell the creature adored her. If only he could be the one waddling after her swaying skirt. Young Anna Liese's skirt had bounced rather than swayed. He found he could not look away.

Arriving at her front door, she turned about and caught him staring. Laughing, she went inside. It was only eight in the morning. He feared it would feel like for ever until ten o'clock tonight came.

It was nearly the perfect time to meet with Peter. With the household bedding down for the night, no one would notice her going outside.

Except that it was raining—not a downpour, but still a steady drip which might keep Peter from coming out even though he was the one who had told her to bring an umbrella. A spot of wet weather was certainly not going to keep her from venturing out.

Anna Liese tiptoed to the kitchen, prepared a jug of hot tea, then gathered a pair of pottery mugs. Even though the tea was likely to be cooled by the time they drank it, it seemed sensible to bring it along. Even now she felt the lingering touch of Peter's hand from the other day. It would be wise to keep her hands occupied with holding the tea.

Peter had seemed anxious to spend time with her. But was he as eager as she was? All she thought of lately was being with him. Over the years she'd sat upon the bench on the hill, watching stars and listening to night sounds, but it had never been as lovely as when she used to sit there with Peter.

She shrugged on the heavy cloak she kept near the kitchen door, snatched her umbrella from the stand and then went outside. Her heart took a happy little hop to see him waiting on the bridge.

He placed his hand under her arm, then they hurried to the top of the hill. Neither of them spoke until after Peter had spread a dry canvas over the bench and they sat down. With their umbrellas forming an arched canopy, they had a rather snug and cosy shelter.

She poured tea, then handed him a mug. Having cooled a bit, the vaporous twirls of steam weakly curled up into the night, then drifted away.

'Isn't this like old times?' she asked.

'We would have been forbidden to come out in the rain when we were children.'

'So true. We were not forbidden much back then, but had our parents known we sneaked out at night to sit up here, we would have been.'

'I miss those days.'

She took a short sip of tea, nodding agreement while gazing down at the village. Streetlamps were still lit, causing raindrops streaking through the light to resemble tumbling diamonds.

This moment held all the magic that a starry night would—perhaps more, even. This night held a sort of enchantment which had been absent years ago. As children gazing at the stars, the focus had been upwards towards the heavens.

At this moment, her focus was on the man sitting beside her. She had a strong urge to lean in close, to feel his warmth and imagine what it would be like if he put his strong arm around her shoulders and drew her closer.

'The funny thing is, here we are running about together as if we were those children still and I cannot bring myself to feel improper about it. What do you think?' He arched a brow, giving her a sweet, crooked smile. 'I'm not wrong about this, am I?'

'To me it does not matter and we do breakfast in town openly. If we were to be caught out here, alone in the night? That would matter.' Each of them took a long, thoughtful sip of warm tea. 'But I, for one, do not intend to tell.'

'You can count on my silence, Miss Barlow.'

His funny, oh, so Peter-ish grin made her laugh, which gained her a laugh in return. Looking at each other, they became caught up in a fit of merriment which somehow morphed into side-splitting humour. It made no difference that nothing was all that funny—it simply felt good to laugh.

'We used to do this all the time.' He sighed softly, as if in his mind's eye he was looking at who they were once upon a time. 'Share a memory you have of us from before.'

There were so many they crowded her mind all at once.

'Well, there was the time we were sitting here one night and you felt something fall on your head from the branch above us. You jumped about, yelping and screeching. It turned out to be a kitten, a very small one, in fact.'

'Ollie! I remember Ollie. You took the little chap home with you. Whatever became of him?'

'He grew to be a sassy fellow and industrious at keeping rodents out of the stable.'

It had been a long while since she had thought of her cat. What a nice thing it was to sit here and remember, the steady *plink-plop* of water off the umbrellas notwithstanding.

'What do you remember, Peter?'

'I remember going into my mother's kitchen one afternoon—it was a few days before Christmas and raining then, too. You were there with her, standing on a stool and putting candy eyes on the gingerbread men you were making. I really wanted to eat one.'

'You did, too. Your mother was about to forbid it, but you dashed forward and snatched one up so quickly that you had it half gobbled before she got the words out.'

'I grabbed two of them, as I recall, and they were delicious.'

Back and forth they went, sharing stories, sighing over some and laughing over others. And some, the sad ones coming at the end of their time together, avoiding all together.

'I wish we could sit here for ever, sharing memories,' he said. 'But the wind is rising. We ought to go back.' He stood. With his umbrella clutched in one hand, he extended a hand to help her rise.

Coming up, she placed her hand in his. She had never felt anything like it before—so large and strong—so intriguingly male. She could not look away from his face. His eyes held an interesting expression. One which a young boy would not have.

She wondered if perhaps he meant to kiss her, but then he did not.

'Have you invited my stepsister to your ball yet?' she asked while they walked down the hill. 'If you haven't, she and my stepmother will be fishing earnestly for an invitation.'

'I shall be delighted to invite them, as long as you agree to attend along with them.'

She would like that, more than anything. But at the same time—London and its bustling streets? Ladies and gentlemen of society wherever one looked? She was not sure.

Even though, as a baron's daughter, she had been born to society, she was a country mouse.

'I really do not think—'

'Do not refuse me, please. I fear I cannot face the occasion without you.'

'Well, perhaps a ball would be interesting. But surely you are used to attending them.'

'As true as that is, I have never attended one in

which I am actively searching for a bride. And the worst of it is, word will have got around that I am.'

'If that is the goal of your ball, so much the better. But you make it seem as if you do not wish to marry.'

'What I wish is irrelevant. It must be done, after all. It is the ball itself which will be a trial. The affair might look Christmassy—good will and peace on earth— but the truth is, in between the carols we will be merrily singing, battles between the ladies will be waged.'

'I'm not sure what I can do about it by attending.'

'Not much, I'll admit. I dread to think it, but imagine a ballroom packed with young ladies and their mothers, every one of them as ambitious as the Baroness and Mildred. Having you present, my friend, will keep me sane through the ordeal.'

Perhaps, but at the same time it would break her heart. Did he believe she could watch him searching out a bride when she herself had once wanted to be that bride? It had been her childhood expectation. She had even imagined her wedding gown being made of rose petals and dew drops. Now that she was a woman with a mature outlook... What? She still wanted rose petals and dew drops!

She had been fantasising about his return for years. And why was that? So that she could say, *Oh, how lovely to see you again and did we not have a fine time as children?* She would be fooling herself to believe it. The reason she had turned down suitors, hidden away from them even, was not only that Stepmama was forcing them upon her. No! It was because none of those men had been her Peter.

Every man she met had been judged by the friendship the two of them had shared. Every time they had been found wanting. She had not been aware of doing it, yet she had, which only went to point out how deeply he had always been a part of her. Of how loving him over the years had formed who she was then as well as who she was now.

She could not possibly attend his ball only to witness him pick someone else, no matter how badly he needed her to be there. Suddenly, the tea which had been so sweet a moment ago turned sour in her belly.

'Now that I have admitted to you that I have no genuine wish to marry, it is your turn to tell me why you have not chosen a husband. There must have been dozens of men infatuated with you over the years.'

'There is a vast difference between being infatuated and being in love, Peter.' Surely he knew that. 'We grew up as children of love matches and were lucky in that. But after that I grew up a home where there was no love match. Since I understand the difference, I will settle for nothing less than my true love match.'

'It is not the same for me. I will wed properly, as society expects me to. I have put it off too long as it is.'

What nonsense! She stopped walking, clutched his arm and looked him hard in the eye.

'Peter Penneyjons, do you truly believe that society will suffer if Viscount Cliverton waits until he finds a woman who will make him happy in marriage? One who makes his heart sing?'

'The ladies awaiting my title might suffer. They have been waiting anxiously for me to do my duty.'

'You make it sound as if you are a commodity and not a man.'

'That is not so far from the truth, Anna Liese.' He stepped closer. Their umbrella brims clicked. 'You confuse me.'

He confused her, too. 'How do I confuse you?'

'You…' He touched her cheek with his rain-slicked fingers. 'Well, you—you are—'

'Waiting for true love…' Was he going to kiss her this time? Would she allow it, knowing that love was not important to him?

Inch by slow inch, he dipped his head. She wanted this kiss more than she had ever wanted anything. She feared it even more. A kiss would make her fall in love with him in a vastly different way than the way she always had been.

Until this moment she had loved her young, childhood friend. In a blink, a touch, he would change everything. If his lips touched hers, it would all be different. The boy would be replaced by the man for ever.

What was she to do? How was she to resist what she wanted most? But, no! This was not what she wanted most. When she did kiss him, she wanted her love returned. She wanted him to look at her with love in his eyes. There was something in his eyes, something simmering and compelling. Whatever it was, it was not love.

She ought to step back, to run for home, not take a risk. She would if her feet were not rooted to the wet ground, her legs not leaden and useless. If her heart were not balanced on the head of a pin, unsure of which way it would leap.

His lips dipped slowly towards hers. She felt the heat of his breath, breathed in the scent of his skin.

This was her dream come true and it was her nightmare. She turned her face so that his kiss connected with her cheek.

'I beg your pardon.' He set her at arm's length, breathing hard. 'I regret taking advantage of you.'

Not as much as she regretted not allowing it. She took a quick step away. Hopefully quickly enough that he did not taste the one tear that had escaped and run down her cheek.

What she needed to do was to make light of what had happened. If she did not, how could they go on? And she did want to go on. The thought of not spending time with him was horrid.

'Do not take it to heart, Peter. You did not take advantage.' It shattered her, wondering if he really would not take it to heart. 'We have been playing about at this kissing business. I suggest we put it behind us and carry on as the friends we have always been.'

She could scarcely believe her voice did not quaver while she lied.

'Thank you for not taking my indiscretion to heart. I do not deserve a friend like you, Anna Liese.'

If he assumed she had not taken it to heart, he didn't know her at all. What had just happened—or not happened, more to the point—was for the best.

'Goodnight, Peter. I will see you in the morning. We shall discuss what furniture to purchase for the cottage.' She sounded so ordinary, so every day. He would never guess how she wept inside.

Had they kissed, her world would have changed. His would not have, although she thought he was not unaffected by what had happened. Knowing him as she did—and she did know him—he had felt a moment of confusion where past and present collided.

The same had happened for her.

Unlike Peter, she was not confused about what it meant. She wanted to marry him now the same way she had when she was a child. Only, not at the cost of giving up true love.

Chapter Nine

The next morning, Peter bicycled back from the village with a box precariously balanced on the handlebar. The scents of breakfast wafted out and made his stomach growl.

Even though it was no longer raining, it was as cold as the dickens out here. What a relief it would be to get inside the cottage where he had built a fire in the hearth before peddling off to town.

Not certain what time Anna Liese would arrive, he wanted it to be warm when she stepped inside. It had taken him an hour or more last night to stop shivering after being out in the rain for so long.

If, in truth, it had been the weather causing his shivers. Facing facts, he had to admit to being nervous. He had done the unthinkable last night and came within a breath of kissing his childhood friend—again.

She would be within her rights to be incensed— to not wish to be alone in his company again. No one would blame her for it. Although she did say they should think no more about it and put the incident behind them.

In the moment he was finding it nearly impossible to do. Even though their lips had not met, their breath had mingled. He had breathed in and caught the scent of her desire.

What a surprise it had been when she turned her cheek to him. What he could not get out of his mind was her tear. He had seen it slip down her cheek, then tasted it when she turned away from the kiss.

He could hardly blame her if she did not come to the cottage this morning as they had planned. If she did, he would treat her with the respect she deserved, behave as the gentleman she expected him to be—treat her as the lady she clearly was.

Last night it had been pointed out quite clearly that his Anna Liese was now a woman. It was not as if he hadn't noticed it before—how could he not? But the difference now was that he felt it.

Ah, but what must she think of him? It was troubling to him that she might believe he kissed every woman he happened to be alone with. Far from it! He was exceptionally careful not to be caught in a compromise.

Stashing his bicycle on the back porch, he walked around to the front door, carrying the box of food. He stopped for a moment to sniff the air which was crisp and redolent of evergreen trees.

He glanced towards Maplewood Manor, hoping to see Anna Liese coming out. She was not, but someone was. Mildred stared at him. From this distance he could not see her expression, but she waved her hand vigorously. He waved back, feeling her eyes on him even after he closed the door.

'Do not come over, please do not.' he mumbled.

But what was that? Singing—a voice so pure, so ethereal it felt like breath whooshing around and through him. The shiver that had taken him last night raced over his skin again—but pleasantly warm. Oddly, the scents of pine and cedar, which he had only a moment ago been admiring, filled the cottage.

Following the sound of Anna Liese's voice, he entered the drawing room. What on earth?

She turned to him with a wink and a smile which warmed him more thoroughly than the fireplace she stood in front of. 'Do you like it?'

'You have "decked my halls with boughs of holly"!'

Swathes of greenery draped the windows on either side of the fireplace. Pinecones and holly made an artistic arrangement on the mantelpiece.

'Fa-la-la-la-la,' she answered, giving a quiet laugh.

'It is beautiful.'

More than that, it indicated she did not hate him for last night. That they remained friends despite what he had done.

'But is it not too early to decorate for Christmas?'

'Not when one will be leaving to choose a bride before then,' she said brightly and handed him a garland of pinecones dotted with gold beads. 'If we do not decorate now, you will not be able to enjoy how festive the cottage can be at this time of year.'

She pointed to the newel post and indicated he was to twine the garland around the bannister.

'I will be coming back before Christmas. And I will bring my cousins and their families.'

'These will be dried out by then.' She tapped her finger on her chin. 'You mustn't worry, though, I will refresh them while you are gone.'

Clearly, this was her way of saying she would not be attending his ball. If she did not wish to come to London, he could hardly press the matter.

For instance, he would not point out that she would meet many fine gentlemen in the city. Perhaps one of them would be the man with whom she would make her true love match. If he tried to utter those words, he feared he might choke on them. Which was absurd. Didn't he want her to find what would make her happy—or rather, who would?

Since she apparently wished him well on his marriage quest, she merited no less from him.

'I've brought breakfast,' he said. 'Over which I will apologise profusely for last night.'

While he dragged the small table in front of the fireplace and withdrew the contents of the box, he thought who among his acquaintances he would introduce her to if he had the chance. One after another, faces appeared in his mind and he rejected them.

Watching while Anna Liese sat down across from him, then fluffed her skirts until they were arranged to her satisfaction, he decided his sweet friend was too good for the lot of them.

'Thank you for breakfast, Peter. I am hungry. But please do not apologise for anything. Let us move past it and go on.'

Apparently in her mind the issue of kissing had been put aside.

'Very well. I'm hungry, too.'

She did look as though she had put the incident behind her. While he had been restless into the wee hours, she looked as fresh and cheerful as the bright bow she had fastened to the garland.

'Maplewood is sparkling in your honour, Peter. The house has not been so well adorned for Christmas in years.'

'I am looking forward to it, Anna Liese.'

'The affair is the talk of the village, you know. Woodlore Glen does not typically have such a grand visitor.'

'I am not grand and you well know it.'

'Oh, please, surely you have noticed how people fall all over themselves to do your bidding.'

One could not fail to since their attentions were pronounced. Here in Woodlore Glen he stood out from the average villager even though he never dressed in his London finery.

The only person to treat him as a genuine human being was the woman sitting across from him. To her he was simply Peter Penneyjons, her friend—the boy who had grown up across the stream from her. One could hardly romp through green fields, catch tadpoles in the stream and afterwards put said friend on a lofty pedestal. She knew his secrets and he knew hers.

'I'm glad you do not treat me that way.'

'We are too old of friends to observe society's nonsense.'

Indeed, she would not be sitting across from him having breakfast if that were the case.

'Anna Liese, I hope you know how much I value our friendship.'

'As do I, Peter.'

'The reason I say so is because—it is only that I hope that, once I am married, what is between us will not change.'

A delicate blush rushed up her neck and pulsed in her cheeks. Perhaps it was only the fire reflecting off her skin that made it appear that way.

'I'm certain—'

Whatever she was about to say was cut off by a loud rap on the front door.

'Mildred,' he muttered. 'She saw me come in.'

'She is up and about early today because the modiste is delivering her gowns.' She stood up when the pounding became more urgent. 'I will leave through the back door.'

'I hate for you to go so soon.' He had the strongest urge to restrain her with a kiss. Apparently, he was not doing a grand job of putting the thought behind him. 'We have yet to discuss what furniture I need to purchase.'

'Later. Perhaps once the dinner party is past.'

'Lord Cliverton!' Mildred's voice sounded strident, even though muffled by the heavy wood door.'

'Goodbye, Peter.' To his surprise she went up on her toes and gave his cheek a quick, friendly kiss. 'I will see you in a couple of days.' With that she rushed out of the room, through the kitchen and out the back door.

He went to the front door, wondering if one slightly plump lady could actually batter it down.

'Good morning, Miss Hooper,' he said, opening the door and glancing at her knuckles in the hope that she had not rubbed them raw.

'Good morning, my lord,' she said, peering past his shoulder as if she were looking for someone, then shifting her gaze to his face. 'Is there something wrong with your cheek?'

He jerked his hand way from the spot Anna Liese had kissed. Apparently, he had been caressing it without being aware.

'No. Just a—' He shrugged, stalling while trying to think of something. 'I hurried to answer the door so quickly I collided with a—door frame.'

She frowned, no doubt trying to picture such an unlikely occurrence.

'Do not worry, my lord, it does not appear that it will leave a mark.' She lifted a napkin which had something wrapped inside. 'I saw you coming back from the village and thought, since your own cook has not yet arrived, you would like a bit to eat. It is apple cake and I promise it is delicious.'

'How thoughtful of you to come out in the cold and bring it. Thank you for your trouble.' He nodded, starting to close the door, but she placed her palm on the wood. 'I shall enjoy every bite.'

'I did not realise how cold it was until I was halfway across the bridge. Perhaps I might come inside? There is enough cake for us to share.'

For a moment he could not help feeling some pity for her. Even though she and Anna Liese had grown up in the same household, they were quite different people. Despite everything Anna Liese had been through, she was a lovely, caring person. Mildred, by comparison, had grown up to be disagreeable.

The reason for the difference might be what Anna Liese had pointed out last night. Being a child of parents who loved one had a great deal to do with one's outlook on life. Mildred could not help that she had not been so blessed.

Looking at her rather desperate expression, he determined to treat her with kindness. Not that he would allow himself to be trapped by her, but he would be polite, have compassion for the past she had been formed by.

'I'm sorry, but I was just going out again. I have business in the village. Perhaps you would care to accompany me?'

If she were as cold as she claimed to be, she would refuse, but the offer was sure to show his appreciation of her bringing him apple cake.

'How delightful! I would enjoy a few moments out from under Mama's thumb. It is not enough that she orders the servants about, she is doing it to me as well.'

The question in Peter's mind was how hard was the Baroness making Anna Liese work, the true daughter of Maplewood.

It did not set well that she was doing so in the cause of honouring him. He would rather not be honoured if that were the case.

'Wait one moment, Mildred. I will bring a second coat for you.'

He recognised his mistake when her face bloomed

in undisguised pleasure. What a great blunder to call her Mildred instead of Miss Hooper. Please let her not consider them a step shy of becoming betrothed.

Having retrieved the coats, he set off at a brisk pace across the bridge. Clearly this was not the pace she preferred because she dragged her feet in a leisurely stroll. She slipped her hand into the crook of his elbow, no matter that he had not offered his arm.

A short distance along the path, she began to speak in a tone so low that he had to incline his head towards her in order to hear. He imagined they presented an image he did not wish to portray. Anyone who did not know better would think they were enamoured of one another and indulging in romantic conversation. He could only pray there was no one about to make such an assumption.

'Oh, look,' Mildred said. 'There is my stepsister standing over there near the stream, holding that goose of hers. She looks rather pathetic, don't you think? As pretty as she is, you would expect her to have wed by now. I think perhaps she is afraid of men. But do not worry, my lord, I have no fear of you.'

She might have no fear of him, but he certainly did of her. He was also worried that Anna Liese might misunderstand what she was seeing.

Mildred lifted her arm and waved energetically while leaning closer to him than was acceptable. Clearly, her intention was to make sure that Anna Liese did misunderstand what she saw.

Rather than returning her stepsister's greeting with an answering wave and her customary smile, Anna

Liese offered a curt nod, then hugged her pet closer to her heart.

'It is rather sad, don't you think? Having a goose as your closest friend? It is not even a sweet goose. I cannot tell you how many times it has attacked the ruffles on my skirts. Perhaps I should speak with my mother about getting Anna Liese a dog instead.'

The goose had attacked him, too, but only in the cause of protecting Anna Liese.

Which was more than he was doing in the moment. He ought to be defending her against Mildred's spiteful comments and would be if his companion would give him a chance to speak. The woman chattered on as if this were a monologue and not a conversation.

Whatever business he came up with in town, it would be short. He would probably need the whole of the afternoon to recover from a few hours spent in Miss Hopper's company.

Exclamations of delight issuing from the library gave away the fact that the gowns had been delivered and none too early, given that the dinner party was tomorrow.

Anna Liese felt no great rush to see her own dress since Stepmama would have given special instruction for it to be drab. Just the same she did enjoy gowns, seeing the bright colours and pretty fabrics, even if they were not meant for her.

Standing in the hallway where she had a view of the library, she watched Mildred pose on the dais which was always kept at the ready for the frequent fittings her stepmother and stepsister indulged in.

Mildred's gown did have a nice swirl to the fabric and might have been lovely were it not for the abundance of bright green flounces and ruffles.

Although the modiste had done her best, Stepmama had insisted on getting what she wanted no matter how ugly the result was. No doubt Mrs Creamer cringed, imagining people would judge her work by her customer's taste, but business was business and the Baroness must be satisfied.

Which, given her stepmother's gushing exclamations, she was.

Spotting her, Mrs Creamer excused herself and hurried towards where she still stood watching from the hallway.

'Your gown is to your stepmother's specifications, my dear, and I am sorry for it. But there is another gown. I have given the box to your maid. She has taken it to your room. The Baroness knows nothing of this one.'

'I cannot imagine how I will pay you for it. The Baroness handles the finances.'

'No need to worry, my dear, the cost of your gown has been absorbed by the others. It is an easy thing to hide when there are so many of them.'

'I am grateful, Mrs Creamer. Although I'm sure the gown you made at the Baroness's request is lovely.'

'Oh, it is, indeed, for an afternoon at home. And not a thread of chartreuse in it.' She laughed quietly, careful not to be overheard. 'Come, let us go in and do our best to gush and pretend Mildred looks like a princess.'

Her stepsister had changed gowns and the one she

now wore was pretty, being pale yellow and a nice cut for her figure.

She did not want to wonder, yet one could hardly help what one wondered about. But—would Peter think Mildred attractive when he saw her wearing it?

Earlier this morning, she had been stunned to see him strolling with her stepsister. His head bent down to hers, they had appeared companionable. She had thought Peter would have sent Mildred away rather quickly. Could it be possible that he was developing fond feelings for her? Had she tricked him into seeing her as a person she wasn't?

Perhaps not. But the day would come when she would see him walking with a woman. Peter would be bringing his future wife to Woodlore Glen. The only way she would avoid witnessing his possible marital bliss would be to accept the attention of a man she did not love, to marry him and move away from her home.

No—that was unthinkable. The best she could do was deal with the pain of seeing him with a woman who was not her. Better that than dealing with the anguish of giving up Maplewood where she relived happy memories of her past wherever she looked.

Moving away from home would not even help greatly since she could not move away from her mind. Just because she did not see Peter and another woman with her eyes did not mean she wouldn't imagine it.

Seeing her step into the library, Alice plucked a gown off the back of a chair and carried it to her.

It was a well-made dress, the stitches straight and even. The fabric was sturdy, durable and a shade of grey that ensured to make her blend into the background.

'I shall try it on in my room,' she said, lifting it from Alice's arms.

'Please let me know if it is suitable, miss,' Alice answered, giving her a discreet wink.

'I cannot say how grateful I am.' She glanced at Mildred before she exited the library, only to see her dressed in the bright green gown again. 'You are sure to catch any gentleman's eye, Mildred.' It was the truth, only not in the way her stepsister dreamed of.

'Do you think so, Anna Liese? Really?' The question seemed sincere, the look in her stepsister's eyes hopeful.

'You look lovely.' Despite the gown.

She hurried up the stairs and burst into her room to see Martha holding up the most exquisite gown Anna Liese had ever seen. The fabric was a pure sky blue and shimmered as if caught in a ray of sunshine. She had not seen this material among the ones the modiste had brought for the fittings.

The gown was so pretty, looking at it made her feel breathless. A princess could wear it and be utterly admired. The bodice was ruffled and tucked in such a way that it would appear to float about her bosom and shoulders. Attached to the sheer fabric were small silk butterflies and lace rosettes. It was hard to imagine how the cost of this gown had been absorbed by the others.

'Oh, my dear!' Martha exclaimed. 'You will appear an angel tomorrow night.'

'I do not dare wear it.'

If only she were bold enough to march boldly into Stepmama's presence without fear of something 'happening' to her beautiful gown.

'I suppose you are right—but put it on so we may appreciate Mrs Creamer's vision.'

It would be thoughtless not to do so. The ladies had gone to a great deal of trouble on her behalf.

Martha helped her into the gown.

Holding the skirt in her hands, she twirled in front of the mirror. It felt like a dream, as if she were whirling about in blue mist.

'You are a vision, my dear girl. Some day you will wear this gown and bring every gentleman in the ballroom to his knees.'

'It is nice to imagine such a thing. But I doubt I will be attending any balls.'

'Lord Cliverton is hosting a ball. Surely you will be going?'

'Help me out of the gown, if you please.' She maintained her smile with difficulty because she would rather not have Martha see what was in her heart. She certainly would not be attending a ball in which the man she loved would be picking a bride. A heart could only take so much misery.

She blinked, then blinked again. She did love Peter Penneyjons, loved him more each time she saw him. Funny how the understanding of it had not hit her as a grand revelation. Probably because love for Peter had always been a part of her, a bright and never-forgotten part of her soul.

She was not sure how it had happened, or exactly when, but the little girl's love for a friend had become a woman's love for a man. A man who did not return her feelings, not in the way she needed him to.

'We must hide it away. I do not want to know what would happen if my stepmother discovered it.'

'I shall keep it in my quarters above stairs. It will be safe enough since neither she nor Mildred visit the servants' quarters.'

'Thank you, Martha.'

'Now, let me see what you will be wearing tomorrow night.' She picked the grey gown from the back of the chair where Anna Liese had dropped it and grimaced. 'You might as well not attend for all that you will be noticed wearing that.'

Peter would notice her regardless of what she wore. She was certain he would. Even though he was a viscount, he was not one to be swayed by fluff and frills.

Doubtless her stepmother's message in presenting her with such a gown was that she was not welcome at the event. An event to be held in her own home to welcome her very dear—friend.

No matter what Stepmama's feelings on the matter, Anna Liese was attending. And she would not blend into the wall. She did have other gowns, after all.

She must simply make sure no one sent them to be laundered.

Chapter Ten

The event so anticipated by everyone from Stepmama to the scullery maids, from the village lamplighter to Alice, was at hand.

Descending the grand staircase, Anna Liese paused halfway down, glancing about with pride at what the staff's and her own hard work had accomplished.

Maplewood sparkled as it had not since her parents were alive.

Garlands of red and green were draped over windows and doorways in the drawing room. Through the wide doorway of the grand drawing room she admired pine and holly wreaths hung on the mantelpiece and in windows announcing that Christmas was around the corner.

The sounds of the string quartet, along with the muffled conversation of guests who had already arrived, wafted out of the drawing room door. She closed her eyes, simply listening to the lovely strain of the instruments playing 'Good King Wenceslas'. One could nearly feel the excitement of the season dancing on the air.

Coming down the rest of the steps, she glanced about for Peter. She was beyond anxious to share this with him. They had spent so many happy hours at Maplewood when they were young. Just imagining his smile made her want to skip instead of walk. No matter what scheme Stepmama might have in mind to drive her away, she would not fall prey to it.

Apparently he was not here yet so she greeted the neighbours with one eye on the doorway.

She was not the only one to have an eye on the hall. Everyone was anxious to meet the Viscount in their village. Stepmama and Mildred stood in the hall near the front door, heads together in conversation. It would be best to know what they were saying. Forewarned was forearmed she had come to learn.

Anna Liese walked towards them, but then hung back from the doorway. She was not yet ready to have her stepmother see her wearing not the drab grey gown, but one of her old gowns which was a lovely shade of dusty rose. It was a pretty, festive dress of lace more appropriate for the Viscount's welcome.

'You ought to have seen how he admired me, Mother.'

'Perhaps he was simply being polite. You should not have shown up at his front door as you did. He might have taken you for over-eager. You must appear uninterested. It is a trick to get them to want what they believe to be forbidden.'

As if he would succumb to such trickery.

'He called me Mildred. That has got to mean something.'

By mistake, perhaps—Anna Liese hoped so at any rate.

'It well may. However, you must still charm him. Smile, laugh quietly and, whatever you do, make sure not to eat too much.'

'What if I get hungry?'

'After you are wed you may butter your bread as thick as you like. Until then you will pick at your food like a bird.'

'I can be as charming and hungry as can be, but if Anna Liese comes downstairs Lord Cliverton will see no one else.'

Truly? Is this what Mildred believed? How interesting.

'If she does come down, she will not stay.'

'I fail to see how you can prevent it. Especially if the guest of honour wishes for her to stay.'

'Put away that pouty expression. You may trust that I have taken steps to ensure she will not be here.'

'What steps?'

'Never you mind. Your job is to be pleasant to the Viscount.'

'But I wonder if—'

'Hush now, we have guests.'

Whatever the scheme, Anna Liese would not fall prey to it. She would do nothing which would take her away from Peter's welcome dinner. Mildred would simply have to shine enough to attract Peter's attention. Anna Liese had no intention of getting out of the way in order to make it easier for her. If Peter held tender feelings for Mildred, Anna Liese's presence would make no difference.

It was time to make her presence known. She swept inside, making a grand sweep of her lacy skirt. She would be happy to wear the sturdy grey gown—tomorrow.

'Everything looks fit for a viscount, Stepmama. Lord Cliverton will be delighted by all you have done to welcome him.'

Not that her stepmother had lent a hand, only ordered people about. But in the end, Maplewood was as festive as she had ever seen it. Or heard it. The Christmas carols wafting softly through the rooms—it was enchanting.

Some of the enchantment had to do with knowing Peter would be here soon, knowing she would have the evening to spend with him.

'Why, Anna Liese, what a lovely gown.'

'But do you not have a new one?' Mildred asked, casting her frown over the delicate pink lace. 'Do you not think it disrespectful to wear something old?'

'I cannot imagine he would think so. We are childhood friends and such things between us are trivial.'

So she said, but Anna Liese did want Peter to see her dressed in lace and looking pretty.

Footsteps thumped across the floor.

The three of them turned to see the footman, Thorpe, striding towards them.

'This was delivered by messenger for you, Miss Anna Liese.' He placed the tightly folded note in her hand.

'Who is it from?' Stepmama asked.

'I cannot say, my lady.' Turning about, he left them as quickly as he had come.

'Well, my dear, I imagine you would like some privacy to read this mysterious missive. Come along, Mildred. We shall wait for the Viscount with the others.'

Mysterious was a mild word for the folded paper in her hand. And why wasn't Stepmama more curious about what it was? Anna Liese might have expected her to be reading it over her shoulder. Something felt wrong, but she would not know if it was or not until she looked at it.

The only person she could think of who would send her anything was Peter. Why would he not just wait and speak with her when he came? Unless something was wrong. That sent a shiver along her neck.

She glanced out the window, hoping to see him crossing the bridge. He was not and the lamps were still burning in his front windows.

What on earth?

She opened it and read, 'Anna Liese, I am suddenly feeling unwell. I fear I will not be able to attend. Please give the Baroness and Mildred my regrets.'

It was odd that he not had the note delivered to his hostess. It might be a scheme to somehow make her lose interest in the party and go to her room. She had overheard Stepmama say she had some sort of plan.

On the other hand, Peter was not here and the drawing room lamps in the cottage were burning. If only she knew what Peter's handwriting looked like. Since they had never corresponded, she did not.

There was nothing for it but to cross the bridge and find out for herself. Opening the front door, she went out, leaving the lovely strains of 'Silent Night' behind her.

Just before she got to the bridge, she heard a voice calling after her.

'Miss! Your cloak!' It was Thorpe hurrying towards her with it slung over his arm.

Well, that was odd. How could he know she would be going out, let alone retrieve it so quickly and come after her?

He could not.

She started to run for the cottage, to shout for Peter, but Thorpe tossed the cloak over her head, trussed her up in it, then slung her over his shoulder and carried her away from the manor house.

She wriggled and squirmed, cursed even, to no avail. At one point she was bound by a rope, then put in the back of a wagon and carted off by someone else. Kidnapped. Nothing but fear for Peter's safety could have made her act without caution.

But whoever had done this was not going to find her a compliant captive—and she had a good idea who was going to discover she was not. Trussed up as she was in the moment, she really did not wish to be in Hyrum Grant's shoes once she no longer was!

Entering Maplewood, Peter felt propelled back in time. Something, an echo of times past, enfolded him in a sense of well-being.

Perhaps it had to do with the melodies played by the string quartet. Music had always been a part of the Maplewood he remembered. Anna Liese was not the only one of her family to be musical. Her father had

had a beautiful singing voice. And her mother—yes, he remembered now that she had played the violin. His family and Anna Liese's had spent many evenings together just this way. It was somewhat similar, but back then he had not been a viscount and the gathering intimate rather than grand.

But something of the feeling of how it had been in those days lingered. He could scarcely wait to find out if Anna Liese felt it too.

'Lord Cliverton!' The Baroness bustled forward, her hands extended in welcome. 'It is an honour to have you grace our humble home.'

Humble was not how he would describe Maplewood. In his mind it was large, yet at the same time warm and inviting.

He thought the appeal had to do with Anna Liese. This was her home and, even though the Baroness and Mildred lived here, it was Anna Liese's presence giving it a sense of home. He understood how much she loved Maplewood. This was the place where she nourished memories of her past, kept them fresh and alive.

Now that he was in Woodlore Glen and had his own memories returning, he knew he ought to have been more like Anna Liese over the years. Rather than avoiding pain by forgetting, he ought to have sought solace in remembering.

He glanced about. Where was Anna Liese?

Mildred hustled towards him, looking flashy in a wealth of green. Bright, shocking green. He was not one to notice fashion even though he had grown up with women wanting his opinion on it, but this gown was—it was one to be noticed was the kindest way to think of it.

'How nice it is to see you again, my lord.' It was apparent that Mildred wished to reach for his arm and escort him to another room but withheld the impulse. 'I told dear Mother what a lovely walk we had yesterday.'

'I do feel the motherly need to scold you for taking my daughter off without a chaperon, Lord Cliverton. But I shall overlook it this one time. Young people will be young people, will they not? It is easy to get carried away when hearts are calling to one another.'

Young people? They were hardly all that young.

And hearts calling? This was far from the case.

The Baroness placed her hand in the crook of his arm and led him towards the large drawing room. The home had two as he recalled. A large one for entertaining and a smaller one for family. 'Come along, I will introduce you to the other guests.'

Mildred started to place her fingers on his arm then received a sharp glance from her mother.

'We are a small group tonight, my lord,' the Baroness declared. 'I prefer an intimate gathering where we can get to know one another more easily.'

'I prefer it, too.' He greatly looked forward to being able to spend time with Anna Liese in the same place they had as children. How many more memories would come back to him? he wondered.

Coming into the drawing room, Peter nodded to several guests who were seated about the room in comfortable-looking chairs, conversing and looking at ease. It was clear these people had known one another for a long time, if not all their lives.

Newcomer to Woodlore Glen that he was, he was anxious to know them as well as they knew each other. He intended to make this his home away from the city after all. It would be good to be on neighbourly terms with the people here.

The Baroness promenaded him in a circle about the room, introducing him.

In front of the fireplace there were three unoccupied chairs. Baroness Barlow indicated that he should sit on the one in the middle.

The ladies sat down on each side of him.

Where was the chair for Anna Liese? It only seemed right that she should be in this apparent place of honour with the rest of her family.

'Thank you for this fine welcome, Baroness. I do appreciate having the chance to get to know my neighbours.'

'Oh, but we are so humble here in Woodlore Glen. Please, you must tell us all about London,' she said.

'Oh, yes, please do!' Mildred clapped her hands. 'I would love to hear about the grand balls. I have been to so few of them. Here in the countryside they are rare.'

'Have you never been to London, Mildred?' he asked, making polite conversation while glancing at the doorway whenever someone entered the drawing room.

Where was Anna Liese? Given all she had done in preparation of the event, he found it odd that she would be late.

'On the rare occasion and then only for a short stay.'

'But now that we have a friend who resides in the city, we shall make an effort to go there more often,' the Baroness said.

'Oh, yes, Mother!' Mildred spoke to her mother but stared at him while she spoke. 'I would love to see a grand ball. Even if we did not attend, I would be content to watch from the kerb while lords and ladies came and went.'

That was the last thing Mildred would be content with, in his opinion. Anna Liese had warned him that they would be casting about for an invitation to his ball. He would rather wait until she arrived and then offer it to all three of them at once. She had clearly said she did not wish to come. Still, he would give the offer one more go.

But where was she?

He was beginning to feel uneasy about her absence. Something about it felt wrong. Conversation stalled while Mildred stared at him, blinking and smiling. Better to get it over with, then. He would formally invite Anna Liese when he saw her, which he hoped would be soon.

'As it happens, I am hosting a ball. It is to be just a few days before Christmas. I understand this hardly gives you time to plan, but if you can manage, I would be delighted for you to attend.'

'Oh, my.' The Baroness frowned, as if she had not been trying to extract this from him all along. 'It is rather late notice, with everything to be done in order to be made ready. I suppose I will need to give you my answer once I give the matter more thought.'

An hour passed by before dinner was announced and still there was no sign of Anna Liese.

He stood up to go to the dining room and was immediately latched on to. Each of his arms became possessed by Lady Barlow and Mildred. They led the way to the dining room with the other guests coming behind.

'Will Anna Liese be joining us for dinner?' Given how jealous these two were of her, he ought to have referred to her as Miss Barlow, but doing so would have felt unnatural in the extreme.

'I rather think not, my lord.' The Baroness sniffed as if there was something unpleasant in the air. 'She received a rather odd note earlier and I have not seen her since.'

'Perhaps it was bad news and she retired to her room,' Mildred suggested.

'How long ago did this note arrive?' Something was not right. He felt the wrongness down to his bones.

'Oh, well, let me see.' The Baroness tapped her chin. 'More than three hours ago.'

'Has anyone been up to check upon her?'

'I asked Thorpe to send an enquiry to her maid, but I have not heard.' She glanced about. Waved over the footman. 'Thorpe, is Miss Barlow in her chamber, do you know?'

'I cannot say, my lady. I took her cloak to her when she went outside without it. I did not see her return, but she must have done.'

'Well, I'm certain she has. Thank you, Thorpe.'

'I find it odd that Miss Barlow would work so hard and look forward to this evening so much to spend it in her room.'

'One never knows what my stepdaughter will do. She does tend to disappear without word on occasion.

Ah, here comes the meal,' declared the Baroness, apparently satisfied that her stepdaughter was safe.

On this occasion? It was not likely.

'Should someone not check to see if she is ill?' Mildred asked.

'We saw her only a few hours ago and she looked quite well,' the Baroness answered.

Peter had not seen her and so could not be sure she was well. Until he was, he would not be able to stomach the meal.

'Thorpe,' he said. The man had not gone about his business, but lingered by the table. 'Will you send for Miss Barlow's maid? I would like a word.'

Moments later the maid arrived, but she did not enter the dining room, but rather stood by the door looking concerned.

'If you will excuse me?' He stood.

'Surely you are not leaving,' the Baroness gasped. 'I'm certain that even if Anna Liese is not in her room, she is well enough. She dislikes society, that is all.'

'She does not dislike my society.'

'Perhaps someone else might speak with Martha?' Mildred suggested. 'It is not your place to—'

He did not know what else she said because he was striding towards the hallway where Anna Liese's maid waited for him.

'No, my lord, she is not in her chamber. I have not seen her since she went down. Thorpe came to collect her cloak quite some time ago.'

'Do you find it odd that she wished to go out?'

'Most odd, but Thorpe said she had received some sort of note.'

What the note had to do with anything he could not imagine. The fact was that Anna Liese had gone out in the dark and the cold and she had not returned.

Hurrying into the hall, he instructed the servant in attendance to bring his hat and coat. Shrugging into his coat, he asked the man if he had seen Anna Liese go out or return.

In the hour he had been in attendance he had not seen anything.

Standing on Maplewood's front porch, Peter took off his hat and scratched his head. Which direction would she have gone? And what, if anything, did the note have to do with it?

He walked the path towards the bridge in case she had been coming to see him. Perhaps there would be some clue to where she had gone.

Suddenly the wind picked up, blowing dry leaves across the path. But wait—not only leaves! A few feet away from where he stood, a scrap of paper blew towards the stream.

He rushed for it and caught it up a step before it tumbled into the water.

He went cold, reading it. It was supposed to be from him. Not only had he not written it, he was not sick! Or he had not been until he read the thing.

Shoving it in his pocket, he cursed. Someone had lured Anna Liese away by trickery. He meant to find her and discover why.

Anna Liese glanced about her cell, which happened to be the back room of the bank.

'I've finally got myself the Barlow lady. It has not

been easy, I can tell you,' Hyrum Grant said, smiling as if he were quite proud of the nasty accomplishment.

'If you believe it will be any easier now that you have me, you are greatly mistaken.'

'I'm glad it is you and not the other one. Mildred—I cannot imagine being wed to her. I imagine your fine Viscount is enjoying her company.'

That was no doubt what Stepmama had in mind in instigating this outrage.

She was going to fight energetically to make sure she did not get away with it.

'You are wasting your time if you think to be wed to me.'

'I hardly think you are in a position to refuse me.'

Her strength pitted against his, this was true. She, however, would use a different weapon. For all that the man was stronger than she was, he was not very clever.

'I will procure a special licence in the morning,' he said with an arrogant smirk. 'Do not worry, my dear, you will be a respectably married woman in a day or two.'

'A special licence in Woodlore Glen? I cannot imagine where you will find one.'

'I do have many connections.' He grinned, showing off his straight, white teeth. 'But once I am your husband, I will gain many more influential contacts.'

'There are not all that many connections in our small village which you have not already made. I doubt if I will be much help to you in that.'

Anna Liese glanced about the back room. The curtains were drawn against the night. As far as she could tell there was no easy way out. Even if she screamed no one would hear her. The village shops were closed and, even if they were not, the back door of the bank faced the little-used rear road.

The very road on which Peter taught her to ride a bicycle, where she had fallen off and landed in the bush and he had nearly kissed her. But the tender moment had been interrupted by this man—the one who expected she would meekly go along with his demands.

Well, they would see who was whose captive.

'If you think I will be married in anything but a proper gown, you are greatly mistaken. I am the daughter of Baron Barlow. It will bring shame upon you if I wed in rags.'

'You are not wearing rags. Besides, you have other things to worry about than fancy gowns.'

'What might those be? Gowns are of utmost importance to a woman of my position.'

Behind the curtains, she saw the shadow of bars on the windows.

'After we are wed, we will discuss what you will wear.'

'Can I be honest with you, Hyrum?'

'No, I would rather—'

'Being married to me might not be worth the supposed influence to be had.'

'It's not only that. Your stepmother has offered me a good sum of money to get you off her hands.'

'Surely you do not think she has enough to make this worthwhile.'

'I need a wife anyway. Why not get paid for it? It makes life simpler, two birds with one stone and all that.'

Upon their last meeting, Hyrum had indicated that he expected obedience in a woman.

Very well, let the battle begin.

'If you believe that being married to a woman who is forced into it will be simple, you are mistaken.'

What a nasty, arrogant smile he had. She wished to punch it so intensely that she had to sit on her hands. If she did end up doing so, it would be strategic and not an impulse.

'I think you will do.'

'Tell me then, what is it you require of a marriage, Mr Grant? Because I am certain you will not get it from me.'

'I'll need food on my table and my clothing washed. My house kept clean. I do not care much for children, though.'

'We shall have a large staff to see to those things. I will care for the children myself. All six of them,' she added when he stared at silently at her. 'Do you wish to know what I require of marriage?'

'Not that it matters, but I assume you are going to tell me.'

'I require a true love match. Will you be able to give me that?'

'Believe it or not, I have long admired you.'

She did not believe it, not for a moment. It was money and prestige he admired.

In that moment she wished for Peter's presence more than her next breath. If he were here, he would give this man his due. She would fear nothing if Peter was here.

For all that she pretended not to be, she was quite frightened. She was this man's captive and as much as she told herself she was capable of handling it, she really was at his mercy. Perhaps if she imagined Peter's arms tight and snug about her she would find the courage she needed to get through this unscathed.

'I do not believe it.'

'It doesn't not matter to me whether you do or not. The outcome will be the same. You will be my wife.'

'I'm hungry. Since I am your captive you must feed me.'

'Very well, Princess. Perhaps you should relax and get used to your new home while I am gone.'

'There are bars on the windows, Hyrum. I will never feel at home as long as they remain.'

There was little chance of him removing them, but it did bear pointing out. What she would be doing while he was gone was trying to work out a way out of here. If there was a way to be found. Banks were known for being secure.

'Feel free to explore, my dearest.' Oh, but that sneer made her want to strike him. 'Just keep in mind you will be wasting your effort looking for a way out. This door locks from the inside and the outside. And, as you say, there are bars on the windows.'

'Do you have bars on the windows of your home? If you do, I will insist on removing them. They will scare off our many guests. You do enjoy entertaining? I shall invite a dozen callers every day.'

She knew he did not enjoy the company of a great number of people—it was a well-known thing about him. It was odd since he wanted status, which by nature involved the society of others.

What else did he dislike?

'And we will have cats.' Many people were allergic, she could only hope he was one of them. 'Only two to begin with, but I do hate separating kittens from their mothers so the house will soon be overrun with the sweet creatures, although I imagine we will have to deal with fleas.'

With an ounce of luck, he was beginning to believe she was a shrew and no amount of money would be worth living with her.

Grumbling, he opened the door and let in a whoosh of cold air.

'Do not forget to bring dessert, Hyrum. I adore sweets.'

And Peter—she adored his strength and his honest nature. He was everything that Hyrum Grant was not. Even if the banker did manage to ruin her reputation, she would not marry him.

He slammed the door going out. The lock clicked sharply into place. She really was stuck in here. What was she to do now?

Escape seemed impossible, which meant she must carry on with the weapons she had: her tongue and her superior wit. So far, her captor did not seem prone to violence. But she had no idea how far she might push the man until he was. Still, she had no choice in the matter. It was vital she give the impression that life married to her would not be worthwhile.

Seeing a desk, she crossed the room and opened a drawer. Perhaps it held something that might be used as a weapon. It would need to be small or he would see it. Drat, all it contained were pencils and other clerkish items. Scooping up the pencils she dribbled them on the floor. With any luck Hyrum Grant would slip, where-upon she would snatch his key and make her escape.

'Look at this,' she said to no one.

She withdrew a bottle of ink and opened the stopper. Since she did not wish to damage her gown, which had already taken abuse during the drama of getting her here, she did not dribble it on the floor. Instead, she poured it on the seat of the desk chair. A lovely black splotch bloomed on the navy-blue cushion.

'I would not want to marry me, especially after all these papers get scattered across the floor. They will be too crushed to read, I imagine, once I begin to pace about. He might begin to wonder what damage I will do to his home and regret this decision.'

Think, she told herself. *Think*. What in here might be used for a weapon?

Going to the window, she inspected the bars, yanking them one by one. Bars only went to point out yet another flaw in Hyrum's character. His judgement was off. Why on earth did he think he needed bars in Wood-lore Glen? He was the least scrupulous of the souls living in the village. Was he barring windows against himself? She went from window to window, trying and failing to get out.

'Ouch!' A splinter pierced her finger, but she had no time to tend to it. She could not imagine where her captor was going to get dinner, but it might not take him long to do it.

And then something snapped. When she glanced at her hand a small bar was curled in her fist. It was only ten inches long, but it was a great deal more useful than a pencil.

* * *

Running across the bridge to get his bicycle, Peter could not recall ever being so worried. Or so angry! He swore his heart crept up his throat and the panicked beating was choking him.

Thorpe had been the person to give Anna Liese the note so Peter had sought him out. The man hadn't stood up to Peter's inquisition and admitted that he had delivered Anna Liese to the banker. Thorpe swore he did not know where Grant was taking her.

He'd let the footman go without punching him the way he had wanted to. The man already had a bruise swelling under his eye and he could only hope that Anna Liese had given it to him.

Whatever Grant had in mind for Anna Liese, it would not be to her benefit. He did not know that Grant would resort to violence against her, but neither did he know he would not. What Peter did know was that he, himself, would not hesitate to resort to violence if need be.

Although he had never had occasion to pummel anyone before, he knew he could. His hands clenching on the cold metal handlebars told him it would not be a difficult thing to use his fists in defence of his friend.

For all that he was running on pure emotion, he needed to act with logic and work out where the banker would have taken her. Somewhere secure where she would not be heard and where she could not get out. The bank would fit all those requirements. And Grant had the only keys to the place.

As fast as he was flying along the path, he risked

going down. Uneven stones and pebbles hitting his front wheel made the bike wobble.

What did not wobble was his resolve to free Anna Liese.

To Anna Liese's surprise, the dinner Hyrum came back with smelled delicious.

'What is that, Hyrum? Did you find it in a rubbish heap? It smells rotten.'

He plunked the dinner tray on the desk, casting her a sneer.

'What has happened here?'

'It was an accident.' She glanced at the floor and shrugged.

'It looks like—what have you done?'

'Sit down here in the chair,' she said pleasantly. 'You might as well eat the food even though it is not up to my standards. Once we are wed you will need to do better.'

'Do not test me, Anna Liese.'

Oh, but he did sit down! He must be wondering why she, his captive, was grinning so broadly. She felt rather good about having the bar tucked into the pocket of her skirt. Now she only needed to discover a way to use it.

'Test you? I am not doing that. It has simply become apparent to me that I am trapped and will soon be your wife.' She nudged the tray towards him, smiling as prettily as she knew how while he scowled at the mess she had made of his shiny floor.

That was funny, really. If Peter were here, he would laugh. He would also rescue her. But he was not here and so she would wrap the thought of him around her as a buffer against fear.

'As a dutiful wife, and I believe such a lady is one you require, I merely meant to help.'

'Help?' he grumbled.

She nodded.

Still seeming to be unaware that he was sitting in ink, Hyrum began shoving food into his mouth.

She thought he cursed behind a mouthful of bread while he shook his finger at the floor.

'Well, I did get rather bored while you were gone. You should know that I require entertainment in order to keep myself in bounds—rather like a puppy, or so I have been told. You will need to make your own judgement about that in time. Well, I found the correspondence in the drawer, all these letters needing to be answered. When I picked them up, I slipped and they all flew out of my hand and then…well, you see for yourself what happened.'

'If you dislike tonight's dinner, you will detest our wedding feast. I am partial to goose and you have one, I believe.' He slanted an evil, narrow-eyed glance at her.

Was he now about to burst into a fit of violence? What a lucky thing there would be no wedding feast. Although, so far, her portrayal of a being shrew did not seem to bother him. Perhaps once he noticed the ink on his trousers…

Oh! But wait. Just there—a shadow moved across the curtain from the outside. Her heart went still, then pounded so madly in her ears she thought her captor could not fail to hear it. Apparently, he did not, noisily chewing on some sort of meat.

She recognised that beloved shadow, although it seemed impossible that Peter could have found her. She knew the way his shoulders moved when he walked and the way his head tilted when he was thinking hard about a matter. She was certain it was him—who else's presence would she react to right through the walls of this building?

He had come to rescue her. Although in order to be able to do so he would need to get inside. But this being a bank, there was really no way to do it. The door would need to be opened from the inside for Peter to rush inside and free her.

'I hate to bother you, Hyrum. And I would not mention it if the matter was not urgent. But you did not supply a chamber pot. You ought to have done so because I—'

'I am beginning to think I do not admire you all that much after all.'

He stood up. He would not admire her in the least once he noticed the seat of his expensive-looking trousers.

'It does not matter a great deal if you admire me or not because did you not say it was only the money which mattered? But the fact remains, I do require a way to relieve my needs.'

'Can you not wait until after I finish eating?' he asked with a regretful glance back at the half-eaten meal.

She shrugged, shifted her weight from one foot to the other and bounced up and down for effect.

'Are you willing to risk it? The floor is a mess as it is—my dear. I shall begin calling you that in order to be used to the endearment when we recite our eternal vows.'

He yanked the key from his pocket and marched towards the door. She followed close behind, curling her fingers around the hidden ten inches of bar.

She only prayed that Peter would be on the other side of the door when Hyrum opened it.

'I think that our wedding night would be more interesting if you continued to admire me, my dear,' she said, watching while he turned the key. Now was the time to keep his mind fully distracted. 'Would you like to know a secret, Hyrum? I do not know a thing about what goes on in the marriage bed except that it is better when the couple are—well, naked. I have heard that some sweating occurs, but that sounds odd to me. I will need your instruction on what to do, so—'

He glanced back at her, arching one brow while slanting her an unattractive smile.

The door crashed open.

There stood Peter, looking magnificently heroic. He balled his fist, ready to deliver a blow to Hyrum's razor-straight nose. Oh, dear, the cad began to close the door, which would land the blow on solid wood.

Whipping the bar from her skirt pocket, she smacked the banker smartly on top of his head. The surprise gave Peter the opportunity to punch Hyrum's pointy chin. And then his stomach.

Ducking past the men, she ran a short distance and then glanced over her shoulder. She stopped and spun about, stunned to see Peter gripping Hyrum's collar and lifting him off the ground. My word, she had no idea he had grown to be so strong. If her heart had not already been galloping, it would now be, but for an entirely different reason.

Peter was shouting something in the banker's face, to which Hyrum was nodding vigorously. Once Peter set him back on the ground, the scoundrel scurried into the bank.

Watching Peter stride towards her, rolling his bicycle with him, she slipped ever deeper in love. She had never been rescued before and it made her feel—cherished.

Even after what she had just endured a sense of comfort wrapped her up. This sense of well-being had been lacking in her life ever since her father died. All she wanted was to stand still, right here on the path, and capture the sensation.

'He will not be bothering you again.'

'It appeared that you gave him a vigorous warning. I only hope he remembers it.'

'Don't worry, Anna Liese, he'll remember.'

'What did you say to him?'

'I reminded him of who I was—and who he was.' He grinned, his eyes sparkling and stern all at once. How did he manage such a glance? 'I made him understand that you were under the protection of a viscount. That if he bothered you again, I know people who could ruin him financially.'

She had heard of knees going weak and now knew it to be true. Her heart and brain felt mushy, too.

'You are my hero, Peter.'

What would she not give to kiss him and demonstrate her affection, her deep and growing affection? More than that, her love.

He drew her cloak from across the handlebars of the bike. 'I found it on the path further back,' he said, laying it across her shoulders and buttoning it under her chin. His large warm fingers lingered over the task for a moment.

She dug her fingers into her skirt. Peter was not in love with her. She would not kiss him again unless it would be answered with the same passion with which she offered it.

He shook his head, let his hands fall away from her. 'Do you wish to stay at the cottage tonight? I will take a room at the inn if you do.'

'I need to return to Maplewood. Would you mind taking me back?'

'It isn't that I mind, but after what your stepmother did—and I know she was behind this—are you certain you want to?'

'I must.' It was really the last thing she wanted to do, but she needed to let her stepmother know she had failed once again to be rid of her.

And how wonderful would it be to walk back into the party on the arm of her hero? To see Stepmama's face when she realised she had done nothing to keep her away from him.

'If you are certain, then,' he said.

'I do not wish for her to think she has intimidated me. Stepmama must be made to understand she must stop this manipulation.'

She was firmer in her determination to marry in a true love match than she had ever been. How could she not be when her true love was walking beside her, making her feel as if she were melting into her muddy party shoes?

It hit her that, unless Peter felt the same way about

her, she might never have her love match. It was unlikely that she could transfer her feelings to someone else as if she were changing shoes.

'Let's go then,' he said with the grin she had always adored.

Even after what she had been through over the past few hours, going back to dinner with her skirt muddy, with her hair mussed and tumbled down her back, felt delightfully like mischief. It was almost as if she and Peter were children again, merrily bedevilling their parents.

'I'll just put the bike away.' Peter said. 'I imagine your stepmother will be glad to see you safe and hale.'

'She will be horrified.'

And for some reason a situation which ought to have been awful made them both laugh.

Stepmama was going to more horrified than Peter knew because in the instant she spotted her with the Viscount, she would read how very deeply Anna Liese loved him.

By the time Peter escorted Anna Liese into the grand drawing room, dinner was over, and people had gathered for drinks and conversation.

Conversation which ended abruptly when he strode inside, with a dishevelled Anna Liese on his arm.

'Baroness Barlow,' he announced, enjoying the stretch of a grin cutting his face. What had happened was not humorous in the least. Anna Liese's future had been threatened. But this! Watching the Baroness turn the shade of a bleached sheet on washday was satisfying. 'You will be relieved to know the note Anna Liese received was nothing of concern.'

'Indeed, it is a relief.' The drink the Baroness held sloshed in the flute and came close to spilling. 'I hate to think she might have received bad news.'

'It seemed at first that it might have been the case,' Anna Liese said, letting go of his arm and taking a step away from him. 'For some reason, Hyrum Grant was under the impression that the Viscount had fallen ill.'

'Hyrum Grant? I wonder why he would think that?' Mildred asked.

'As do I, how very odd.' The Baroness set her drink aside, no doubt fearing her scheme against Anna Liese was about to be exposed in front of her guests. 'I cannot imagine why he would think such a thing.'

'Or why he would send a note to Anna Liese?' Peter looked hard at Lady Barlow while he spoke. 'It is peculiar. I wonder how Mr Grant, being in the village, would come by any knowledge regarding my health, or be concerned about it.'

Mildred shook her head, taking in Anna Liese's appearance with a frown. 'What happened to you?'

'As anyone would, when I got the note, I walked over to the cottage to see for myself.'

'But I was already here and you know how concerned I was when Anna Liese was absent from our gathering. Well, I discovered from Thorpe that she was with the banker, discussing the meaning of his note.'

'And did you discover it?' The Baroness seemed to be holding her breath, staring hard at her stepdaughter while waiting for him to answer.

Anna Liese was the one to answer.

'I did not, even though he insisted I accompany him to the village to discuss it. But then Peter came along and—' she gazed up at him, her eyes warm and shining '—and insisted forcefully to know the reason for it.'

'But what was it?' Mildred asked looking puzzled so he thought that she, at least, had nothing to do with it.

'Mr Grant thought he heard someone say so, but try as he might, he cannot recall who. If he remembers, he promises to let me know.'

He did not wish to reveal the truth and make this uncomfortable for Anna Liese, especially with people looking curiously on.

'But, Stepmama,' Anna Liese said, 'you will be glad to know that he has promised not to cause us further trouble—with his notes.'

'He made me a particular vow about it.' Peter let his frown settle on the Baroness, letting it rest upon her until she slid her gaze away and stared at the flute on the table beside her.

Good, he believed she understood.

'But that does not explain what happened to your hair, Anna Liese,' Mildred half whispered, half hissed.

'It is nothing that cannot be repaired.' Lady Barlow shot her daughter a glance, clearly ordering her to carry the question no further.

Glancing at Anna Liese, he saw she was sucking on the tip of her finger.

'What happened?' he asked. He had not noticed her favouring her finger until now.

The Baroness stood up, looking a shade paler than she had.

'I clearly instructed him not to—that is, what I mean

is that I will instruct Thorpe not to deliver notes without coming to me first. Were you injured, Anna Liese?'

'A splinter, that's all.'

Beckoning to Martha, who was standing near the doorway looking concerned at what was happening, Anna Liese's stepmother waved her over.

'Come, take your mistress upstairs and see to her finger.'

'Do not bother.' Peter nodded to Martha. 'I shall see to it.'

With that, he led his frazzled-looking friend out of the drawing room. They had done what needed doing in letting the Baroness know her scheme had failed. The sooner they were out of her company the better. As welcome dinners went, this one was memorable.

The last thing he heard going out was Mildred's whine of complaint.

'My stepmother will be in a mood now,' Anna Liese said while sitting on a stool in a quiet corner of the kitchen.

'That is for her to deal with. She needed to know she had not got the better of you.'

Easy for him to say, but she would be the one left to deal with the aftermath. Ah, well, it was not as if she had not done so before. Trying to avoid her stepmother's moods was not easy even at the best of times.

A few of the staff bustled about, placing pastries and drinks on trays to be carried out to the guests.

One of the scullery maids cast Anna Liese a puzzled glance while she scrubbed a pot.

'Please carry on, Lucy.' The last thing she wanted

was for the girl to have to work later than necessary in order to give them privacy.

Martha hurried across the kitchen, then placed a clean towel, a bowl of steaming water and a pair of tweezers on the small table next to the window where she and Peter sat. Wind blew against the diamond-shaped panes, making one of them rattle.

Martha returned with a small lamp and set it on the table. 'Be gentle with her, my lord.' Martha gave them a smile, a wink, and then hurried away.

Peter picked up the tweezers, turned them this way and that so they glittered in the light, then he set them down. He held his palm open for her to place her hand in.

'Don't be worried.' He held her finger to the light, examining it, then dipped a corner of the towel in the warm water, wrapped it around her finger and gently pressed.

'Does it hurt?'

'It is tender, but I will do.'

'I'll make quick work of it.'

'You have done this before, when we were children.'

Then his hand had been slender and boyish. Not like now—now it was large, masculine and the fingers brushed with coarse hair. She hoped he did not make terribly quick of work of removing the splinter.

'I haven't removed one since then. Let us hope I have not lost the skill.'

'I remember once you pulled one out of my thumb with your teeth. Still, I shall try my best to be brave.'

He looked into her eyes for a long silent time while

he pressed the warm cloth to her hand. The only sound was the loose pane of glass shivering the wind.

'You are the bravest person I know, but I have to ask. Anna Liese, you were with Grant for a long time before I got there—did he… What I am trying to ask is if he hurt you?'

'I do not imagine you had time to notice the condition of the bank while you were punching him in the jaw.'

'I've a vague impression of papers scattered on the floor as if there had been a fight.'

'He did not harm me, Peter, only scared me. But in the end, I think I scared him more.'

'How could you possibly?'

'I let him get a glimpse of what it would be like to be married to me. I can't think he would enjoy being trapped for ever with a nagging shrew.'

'You are clever, my sweet friend,' he said while picking up the tweezers. 'Perhaps you did not need me pedaling to your rescue.'

'I did, you know I did. He was bound to become angry after what I did to his paperwork, not to mention his trousers.'

'You came in contact with his trousers?'

His touch on her finger remained gentle, but his eyes sharpened in a way she had never seen.

'Not directly. I poured ink on his chair and encouraged him to sit on it.'

He grinned, but said, 'That was too risky. You should have been more cautious.'

'It would have been worse to cower and I did need to know how far he might be pushed.'

'Luckily, no harm came of it.' He lifted the tweezers to the light, showing her the splinter nipped in the small tongs. 'But there is still your stepmother.'

'She was chastised tonight, but honestly, Peter, the only thing that will make her stop will be for me to marry, or for Mildred to.'

'I cannot help but think marrying would be better than being under constant worry. If you did wed, you could make a choice about your husband rather than having one foisted upon you.'

That not the case. She was kept away from any man worth consideration. And, more importantly, the only man she would choose had just let go of her hand. The man she would choose had an eye on a society wedding in which he would not be required to involve his heart. Such a choice made no sense whatsoever since he had the kindest and most giving heart of anyone she knew.

'I am exhausted, Peter. Go back to your guests if you wish, but I'm going up to bed.' She leaned across the small table, kissed his cheek and let her lips linger a bit longer than friendliness required. 'Thank you for capturing the splinter—and for saving me from having to marry Hyrum Grant.'

I love you, her heart declared while her lips said, 'Goodnight, Peter.'

She stood up, recognising by his frown that he did not wish to go back to the gathering in his honour.

'In case you have forgotten, the kitchen door is that way.' She pointed to a hallway which led to the butler's pantry and then outside.

'Ah, yes, it comes back to me now. So much is coming back—goodnight, Anna Liese.'

He strode down the hallway, but stopped halfway and turned about. He went back through the kitchen again.

'I suppose I must go back,' he mumbled in passing. Then stopping, he said, 'Will you come bicycling with me tomorrow? I believe we could use some fresh air to cleanse this evening from our minds.'

'Meet me on the bridge in the morning.'

He nodded and continued on his way towards the grand drawing room.

She smiled after him because she did not wish to cleanse everything from her mind. Parts of the evening had been harrowing. Had Peter not come to her rescue, she might be facing wedded misery with Hyrum.

But he had rescued her and she would never forget how brave and handsome he had been while doing it. Not every woman had a hero. Many had husbands, yes, but she had her knight in shining armour. No matter what happened in her lonely future, Peter Penneyjons would shine in her heart.

Chapter Eleven

The evening finally ended, Peter opened his front door and then decided he was still too restless to sleep.

Closing the door again, he turned and walked along the back path and then up the hill. At the crest, he sat down on the bench. How many times had he and Anna Liese sat on the bench, watching the folks of Woodlore Glen going about their lives?

Down below, the village was shut up for the night. Only a few lamps shone out of the windows below. It all looked so peaceful—so idyllic.

He might have been content with the image of perfection had it not been for one thing. The back door of the bank, although distant, was in his line of vision. Illuminated in the lamplight of one window, he thought he spotted a figure going past the barred glass. Grant was probably sweeping up the mess of papers Anna Liese had left on the floor. Peter could only guess he was hopping mad about it.

While it had been clever, tricking him into sitting

in ink, the situation spurring Anna Liese to take action had not been humorous.

A while ago, they had made light of the encounter simply because it was easier to do than to openly confront the danger she had truly been in. Which did not mean he was unaware of the evil that had nearly happened.

Had the man got away with what he had intended to, Anna Liese's future would have been a grim one. She had told Peter what she wanted of a marriage. For her it would be a love match or nothing. What the banker would have forced upon her would have been the opposite.

Wind blew briskly from behind, pushing his hair in his face and obscuring his vision. He gathered it in a clump on top of his head and held it there.

Overhead, gusts whipped through bare branches, sounding like a chorus of moans, as if it were singing a song of ill will—of impending doom. Feeling this maudlin was unlike him, but staring at Anna Liese's precarious future made him ill at ease.

For as long as he remained in Woodlore Glen, he would be able to watch over her. But who would do it when he returned to London? She had no man to stand up for her. Her maid, Martha, would do what she could, he thought, but she was a mature lady. What could she do other than report trouble to the Baroness who was the cause of the trouble to begin with?

Because of the wind, the sky was clear, the stars cold and sparkling. He gazed at them for a long time, hoping some solution to this problem would come to him. Short of going down the hill and strangling the man, he did not know what it might be. Since it was not in him to do murder, here he sat, as confused and troubled as he had ever been in his life.

If Aunt Adelia were here she would know what to do. The woman was as clever a lady as he had ever known. He could not recall a social drama she had not been able to sort out. This was not precisely a social drama, but if he pretended to be Aunt Adelia for a moment, thought the way she might think, an answer might come to him. Drawing upon her image, he imagined her sitting beside him, smiling while she tapped her finger on her chin in thought.

'Peter Penneyjons, you do know what to do,' her pretend image told him. Odd how her imagined voice sounded so real. He had to blink to bring her image in and out of focus to be certain she had not inexplicably appeared on the bench.

'No, Aunt, I do not,' he spoke aloud since he was alone on the hilltop.

'It is as simple as keeping her with you, my boy,' his imaginary advisor said in that vivacious way she had about her.

'There is nothing simple about that,' he grumbled. 'I live in London and she lives here.'

'I find marriage to my liking, Peter.'

What? This was his imagination he was conversing with—how could it possibly take such an unexpected turn? Just because Aunt Adelia had found her late-in-life marriage to her liking did not mean that he would find the same in his.

'Goodnight, Aunt Adelia. I will see you at the Christmas ball.'

What he needed was advice from her lips, not what he thought she might say.

A huff of wind bussed his cheek. Odd what one's mind could conjure. He imagined this gust was warmer than the others and that it had been a parting kiss from his aunt—who was not here.

He stood up, stretched and thought he might be able to sleep after all. Because present in the flesh or not, he thought his aunt had given him the answer to his problem. An answer he rather liked the idea of. Coming down the hill, he felt hopeful about it.

Once inside the cottage, he got into bed, looking forward to the morning and being with Anna Liese.

Surely she would agree that what he had decided to do was brilliant and a benefit to them both. With a great yawn, he crossed his hands over his chest and smiled.

Coming outside, Anna Liese decided it was not ideal weather for touring about on bicycles. Dark clouds skimmed the hilltops all about Woodlore Glen. She would not be surprised to see snowflakes at some point today. What a stroke of luck that the wind had stopped blowing.

Peter waited for her on the bridge, flanked by bicycles.

He looked fine and manly bundled against the weather. Watching his welcoming grin, she sighed inside at the way the way the brackets at the corners of his mouth deepened. The sight of him chased away some of the chill.

Not all of it, though—her nose and lips still felt icy. A kiss would warm them. A kiss which was not going to happen. She would have to be content imagining the heat that would simmer inside her—suffuse her from head to toe.

'Brrr...' Peter said, stamping his feet as if to warm them. 'May I suggest we ride no further than the village?'

'Please do say we will go no further. Sitting in front of the fireplace at the village tearoom would be wiser than freezing our toes off.' Sitting astride the bicycle and tucking in her skirt, she glanced up. The clouds looked darker than they had seconds ago. 'Do you think it will snow?'

'I wouldn't mind if it did. We don't see a great deal of it in London.'

'We don't see it much here either, especially this early in the year.'

By the time they parked their bicycles behind the restaurant and hurried inside, Anna Liese was convinced a blizzard was coming.

It was warm and festive inside with holly and berries on the tables and swathes of cedar and pine over the windows.

They had a choice of tables since they were the only customers. Ordinarily at this time of morning there were other visitors, but apparently they had hesitated to come out in the weather.

'I do not remember it ever being so cold,' she said, taking a seat at a table in front of the fireplace. Warmth washing over her from the flames gave her a delightful shiver. The sensation was so delightful that she wondered if the shiver did not have to do with heat from without, but heat from within.

What, she had to wonder, would Peter think if she admitted her feelings for him? How they had grown from those of a child to those of a woman. She would not dare to admit it because she had no reason to believe he felt the same way. She would rather not offer her heart up to be broken. Better to wait and hope.

Which was easier said than accomplished since she had spent the whole of the night imagining how wonderful it would be to be married to him. Each day they would awake with declarations of love and then end the day declaring it without words.

Hmm, her odd shiver probably was not caused by the fire. It skittered over her skin in a pleasant heat which mere hearth flames could not account for.

'I don't either. Since I have not been here at this time of year in so long, I don't remember the weather. What I do remember is how much fun we always had no matter the temperature.' He cleared his throat, seeming oddly ill at ease. 'You do remember what fun we used to have, Anna Liese?'

The serving girl came out of the kitchen carrying two cups of hot chocolate. She set them on the table, smiling. They had not yet ordered drinks, but the girl must assume anyone who was out and about this morning would welcome them.

'I do not need to go back so far to remember, Peter. It has only been a few moments since we had fun.' She took a sip of chocolate, sighing at the sweet warmth sliding down her throat. 'I find bicycling to be greatly entertaining. Thank you so much for teaching me.'

'You should come riding with me in London. Hyde Park is an interesting place to pedal about.'

'Hyde Park? That is for society nobs—oh, but you are one of them. Sometimes I forget it.'

'You are also one of them, my friend.'

'Sometimes I forget that, too.' On the social scale she felt closer to humble than noble.

The waitress returned to take their order for breakfast, then hurried away.

'Anna Liese, after I left you last night, was everything well? I hope the Baroness did not take her frustrations out on you.'

'I retired without seeing her and was out this morning before she rose. I imagine I will need to deal with it later this afternoon.'

'I invited them to London, to attend the ball. I can only hope their attention will be diverted and they will leave you alone.'

Had he wanted to invite them? She could not imagine he did. But in the end, what did two more title-hunters matter? The occasion of the ball was for him to choose among the ladies, was it not? Certainly, he knew enough of Mildred not to pick her.

She imagined a few of the women attending his ball would suit his requirements of a convenient marriage—one which would not be marked with morning kisses and nightly declarations of love. Poor Peter. She did want better for him—although to be honest she did not want him to find it with someone who was not her.

For all that she felt left out at not being invited to his ball, she was relieved for it even more. It was difficult to imagine anything worse than watching him seek a bride—or having him ask her opinion on which of them might suit.

'I meant to invite you last night at dinner, but then you were not there to be invited. Afterwards, a social invitation seemed frivolous.' He reached across the table, curled his big, warm fingers around hers. 'Won't you attend? We will have a good time. I would like to show you what London has to offer. Just think of it, we can ramble about as if we were children again.'

It was crushing to know that was how he viewed her, as the child she had been. Had their relationship not progressed from that? In her heart she thought it had. Was it possible it had only been her heart to have progressed?

My word, but they had nearly kissed twice!

Maybe she ought to go the ball and wear the new gown which was secreted away in Martha's quarters. The flirtatious bodice would put the issue to rest, once and for all. She took a second to imagine what his re-action to her womanly figure would be. Better to let go of that image. A snapping fire in the hearth was quite enough heat.

But, no, she would not be attending his spouse-hunting ball.

'I fear you must find your bride without my help, Peter.' She wriggled her hand out of his. 'You are the only one who can make such a choice.'

'I have always believed my requirements in a bride are simple.' He frowned for a second, then blinked and resumed his smile. Something was shifting about in his mind, but she could not imagine what. 'I shall be content as long as she is companionable and of good character.'

'Peter Penneyjons! That is a cavalier attitude. You

should care very much. You speak of your future as if the lady will make little difference in it, as if one was interchangeable with another. I am certain whoever she turns out to be will resent it.'

'I'm sorry, it did sound callous. I only meant that this is how it is for men of my station. I am expected to pick a bride for her position in society—for her large dowry. Every lady seeking my attention understands it.'

'As noble as you may be, Peter, you ought to know better having arranged love matches for your cousins.'

'I hadn't a hand in any of that. One and all, they chose for themselves.'

This was not a subject she wished to discuss. Let him choose where he would.

A bell jingled over the front door. A tall, dark-haired young man rushed inside. He glanced about while brushing the shoulders of his coat.

His smile settled on the young waitress who was standing on a chair affixing a sprig of mistletoe to a beam.

'It has begun to snow, Catherine!' he exclaimed, grinning at them as well as her. 'We might have a white Christmas if it lasts.'

'I'm working, Glenn.' The girl shot him a grin over her shoulder. The handsome young man hurried over to help her down. 'You must come back later.'

Catherine's smile lingered on Glenn, her affection for him evident.

'Please say you will come sledding!'

'Off with you, now.' Catherine shooed her fingers at him. 'The snow has not yet covered the ground.'

Glenn did not seem to care. He took her hand and

tugged her towards the front door. With the way his blue eyes were twinkling, Anna Liese could not imagine how Catherine resisted the invitation.

What Anna Liese saw in the young man's eyes made her heart yearn for what she was not likely to have in her own life. So far, she had seen no sign of anything like that in Peter's eyes.

In the face of the young man's affection for Catherine, Anna Liese was reminded that in Peter's eyes, she was only a friend—a dear friend—but not a true love.

'Later, then—I'll be back for you when the snow is deeper.' Not seeming to care that there were customers in the restaurant, Glenn kissed Catherine on her lips, quickly, joyfully.

Catherine swatted his arm, gave him a false frown. 'The mistletoe is over there.'

He pulled her under the inviting sprig, then kissed her again.

'I beg your pardon,' the girl said, pressing her fingers to the blush in her cheeks. 'Glenn asked me to be his wife last night and he has not settled from the excitement of it yet.'

With that, she spun about and half skipped to the kitchen. Clearly, Catherine's heart had not settled either. What a joyful thing it must be, to feel so flushed with love, with such hope for the future.

Peter was saying something to her, but she'd quite lost track of what it was. Witnessing the love the young couple shared for one another made her reaffirm her commitment not to marry until a man looked at her the way Glenn looked at Catherine.

Returning her attention to Peter, she found him

blinking at her, his smile indulgent and—and friendly. Clearly, thoughts of mistletoe were not on his mind.

'I'm sorry, Peter, what were you saying?'

'I don't blame you for not hearing me. With the snow coming down harder, it is exciting.'

'We shall have great fun,' she answered, grateful that she did not need to make up a reason for her lack of attention. 'Build a snowman or go sledding?'

'I'm for a snowball fight—have we ever had one? I can't recall. But first I would like to discuss what you did not hear me saying.'

'Of course. By the time we have finished discussing it the snow will be deep enough for play.'

Peter cleared his throat, that odd sense of nervousness she had noticed a moment ago returned.

'Is something wrong?'

He nodded, pursed his lips. 'I am worried about you. I need to know you will be safe when I return to London. Just because Hyrum Grant is not likely to be a threat, someone else might be.'

'You needn't be worried. I have been dealing with this sort of thing for years. You may return to London. Find your bride, Peter. I will get along as I always have.'

Except that she would not get along as she always had. In the past she not been in love. While it was true that she had always loved Peter, that love had been for a child—from a child. Now that she loved the man, nothing would ever be the same.

'Truly? Have you ever been kidnapped before?'

'I will admit, I did let down my guard, but it was only because I thought you were ill.'

'I will not allow that to happen to you again. I have come up with a solution to your problem.'

Had he? She could not imagine how since he did not know what her problem was: that she was in love with him and he was not in love her.

The reason he was unaware of it was because she had not told him. Perhaps she ought to. Right now, sitting here with no one to distract them, she should confess, 'I love you Peter'. In her heart she knew she must. If she did not, the regret would follow her for ever.

Very well, then——

He reached across the table, caught her hand again, held on and squeezed her fingers. 'What if you married me?' he said.

The confession died in her mouth—in her heart.

'Do not refuse me right off. If you think about it, it makes sense.'

Sense! As words of love went—sense was not one. Sense was the last thing a woman—this woman—wanted to hear when being proposed to.

'Have you lost your mind, Peter Penneyjons?'

'Not at all. If we wed, the Baroness will not be able to force you to marry someone you do not wish to.'

'I do not wish to marry you!'

She did, of course. But not unless he loved her, which he clearly did not.

'We already know we get along well.'

'Getting along and being in love are not the same thing.' Her stomach roiled. If she did not lose her hot chocolate, it would only be by an effort of extraordinary self-control.

'Ever since last night I've been thinking about this.'

Given that he was grinning, he was clearly not aware of cleaving her heart in half. 'To go into a marriage already knowing I like my bride will be a great relief. We both benefit from the arrangement.'

'A relief? Because you already like me?' She stood up, clenching her fists so he would not see them trembling.

'You know I do—you are and always have been my dearest friend. Many marriages begin with less.'

'The one I want—' she concentrated on breathing, in and out, slow and steady '—requires much more.'

Peter stood up, reaching for her hand with a pleading glance. 'Anna Liese, you must know how deeply I care for you.'

'I will never accept a sensible proposal from anyone, even you.'

She spun away. Out of the corner of her eye, she noticed Catherine frowning, shaking her head. As young as the waitress was, she knew more than Lord Cliverton did!

'I understand this proposal is not the romantic one you wished for. I suppose I should have used prettier words, recited a romantic poem perhaps. But before you dismiss it out of hand, consider how it will benefit both of us. And is marriage not meant to be a beneficial arrangement for both parties?'

Marching to the door, she snatched her coat from the rack and jerkily put it on. If she did not escape this instant, he was going to discover how deeply he had wounded her.

Beneficial arrangement? Hang beneficial—stamp on it and curse it! Romance be hanged as well. He knew what she wanted of a marriage and yet he... Had the man no heart?

How shallow he made her emotions seem. What little value he placed upon them. Did he not understand that mere romance, hearts, flowers and vain poetry, came and went as if borne on a fickle breeze? It was bone-deep, lifelong devotion she craved. If she could not have that, she would have nothing at all.

And now she knew beyond a doubt he did not feel that sort of love for her. In his eyes, she was still a girl, fit only for laughter and adventuring. Worse—for a marriage of convenience.

'Good day, Lord Cliverton,' she snapped.

It had been on the tip of her tongue to say goodbye, farewell for ever, but despite what he had done she could not manage it. Tomorrow, or the next day, she would tell him goodbye. She would wish him success in finding a bride he would grow to like.

After she regained control over her emotions, she would wish him well in a life that was lacking the very thing that counted most in the world. The very thing she now knew for certain she would not have. Love to endure the storms of life, to withstand hardship and rejoice in blessings, was now unobtainable because, apparently, he was not capable of such devotion.

She had completely misjudged the man young Peter had grown to be.

Closing the door behind her, she went outside. Striding past her bicycle, she forsook the convenience of a quick trip home. She no longer wanted his gift. Huffing, she walked briskly through a hail of snowflakes.

The salt being rubbed in her soul wound was that

Peter was correct. If she wed him, she would be beyond her stepmother's reach for ever. She could not
help but see his point. Also, looking at the situation as
Peter must be doing, he would be saved from the effort of finding a suitable bride. One whom he need not
commit his heart to. It was all so logical.

'Anna Liese, wait!'

Wait for what? For Lord Cliverton to be struck by
Cupid's arrow?

She glanced over her shoulder, saw him pushing
both bicycles through a swirling gust. She walked
faster, but not fast enough.

'Give my offer more thought before you dismiss it!'

'I already have!' she called over her shoulder.

Luckily, no one was about witness this sorry business.

'I will come for your answer tomorrow!'

At which time she would carry through with her intention of wishing him an adequate future without love.

Without her.

Chapter Twelve

That had not gone the way he had imagined it would.

All the way home he had walked several yards behind Anna Liese, trying to understand why she was so angry.

While it was true that she'd told him she wanted a true love match, it was also true that her safety was at risk—her future.

For as long as Mildred remained unmarried, Anna Liese ran the risk of being bound to a man who would treat her badly. There were worse men out there than Grant. Gentlemen who called themselves such, but were cads under it all.

He watched while she crossed the bridge, marched the path towards her front door, then went inside.

If she continued to refuse him, there was still one thing he could do to protect her—although the thing hardly bore thinking about.

Leaving the bicycles at the back door, he went inside, trying to forget the solution to protect Anna Liese which had just popped into his mind. Although once imagined, it was difficult to put aside because, for as awful as it was, it did make sense.

Kneeling to bring the fire in the drawing room hearth to full flame, he hated that wedding Mildred might be the only way to keep Anna Liese safe.

Anna Liese was correct when she told him the Baroness would not cease her efforts until one of them wed. Since Anna Liese refused his logical offer, what else could he do? The idea of marrying Mildred was so distasteful it left a bitter residue in his mind.

When it came down to it, perhaps he could not do it. For all that he did not require a love match the way Anna Liese did, he did require a lady more congenial than Mildred was.

Perhaps if he teased Anna Liese with this second idea, she would not wish him to sacrifice himself for her. Despite her rejection of his proposal, he knew she did care about him. Their friendship was a rare and beautiful thing. It was impossible to believe she no longer felt it.

Still squatting, he poked the flames with an iron, trying to understand why she had seemed so hurt. What had he said that was so objectionable? He had assumed their bond was deep. Even after all the years that had passed, they had easily picked up where they left off.

The moment they'd been reunited, the way they had been in the old days had slipped into place as easily as if the years had not happened. Even though they were no longer children and she had grown to be a beautiful woman, they were still who they had been or so he assumed until moments ago.

He stood up, glancing about the drawing room.

Thanks to Anna Liese's help it was ready for the family to come for a visit. It had been such a pleasure working with her over the weeks. He felt she thought so, too. Surely, she must see what a pleasant life they would share if she married him.

'Curse it,' he whispered, even though no one would hear his frustration.

Wedding Anna Liese was not without risk—he had not thoroughly considered this before proposing. The fact was, he did love her. He always had. To lose his great friend to death would be more than he could bear, even without sharing the grand passion she wanted of him.

He didn't, did he? He had never allowed himself to feel that sort of emotion for fear of the crippling loss. He was not certain he could live through such grief again.

But right now, he did fear losing his friend. No matter what the thing he felt for her was called, he did not wish to lose it. Which, it seemed he was about to do. He must seek Anna Liese out. He needed to convince her of the wisdom of becoming Lady Cliverton before he returned to London the day after tomorrow.

Everything about this was right. They got along. She would fit in well with his family. Most importantly, she would be safe with him. Whatever it took to make her happy in their marriage, he was prepared to do it.

Suddenly he was struck by two thoughts at once. First, he wondered if marrying a woman only because she was appropriate was enough for him. It must be because he had always believed it to be so. He had seen that kind of marriage more often than marriages where love came first. That is, if one did not count one's own family.

And second, quite to his surprise, the thought of Anna Liese being married to her 'true love match' made him feel—queasy.

He strode to the window and watched the snow drift past in whirls. An emotion he had never felt in his life snaked around his gut, flicking a barb at his heart. He thought he might be jealous—of a man who did not exist. The person, her true love, was an idea. Curse the dream lover.

How was he to compete with an idea?

Since it looked as if going out tonight would be impossible given the weather, he would have to wait until morning and then go see what was to be done about vanquishing Anna Liese's dream lover.

Upon rising, Anna Liese knew what she must do and do it without delay. Say goodbye to Peter. He was scheduled to go back to London tomorrow, but she would bid him farewell today.

Putting it off for another day would be too difficult. As it was her nerves felt like jangling bells. She was not sure how she would manage to part from him, but waiting another day to do it would only draw the tension out. She would simply—no, not simply—but none the less get it over with.

Putting on her warmest cloak, she walked to the stable. It was not that she was procrastinating, she merely needed to check on Fannie, make sure the goose had come in from the storm.

This afternoon would be soon enough to speak with

Peter, to accept a future without him in it. Glancing at the cottage on the way to the stable, she wanted to cry. It was not entirely true that he would not be a part of her life. He would bring his adequate wife to visit— and his children who were bound be adorable.

It was hard to fathom how she would manage to be a friendly neighbour, to welcome them all as if she were not desperate to be that woman and the mother of those children.

Entering the stable, she found the stove lit and the space warm. Their occasional stableman must have come from the village to check on the animals.

'Fannie!' she called. She heard straw shuffling. Seconds later the goose waddled out of a stall, giving her a honk in greeting.

'There you are!' Anna Liese stooped down to pet the bird. 'You don't have a mate and you get along fine. You shall be my inspiration.'

Fannie ruffled her feathers, turned about and sauntered back to where she had been nesting.

It was too cold to go back out so soon and she did not wish to return to the manor. Stepmama and Mildred had risen early, buzzing about and preparing for travel. Twice already, Mildred had asked if Anna Liese knew whether Peter would be paying a call before leaving for London. It should not be annoying to hear her stepsister call Peter by his name, but it was. Mildred's obsession with their neighbour was wearing on Anna Liese's nerves.

'I'll need to get used to hearing it,' she explained while Fannie's white tail disappeared around a stall door. 'Very soon some woman will be calling him that. No doubt blinking great doe eyes at him, too.'

It did not have to be that way. She could prevent it by marrying him herself. She could accept his proposal, such as it was and perhaps in time she could make him see her as a woman. Perhaps he might come to love her...eventually. Perhaps...but perhaps not. So far, he hadn't fallen in love with her, even after they nearly shared two very perfect kisses. Perfect in her opinion, but clearly not his. But what if she had actually indulged in one of those almost kisses? Would it have made a difference?

Hoping for love to follow marriage was too great a risk. She did not think she could bear looking into his eyes, feeling so deeply for him and not seeing that love reflected back at her. To see him gaze at her in deep friendship would break her heart bit by bit as the days passed.

But wouldn't that be better than never being able to gaze into his eyes at all? Better than witnessing some other lucky woman gazing into them—wondering if he had fallen in love with her and then all the while be wondering if she, herself, had made a mistake? Would she wonder if the knife stabbing her heart might not be there if she had given him time to fall in love with her?

It was a bit much to think about. There was only one thing she knew of to soothe her stress and that was to sing. Someone had wisely placed a barrel in front of the stove. She sat upon it, let the warmth wrap around her, then began to sing 'The Holly and the Ivy'.

The gentle rise and fall of the tune filled her, took her away to a scene in her head—of a manger with a newborn baby boy lying in it. There were things of greater importance than her love for Peter Penneyjons.

Christmas was nearly upon them, bringing a time for joy and singing, for rejoicing no matter what one's circumstances happened to be.

Lost in her song, she did not hear the stable door creak open, but evidently it had.

'Anna Liese?' Peter's whisper drew her back to this stable and this time.

She did not turn at first because she was not ready to face him. However, she would need to if she were to carry through with bidding him farewell. Pivoting slowly on the barrel, she donned her emotional armour, pasting a smile into place.

'Hello, Peter.'

'I know you too well to believe that is a genuine smile and that you are not still angry with me.'

'You might be right about the smile, but if you believe I am angry, you do not know me as well as you think you do.'

'As well as I know anyone.' He shrugged, then held his hands out as if in supplication. 'And I care for you as much as I do anyone.'

She remained sitting, not trusting her balance overmuch. The man made her dizzy with the desire to show him how mistaken he was about what made for a good marriage. Certainly, he must be aware of the draw between them. It was impossible the attraction she felt was not returned. He was being amazingly stubborn in facing it.

Even with half a stable separating them, she felt the heat of wanting him pulsing under her skin. It was beyond belief that he could be causing her to simmer this way without being aware of it. She was no expert in male–female matters, but she did understand there was some force drawing them towards each other and it was not platonic.

If she had the boldness of a bird, she would give him a kiss to prove it. She would melt all over him and not release his lips until he admitted his passion for her. Unless he did not admit it, but pushed her away instead. She had never been so sure, and at the same time unsure, of anything in her life.

'Since you are here—' she folded her hands primly on her lap, which was far from what she was imagining doing with them '—I will bid you goodbye now and save either of us from having to venture out in the cold later.'

'How very thoughtful of you, Anna Liese.' His attitude seemed to turn as prickly as the one she was faking. 'But you need not be so quick to bid me goodbye. I will be back for Christmas with my family.'

'I am aware. Will you bring your fiancée as well? I shall be delighted to meet her—whoever she turns out to be.'

The oddest look of displeasure crossed his features. She could not recall seeing one like it before.

'I am still hoping she will be you.' He took two steps towards her, then stopped. Leaning his hip against a stall door, he crossed his arms over his chest.

The pose made him look manly, so virile and appealing she had to clench her fingers together. Harder to do, she shut tender yearnings for him away, pretended she was as unfeeling for him as he seemed to be for her.

'Tell me you will reconsider my proposal, Anna Liese.' His gaze softened to the one she was familiar with. 'If you marry me, I promise to be a decent husband to you. I will do whatever is needed to make sure you are happy. I will sacrifice anything to ensure you remain safe.'

'I do not require martyrdom of a husband.'

'You know that is not what I meant. Only that I will not see you shackled to some charlatan. No matter what you think of me for proposing a convenient marriage, I am bound to be a better choice than some man your stepmother has bribed to wed you.'

She was far too insulted to admit he was correct. She would be far better off with Peter.

'I am better off unwed if such are my choices.'

'At some point you will be forced into it. Please, Anna Liese—do not sacrifice your happiness for no reason. Marry me.'

What nonsense! In his opinion waiting for love was 'no reason'? He expected her to give that up in order to gain safe haven? Although, what was the point of waiting for something that was not going to happen? Still—

'No, Peter. Once again, I will not marry you.' She meant the rejection to sound forceful. Sadly, her voice emerged soft...whispery.

'Make me understand, my friend, because I do not. Am I so repulsive that you prefer a scoundrel?'

All right, then! He needed to understand. Words did not seem adequate to illustrate it, so...

Rising from the barrel, she took a fortifying breath,

clasped her hands in front of her to keep them from trembling. Rushing for him before she lost courage, she grasped one of his hands, boldly placing it at her waist. His brows shot up. His handsome jaw dropped.

Undaunted, she took his other hand, curled her fingers through his, then tucked their joined hands behind her back. Lifting up on her toes, she leaned against his chest so that he could not miss the fact that she was no longer the child he remembered, or that her heart raced madly. She kissed his chin, nipping the prickly skin of a missed shave.

He turned his head so that her quick, hot breath mixed with his. He jerked her closer by their joined hands. She was not certain he meant to but, still, he had done it.

Emboldened, she turned her mouth a scant inch closer. She kissed his lips. She felt it when he cast away hesitation. The weight of his body shifted away from the stall while he drew her ever closer and up so that her toes almost lifted off the floor. Kissing her, he stroked the back of her hair, tangled his fingers in the strands.

Drowning in his presence, in his scent, in his heat, she knew she was correct to refuse sacrificing this part of marriage. But would she? This moment was intensely passionate—would he give in to it fully if she wed him?

His fingers felt bold, unhesitating, sweeping the hair away from her neck. When he kissed the tender flesh under her ear, she gripped her hand into the front of his shirt in order to keep grounded.

While she did not actually float off the stable floor,

she was drifting away to a place where dreams came true and love was for ever.

Finally, with a gasp and great sense of loss, she pushed away. She was panting so hard she feared she would not be able to speak. But she must speak if only to keep herself from launching back into his arms.

'That, Peter Penneyjons, is what I will not sacrifice.'

He reached for her, clearly wanting to kiss her again. But any man could kiss a woman and leave her wanting. It was for her to leave him wanting—finally understanding.

'If you marry me—'

She backed several steps away. Watched while his hand clenched, dropped to his side.

'If I marry you, I will be safe. I realise that—but still, I cannot do it.'

Silently, he stared at her, looked as if he would speak and then did not.

'Very well, Anna Liese. I accept that you will not marry me. But do not think I will not do what I must to keep you safe.'

He spun about and strode towards the stable door.

She followed him because—what did he mean by that? She plucked on his sleeve.

He spun around, looking rather like a condemned man. The way he gazed down at her, his lips drawn tight and his eyes shadowed in misery, it was as if she were the one to condemn him.

Oh, no! This rift between them was his doing. She was the innocent party and quite correct to hold out for what she wanted in life.

'I do not understand how you—'

He opened the door. Cold air rushed inside, whirling loose straw into circles on the stone floor.

'But you do, Anna Liese. You said it yourself.'

She shook her head because she could not imagine what he was getting at.

'You said, and were correct about it, that the only way the Baroness will leave you alone is when either you or Mildred marry.'

She had said that and it was true. 'Neither of us are marrying, so I do not understand your point.'

'You are not willing to marry me.' He looked past her shoulder, silent for several seconds. 'I think Mildred will be. I will ask her to be my wife at the ball.'

'You cannot marry—'

'I will do it, Anna Liese.'

And the next she knew she was staring at the wood grain on the stable door. Struck dumb, her thoughts scattered to—to somewhere where they tried to make sense of this, but utterly failed.

There was only a dusting of snow at Cliverton, but what there was, Peter heard crunching under his boots while he came up the front steps of the town house.

He wished he could have remained in Woodlore Glenn a bit longer. He found that the place now felt like his home of old. His old memories were happy ones and he anticipated making new ones there with his family.

Had it not been for the ball which there was no longer a reason for, he would have.

Because invitations had been sent and accepted, he had to carry through with the gala. Ladies would have purchased expensive gowns and whatever went with them in anticipation of being selected as his Viscountess. The ball had not been announced as a bride hunt, but everyone knew it to be one.

It is how these things worked.

He wondered if his family had arrived already. The ball would be worthwhile if only to see them. Especially Aunt Adelia. What he needed more than anything was to speak with her—to get her approval on what he was about to do. As a member of society, she knew what was expected of a man in his position and would set his apprehension to rest.

And he did have a great deal of apprehension.

What would his family think of Mildred? She would become a member of the family and it was important that they like her. Or, at the least, tolerate her.

Tolerate—the word bounced around his brain as if it could not find a suitable place to lodge. Once he wed, that was how it would be—he would begin his day by finding a way to tolerate his wife.

If only Anna Liese had not refused him.

Looking at his future, at the woman he would spend the rest of his days with, he wondered if Anna Liese was correct in waiting for a love match. Living with a person one was in love with could only be a better choice.

The truth was, he did love Anna Liese! But just now, he was confused about what form that love took. After she had kissed him in the stable, he had little doubt of how she felt about him. That kiss had left him shaken to the core...it illuminated dark shadows in his heart.

Ever since going back to Woodlore Glen and renewing their friendship, he had been happier than he had been in a long time. Being with Anna Liese, rediscovering his past, faded memories clicked neatly into place.

Until he had asked for her hand in marriage, life had been complete. Had he been a wiser man he would have asked for her heart rather than her hand. No, not that. What was needed was for him to offer his heart.

He really did need to speak with his aunt. His heart was a three-ring circus with ideas and emotions spinning all at once. Holding Anna Liese in his arms had done something to him. He had been aware of a shift on that rainy night on the hilltop.

But after she had pronounced the near kiss something to be got out of the way, he had backed away from its importance, assuming he had misjudged her feelings.

Perhaps she had not been truthful that night. Would it have made a difference if she had been? Would he have looked at her as a lover and not a friend? There was no way of knowing. He could not blame himself for not responding to a heart that was not offered.

But yesterday's kiss had been different. Not only had she offered her heart in it, but he had responded in a way he had not expected to. The wall he had erected against deep intimacy crashed down on his boots. Which changed nothing about the position he now found himself in.

Anna Liese had stirred him, body and soul. Given time, he believed he would be able to offer her the true love match she needed. That it would be worth the price he might have to pay. But there was no time. She wanted assurance of it before she committed to being wed. What he wanted, needed, was assurance that she would be safe while he was away from Woodlore Glen.

He shivered. How long had he been standing on the porch lost in his thoughts? Long enough apparently for the butler to notice, because the door opened while he reached for the knob. Coming inside, he handed off his coat.

'Welcome home, sir, it is good to have you back.'

'Thank you, Conner. It is good to be back.'

But was it? The house seemed larger than it ever had—quieter.

Perhaps once his family arrived it would feel more welcoming. For a time, at least. The day would soon come when they would return to their own homes and here he would be, once again alone. Until he married and his Viscountess came to live at Cliverton, the house would be like this.

In the beginning, when he thought ahead to his marriage, he hadn't believed knowing the lady beforehand to be greatly important. He needed a viscountess and the lady would have been trained her whole life to become one. The way of courtship was traditional and uncomplicated—satisfactory.

Now he could not help but look ahead and wonder if having Mildred living under his roof would be worse than living alone. It was not as if he would go out of his way to be in her company. More likely he would retreat to his study and she to shopping and social engagements.

Glancing about his tastefully decorated walls, an image of Anna Liese came to his mind. He saw her rushing down the grand staircase, her arms spread to welcome him home, her smile happy and her fair hair streaking behind her.

Since yesterday, his mind pictured her everywhere. How could it not after she, his dearest friend, demonstrated in a poignant way what she would be sacrificing in order to marry him. It was as if he could still smell lavender in her hair, feel the heat of her breath on his mouth and the provocative nip of her teeth scraping his chin.

Yes, something had happened to him in that moment. He did not mean he had a sudden realisation of falling in love with Anna Liese, but more a whispered suggestion that he always had been. Never before had the idea of marrying for anything but obligation troubled him. Duty was duty, he had always accepted that, been relieved that his heart would not be involved in the affair.

Now, he must accept that he had been changed by Anna Liese. Not only by the kiss, but by every moment he had spent in her company. But when she illustrated a slice of paradise and then once again refused his proposal, she left him unsure of everything he had ever believed about courtship and marriage.

It was not right to be dwelling on Anna Liese's lips. Certainly not on the shapely swell of her hip under his hand when he had pressed her close to his—

He was a cad! How could he have lost all sense of propriety while kissing her? Of course, nothing about that encounter had been proper. It had been Anna Liese's way of pointing out where he was lacking.

Feminine laughter from the back of the house caught his attention. Praise the Good Lord. His cousins were home!

Chapter Thirteen

Anna Liese stood at the drawing room window, gazing across the bridge at the cottage.

Peter was gone. When he returned, he would no longer be her Peter.

She had always thought of him as hers. Even though he had rejected her attempt to demonstrate how she felt, she could not let go of feeling possessive of him. Aside from her parents, he was the best part of her childhood. This was not something that could be taken away from her.

What she must learn to accept was that when she next saw him, he would be Mildred's Peter. More than that, he would be Stepmama's Peter, her conquest.

It was going to be extremely odd to live with having the man she loved as a brother-in-law, of sorts. Odd and intolerable.

At least they would be living in London most of the time and she would not often have to witness them together as man and wife. Still, regardless of where they lived, she was going to be miserable.

In the unlikely event that Peter and Mildred were happy together, Anna Liese would feel envious. If they were not happy and Peter was miserable, she would feel responsible for it since she might have prevented it by marrying him.

Mildred fluttered nervously about, ordering everyone who crossed her path to be sure her packing was in order, that her prettiest gowns were put in her trunks.

Anna Liese was glad to see that the butler cast her a wrinkled frown and ignored her order when she instructed him to run upstairs and fetch three of her hats so that she could try them on, each one in the light of the downstairs mirror. The last thing he needed was extra work.

Mildred could not know that it didn't matter what she wore. Lovely or frumpy, she would be Peter's 'chosen one'.

Anna Liese jumped, startled from her thoughts by Mildred's voice suddenly close to her ear.

'What are you staring at? Its only snow and more snow.'

'Nothing, just… I like snow.'

'What a pity you are not attending Peter's ball.' Her sister shot her a smirky little grin. 'But without a proper ball gown, how can you? There is a higher standard for fashion in London than here in the country, you understand.'

Unknown to Mildred, she had the loveliest gown in creation stashed in Martha's chamber. It was sure to be the envy of any woman hoping to win Peter's proposal. If only she had been wearing it in the stable yesterday, perhaps then Peter would have viewed her as a woman and not his dearest childhood friend. Had she known she was going to—well, to do what she had—she would have done it in the gown.

With great flair she would have twirled about in a froth of gossamer blue, lifted her chin while catching his eye, made certain he noticed the swell of her bosom. Then he would have recognised who she was at the heart of her. A woman and not a girl.

But that was not how things worked out. Now Peter was set on making the biggest mistake of his life. And he was going to do it for her sake.

'Tell me true, Sister.' Mildred's softened tone startled her, especially after the peevish comment she had just made. Her voice sounded vulnerable, but at the same time hopeful. 'Do you think there is the slightest chance Lord Cliverton will choose me instead of a pretty debutante?'

'It is not for me to say.'

Although she could put her stepsister's worries to rest if she wished to. But she did not wish to. The thought of Peter giving Mildred the kisses and nuzzles that Anna Liese dreamed of having made her nauseous. She also remained silent in the hope that Peter would come to his senses and not go through with this insane plan.

Staring at the bridge, she allowed herself to fantasise that absence, if only for a day, had made his heart grow fonder. She could see him now in her mind's eye, galloping over the stones on a bold white horse, his formal black ball jacket flapping behind him. He had left the ball behind, dismissed his guests and his potential brides from his mind.

Especially the one standing beside her.

But back to the fantasy—her hero swept her up into his strong arms and carried her off to…to his cottage across the bridge where he declared his undying, true and ever-faithful love.

'I think that without you present, he might see me.'

She could not tell her stepsister that Peter would see only her, even if Anna Liese twirled into the ballroom wearing her princess-worthy gown.

He did not love her the way she needed to be loved and, clearly, nothing she did could change it.

'I realise that Peter will not love me at first, but I do not mind,' Mildred murmured. 'He might come to and even if he does not, I will have finally made Mother happy.'

Her voice forsaking her, Anna Liese nodded jerkily.

'You might look happier about it, Anna Liese, since with me married, you will not need to fear being trapped by Mr Grant or someone like him.'

Oddly, Mildred's voice softened on the banker's name.

'Did you truly like Mr Grant?'

'He was fond of me, I believe.'

'I do not wish to take away from that, but you are well rid of him. His handsomeness is a trick to hide his true nature. I have reason to know he is not a good person. You may be sure that Lord Cliverton will be a better husband.'

'For all that I hope he will choose me, I cannot be sure he will, not with all the others who are younger and prettier.'

'Just smile,' she advised, feeling her heart shred at the words of advice. 'You are pretty when you smile.'

'Ah! There you are, Mildred!' Stepmama's voice interrupted one of the few genuine conversations they had ever had. 'There is no time to waste in idle chatter. The carriage will be ready to travel within the hour.'

This had been far from idle chatter. While Anna Liese did not like hearing her stepsister speak of Peter and her hopes to become his Viscountess, she had at least been speaking from her heart.

'Thorpe!' Stepmama called to the only servant passing by in the moment. 'Have you made certain all of the gowns have been put in the carriage?'

'I will enquire, my lady.'

'Your sister's very future depends upon those gowns,' Stepmama muttered.

It did not. The only reason Mildred had a future with Peter was that Anna Liese had handed it to her. With each passing moment she felt a bit more guilty over what Peter was doing. The man was willing to sacrifice his future so that Anna Liese might have hers. Which was ironic since, without Peter, she had no happy future.

What she had was a great headache. She rubbed her fingers over her brow, not to ease the pain but to hide tears.

'Have a safe journey,' she muttered, then turned and dashed upstairs.

Halfway up she heard Stepmama's harsh laugh. 'I believe we need not fear she will follow.'

No, they need not fear that.

* * *

'My dear boy, what are you doing out here in the dark?'

Peter was standing in the garden, wondering about Anna Liese. What was she doing in the moment? What would she be doing next year or the year after that? Would she find her true love match?

'Aunt Adelia!' Finally, he would have a moment alone with her. 'I have been wanting to speak with you about something.'

'Oh, well, that is delightful. However, do you mind if we go back inside? It looks as if the weather will turn again. But what a lovely white Christmas we will have. London will look like a greeting card.'

Taking her arm, he led her to the drawing room where the yule log crackled with heat.

Glancing about his drawing room with its garlands, ribbons and the grand Christmas tree, he realised it, too, looked as welcoming as a greeting card.

'Apparently everyone has gone to bed early,' he said.

'Are you surprised?' She grinned at him with the twinkle he loved. 'If my husband were here at Cliverton, I would be abed, too.'

His aunt had a charming way about her. No other person he knew could be so sweetly scandalous.

Thinking of his cousins and their husbands, involved in whatever they were probably involved in, made him blush. He felt heat rising from his neck and creeping to his hairline. There were some things better not considered when it came to one's own family.

'Will he join us later, in Woodlore Glen?'

'He has promised to complete his business in time.' She sat down on the sofa, patting the space beside her. 'Tell me, my dear, is there a lady who has struck your fancy? Will you make an announcement at the ball tomorrow night?'

'I suppose I will.' He wished he felt some joy in saying so. 'It is past time that I married, isn't it?'

'You seem less than keen about it. Most young men look at least somewhat eager at the prospect of a wife and family.'

'That is what I was hoping to speak with you about.' He shrugged, not bothering to hide his lack of enthusiasm at the prospect of wedded bliss, since that was far from what awaited him. Hiding anything from Aunt Adelia was impossible anyway. 'What I want to know is, how important in a marriage is it to begin with a love match? I have always assumed that it is not something people of our station can hope for.'

'It is what many believe. But I will tell you what this old woman has learned. My first marriage was an arranged one. Lord Monroe and I barely knew each other, let alone were in love. I thought the arrangement to be adequate because, as you pointed out, those of our position often do not hope for anything else. It was a short but adequate marriage. A few years into my widowhood, I met Lord Helm. We were great friends for a long time. But one day—it was at Violet Townsend's country party, the one where Ginny eloped—I looked at him in a way I never had before. I do not know why. Perhaps romance was in the air, but once seeing him in a romantic light, I could not see him in any other.'

He would never forget what a startling surprise it

had been one morning at breakfast to receive a telegram informing him that not only had Ginny been married at Gretna Green, but so had Aunt Adelia.

'But you were content in your first marriage?'

'I thought I was, Peter, but it was only because I did not understand what it was like to be in love.' She tapped her chin in thought while she looked past his eyes and straight into his heart. 'This lady you suppose you have found, is she someone you love or hope to love?'

Love Mildred? He did not, nor did he hope to. His only question, really, was what was he willing to sacrifice for Anna Liese? Apparently, it was everything.

'I have a reason to ask for this lady's hand, Aunt, but it is not love.'

She shook her head, frowning. 'I doubt you have compromised anyone.'

'No, hardly that.'

Quite the contrary—he hoped to prevent someone being compromised.

'You only have this one life,' she said, seeming uncommonly sombre. 'If you want my advice, wait to wed. No matter that society deems it necessary, wait until you find a lady who will be your best friend in life, a companion you will be joyful with.'

Nothing she said could have shot more at the heart of his trouble.

'My true love match?'

'Precisely. Trust me, dear, it will be worth the wait.'

'May I confide something, Aunt?'

'I adore confessions, although I imagine yours will not be terribly scandalous.'

'I did propose marriage to my best friend and she turned me down.'

'But why would she? You will make a wonderful husband.'

'She is set on a love match and I told her I could not give her that.'

'And so you will now take a bride who will accept you without it? You will end up an unhappy man, Peter Penneyjons. Do you not hope to have the marriages your cousins have?'

'This woman, the one I intend to wed, is not one I would pick unless I had to.'

'Unless you have compromised her, you do not have to.'

'You are familiar with the Cinderella story?' At her nod and sigh, he continued. 'Well, my friend is something of a Cinderella. Her stepmother has often tried to force her into marriage to clear the way for her own daughter to have her pick of gentlemen. Since Anna Liese has turned down my proposal, I will offer for the stepsister so that Baroness Barlow will be appeased and leave Anna Liese alone.'

Why did his aunt's eyes sparkle as if she were about to indulge in a fit of laughter? He had just admitted how wretched he was.

'Do you propose to be the lady's—Anna Liese's—fairy godmother, Peter?'

'I see no other way to ensure her safety. I hope that some day she will find her true love match.'

She patted his cheek indulgently, smiling and shaking her head. 'So, you are willing to sacrifice your happiness for that of your friend?'

He shrugged, nodding. It was exactly what he was doing.

"'Greater love has no man than this,'" she quoted with a wink. 'You are in love, Peter. I suggest you propose to Cinderella again and this time be honest about how you feel.'

Aunt Adelia kissed his cheek, then stood up. 'I'm for bed. Tomorrow is a busy day.'

He stared at the orange glow of the yule log for a long time after she left, thinking about what she said.

Could it be true, in the way she meant it? He did love her and always had. When she had kissed him the other night, he had wanted the moment to last for ever. For ever…as in a true love match and not the natural reaction of a man for a woman? Even if that were the case, what was he to do about it? He had proposed marriage and she had turned him down.

Not once, but twice.

But had she turned him down? Or had she turned down the sort of marriage he had proposed? In the end it didn't matter greatly. Turned down meant there would be no marriage between them.

It also meant there would be one between him and Mildred.

If Anna Liese had not overheard what she had while Stepmama and Mildred waited for the coach to be brought around, she might have slept the previous night. She might be able to pick up her fork and eat a bite of the breakfast set before her. Having heard, she could not sleep or eat—certainly she could not ignore the treacherous words.

They had been discussing a detailed plan to trap Peter, to make it appear that he had compromised Mildred. While Peter did mean to marry her, it would be horrid to have it happen the way they intended.

Why, they were even discussing what type of lace would make up Mildred's wedding gown as, laughing, sniggering, they stepped aboard the coach!

No man was more honourable than Peter. It would be beyond unjust to be accused of something so dishonourable. Had they not been pulling away from the front door, she would have given them a severe piece of her mind. A tongue lashing was what they deserved.

What Peter deserved was a woman who loved him. Which, Anna Liese did! Perhaps it did not matter as much as she had always believed that he did not love her in the way she wished to be loved.

'Miss Anna Liese.'

Oh, dear, how long had Martha been standing there watching her push food about her plate?

'Is there something wrong with your breakfast?'

'I'm sure it is delicious, but, Martha—' Martha was more than her maid. She was the closest thing she had to a mother and so... '—I need your opinion on something. Please be honest with me.'

'But, of course.'

Anna Liese indicated that she should sit at the table with her. With Stepmama absent, there was no one to be offended by it.

'What do you think—is it more important to love or to be loved?'

'That is a rather large question, my dear. I suppose it depends upon who we are speaking of. But in general, we cannot control what others feel for us. It is for us to love because we are in control of that.' Martha nodded at the neglected plate of food. 'If you wish to know the rest of my thoughts, you will eat what is before you. Once you have heard what I have to say, you might need your energy.'

How curious. She began to nibble, but it was delicious so it did not take her long to finish.

'Please, Martha, carry on with your thoughts.'

'We are discussing Lord Cliverton, are we not? That you do not love him in the way he loves you?'

'But he does not love me!' She stood up, pressed her hand to her belly where the food suddenly turned on her. 'He would not be—that is, he would—'

He would not be marrying Mildred if he did. But that was all wrong. He was marrying Mildred because he... Because he cared for her deeply, as one could care for a lifelong friend.

'Martha, he is going to propose to Mildred at the ball.'

'That is a bit of shocking news! I cannot imagine why he would. I thought he would propose to you, but I suppose I was mistaken.'

'He did propose to me.'

'And yet you say he is going to marry Mildred?'

'I turned him down because he does not love me—you are wrong to think he does.'

'Oh, my dear, I am not wrong. In fact, I see the situation clearly. Tell me if I am mistaken.' Martha stood up, took her hand and clasped it in both of hers. 'There is only reason Lord Cliverton would consider wedding the likes of Mildred. Once she is married the Baroness no longer has reason to get you out of her daughter's way. Since you refused the Viscount's protection, this is the only way he knows will see you safe.'

'But I do not want his protection, I want his love.'

'If he is not acting out of love, I do not know what love is. But, my sweet girl, you did ask what was more important, giving love or getting it. In your case, I would say giving love.'

'But I—'

'I think you will find that that you need to act on your love for him and then see what happens.'

'But he is proposing to Mildred tonight.'

'Perhaps he will not do it.'

'He might not have a choice. They plan to trap him into a compromise.'

'Oh, my. The poor man is not as skilled as you are at avoiding their traps.' Still holding her hand, Martha tugged her towards the servants' staircase. 'There is a train leaving Woodlore Glenn on the hour. If we hurry, we might make it to London in time. Come along, we shall do what we can do.'

Chapter Fourteen

'You are a miracle worker, Martha!'

Within moments her maid had stripped her of her day dress, put her in her ball gown, then, quick as thought, arranged her hair in a simple but elegant style.

Squinting at her handiwork, Martha added a blue ribbon to Anna Liese's hair.

'You have always been the silk purse and not the sow's ear, so it was an easy feat. Now, how will we get you to the station on time with the carriage gone?'

Martha placed Anna Liese's blue slippers into a bag which she looped over her wrist. She did not dare put them on until she reached Cliverton.

It would have been prudent to wait to put on the gown, too, but every second was urgent if she hoped to warn Peter of what awaited him. Besides, where would she change into it once she arrived? It was not as if she had time to arrange to stay anywhere.

She did take a moment to twirl in front of the mirror. The delicate gown whirled about her, revealing how wrong her black walking boots looked with it.

No help for it, though.

The gown had no sooner settled about her ankles than Martha draped her cloak of deep blue velvet about her shoulders.

'Hurry now, missy, we barely have time to make it to the station as it is.'

'You need not come with me.'

Martha shrugged into her own cloak. 'It will be odd enough that you are travelling in that gown. You shall not do it without a proper chaperon.'

Stepping outside, she grimaced at the sky. Not only did she need to beat the clock to the village, she needed to beat the weather as well. Unless she missed her guess, it was going to snow very soon. Gathering up her skirt, she would have run, but Martha was past the age for running.

'I do not suppose you know to ride a bicycle?'

'You would be surprised what I do on my day off. I am not overly skilled, but I can make it to the depot.'

Changing direction, they dashed across the bridge and collected the bicycles. Martha helped her gather up her voluminous skirt and petticoats, tucking and folding them as neatly as possible. Balancing the two-wheeled vehicle in one hand, Anna Liese carefully mounted.

'Off we go!' Mildred said with a great grin.

Unless one of them took a wicked tumble on the path, they should make it to the depot with enough time to purchase tickets and board the train.

Cold air blew past her face, tugged at her hair and billowed under her cloak. She could only imagine what a sight she and her maid looked. Hopefully, no one was peering out windows.

Oh, drat! Coming to a skidding stop in front of the ticket office, Anna Liese found someone was looking—or staring, rather—with his mouth open and his eyes blinking wide.

No doubt Hyrum Grant was stunned to see her gripping the bicycle handlebar in one hand while letting down her skirt and fluffing it with the other. He rushed forward. Oh, dear, she did not wish to have to fend him off in her gown.

'Miss Barlow,' he said, looking sheepish. 'May I store your bicycles until you return?'

She hugged her cloak tighter against the chill. In the rush she had not given thought to what she would do with the bicycles.

'We shall expect you not to sell them in the meantime,' Martha said, shooting him a reprimanding glare.

He nodded, took them both, then pushed them towards the bank. Turning, he said, 'Please give the Viscount my regards when you see him, which—' he looked quizzically at the ball gown peeking out from under her velvet cloak '—I imagine you will be doing.'

'Not that it concerns you.' Martha shooed her fingers at him.

While this was not likely to be an apology, it was a peace offering, of sorts. Not peace with her as much as Peter. His threat had been heeded. She was safe from the banker—now she must make sure Peter was safe from Mildred and Stepmama.

Boarding the train, she garnered curious glances. Ladies dressed for balls did not travel by rail. There was nothing for it but to nod, graciously smile and take a seat.

Luckily, she found one she would not need to share since her skirt took up the whole of the bench and would have swallowed anyone sitting beside her. Martha sat across from her and folded her hands in her lap, glancing about at their fellow travellers.

'Good day,' Anna Liese said to an older lady who paused on the way to her seat looking askance at her.

'Indeed!' the woman answered, but then she smiled. 'I imagine my day will not be nearly as interesting as yours, young lady.'

No day she had ever lived was bound to be as interesting as this one. Settling back against the cushioned seatback, she let the warmth of the car wrap her up. With time to think, she realised she had failed to bring a change of clothing for the return trip.

That was a challenge for later. Now she needed to concentrate on getting to the ball before Peter proposed to, or was trapped, by her stepsister.

Glancing out the window, she saw snow beginning to drift past the glass. Hopefully, it would not be so heavy that the train would be delayed along the way.

The man she loved needed her. If she had to leave a stranded railcar and run all the way to London, that is what she would do. Which was a brave thought for all that it was impossible.

She closed her eyes, felt the weight of her slipper bag on her arm and willed the train through the snow.

'This is a beautiful ball, Peter,' Aunt Adelia said. 'Now that Lord Helm has arrived earlier than expected,

I am quite enjoying it. Which, I believe, is more than you are doing.'

She was correct. He could not imagine what man in attendance would enjoy having Mildred constantly trying to draw him under one of the many sprigs of mistletoe scattered about the ballroom.

The woman seemed oblivious to the fact that he had other guests to attend to. Perhaps he ought to pull her aside and get the proposal over with. Once he did, perhaps her attention on him would not be so intense. Then again, it might be worse.

'I adore a Christmas ball. The carols and the festive decor are delightful,' his aunt remarked.

The trappings were beautiful—he must give his staff credit for their beautiful workmanship. The problem was, he did not feel festive. He felt grim.

'Aunt Adelia—' he bent his head to whisper '—have I lost my mind?'

'If you are speaking of proposing to that woman, you have lost it completely. You did not mention how calculating she is when we spoke last night—and her mother? My word, the Baroness is—but here they come again.'

'Heaven help me,' he muttered.

'You will need Heaven's help if you carry through with this madness.'

'What choice do I have?'

'Nonsense. Marry the woman you love. Do you see your cousins over there near the Christmas tree? All of them are in love. I see no reason why it should be different for you.'

'Of course you do. She has refused me. I said so last night, Aunt.'

'You must propose again now that you have realised that you love her. You—'

The rest of what might she have said was cut off by Mildred and her mother returning from the buffet room. The break in their company had been far too short.

Seeing his potential intended with a smear of something on the corner of her lip, which she wiped off with the back of her hand, he felt his stomach sink. If he did not get this proposal out of the way quickly, he would not do it.

It was a harder thing to imagine than it was last night because his aunt was correct in saying he was in love with Anna Liese. He was—desperately and completely in love with her. How big of a fool was he to have not recognised it until it was too late?

If only he had understood what was in his heart in the stable the other night, he would not be in the situation he now was. What would he not give to be announcing his engagement to Anna Liese tonight instead of the woman clinging to his arm as if she had a right to do it.

It had only been two days since he had seen Anna Liese and yet it seemed so much longer. He felt every empty second of those days beating a sad tempo in his soul.

While he imagined Anna Liese, laughing, singing and playing with her goose, Mildred nattered on. He had no idea what she was saying. She had not ceased from gossiping about the other ladies since she came down the ballroom steps, so she was probably continuing with that.

Thankfully, Aunt Adelia had not deserted him.

'Baroness,' Aunt Adelia said, cutting into Mildred's prattle. The interruption was done smoothly. No one could possibly be offended by it because of the twinkle in his aunt's blue eyes. 'When will your stepdaughter arrive?'

'Anna Liese?'

'Yes, Baron Barlow's child. It has been many years since I have seen her, but I recall how lovely she was, even as a small girl. I am anxious to see what a beauty she must have grown to be. I can only imagine how proud you must be to have raised her.'

Lady Barlow blinked in confusion. So did he. Aunt Adelia had visited the cottage when he was a boy, but did she remember Anna Liese?

Lady Barlow and Mildred spoke at the same time.

'She fell ill.'

'She is too shy to attend.'

The women cast each other matching frowns.

'That is disappointing, isn't it, Peter?' Aunt Adelia tapped her chin in thought. One could only guess what she would say next. 'But I imagine your head is spinning with the attention of all the ladies hoping to become the Viscountess, as it is. I cannot imagine how you will pick among them.'

And then—

'Miss Anna Liese Barlow,' the butler announced from the top of the stairs.

Breathing hard, as if she had been running, she stood on the landing, her gaze scanning the guests below. It was as if a spell were cast over the crowd. All eyes were turned upon her. No one spoke. No doubt they were wondering if an angel had descended among them.

An angel in an ethereal gown which shimmered about her as if she were wearing a blue cloud with stars twinkling among the gathers. An angel who, being escorted down the stairs by the grinning butler, wore black boots.

'Mother,' Mildred groaned. 'What—?'

'Indeed.' The Baroness's grin stretched tightly over her teeth. 'What a pleasure it is to see that she overcame her illness and her shyness to join us.'

'But where did she get that gown?'

'Do you not recall that I ordered it especially for her in the hopes she would come?' the Baroness declared, although the only one not to suspect it was a lie would be Mildred.

No, he took that back. His aunt was not easily fooled and, judging by the speculation in her smile, she had not been this time either.

'Peter, my dear. You understand what you must do? Greet your guest and tell her how—' Aunt Adelia arched a brow at Mildred and her mother who had begun to whisper to each other, all the while casting frowns at Anna Liese descending the stairs '—how you feel about her being here.'

What he felt was overwhelmed with love. What had it taken for her to come here? How had she even managed it? Indeed, how was he to find his next breath when she came down the steps, her dazzling gown fluttering about her scuffed black boots?

Her smile while she glanced about the room nearly cut him off at the knees. Wait—he *was* being cut off at the knees. All of a sudden, he nearly went down. Mildred's weight sagged against him when she fainted.

'Quickly, my lord. Take her somewhere private— to your library,' the Baroness ordered. 'I will welcome Anna Liese.'

Winded, Anna Liese stood at the head of the ballroom stairs, searching the faces of the people staring up at her. What a sight she must be. The cab she had hired had got stuck in snow. She had been forced to get out and run the last street with Martha leaning out the window and cheering her on.

Her hair had suffered. She felt loose strands tickling her neck and the blue bow drooping. In the rush to get to Cliverton, she hadn't taken a second to repair it. There had been only an instant to hand off her cloak and shoe bag before she turned to the waiting butler who announced her.

But where was Peter? Glancing about below, all she saw was a sea of strangers gaping at her. And why not? She would gape at herself if she saw herself coming down the stairs with no escort but the kindly butler, clomping down in scuffed boots instead of dancing shoes!

No matter, she had come to rescue Peter. She would not let the man she loved fall victim to her stepsister's scheme because she did not look tip top. Even if he did not love her, she would love him. Martha had been right in asking her to consider which had more value— loving or being loved.

Down below she spotted Stepmama standing beside a woman near her own age. The older lady had red hair and a sparkling smile which was resting on Anna Liese as if they were already, somehow, acquainted. How odd, she was certain they were not.

The woman hurried to meet her at the foot of the steps while Stepmama rushed away in the opposite direction.

Where was Mildred? Please, oh, please, do not let Peter be proposing to her, or worse, being seduced by her.

'I knew who you were the instant I saw you, my dear.' The woman squeezed her hand in greeting. 'The look on my nephew's face gave it away.'

'It did?'

'I am Peter's Aunt Adelia and I am happier to see you than you can imagine.'

She could not imagine, since they had never met that she recalled.

'But where is Peter?'

'That awful Mildred must have overeaten because she fainted. Peter had to tend to her, but do not fear. Now that he has seen you, he will not be proposing to the chit.'

What? How did she know? Time for that later. In the moment she felt that she was strangling on dread.

'Mildred does not faint.' She glanced about, desperate to find him before it was too late. 'Where did they go? Was he alone with her?'

'I believe so. Many people were curious about him carrying her away, but their attention was diverted by your entrance. But her mother went after her.'

'That is bad news! We must find him,' she gasped. 'They intend to compromise him.'

'The man is not easily compromised.'

As she had reason to know—however... 'My relatives are skilled at such schemes.'

Peter's aunt waved to three ladies standing near the Christmas tree, beckoning them to follow. 'Come along. He took her to the library.'

She rushed after Peter's aunt. The three ladies she had signalled to fell in line behind them.

'If the Baroness intends to bear false witness, we shall be five to witness the truth, no matter what we might see with our eyes.'

What would they witness with their own eyes? A seduction or a proposal? Either would result in a marriage which Anna Liese was determined to prevent. She would marry Peter without being loved if that was what it took because she loved him.

And loving mattered more than anything else. What a fool she was not to have realised it sooner. She only prayed Peter did not pay for her mistake.

Peter half dragged Mildred to the sofa because her weight did not allow him to carry her in his arms. He struggled to keep from dropping her while he lowered her to the cushions. The ungainly release did not wake her. He lifted her feet on to the cushions so that she lay flat.

Going to the hearth, he stood there, not seeing the woman on the sofa, but the one who had just arrived at the ball. Anna Liese was here! She had come when she said she would not.

Why?

Why did not matter! All that mattered was that she was here. If only Mildred had not fainted, he would be with her now, discovering the reason for this miracle. He would be telling her how much he loved her and hoping she believed him.

A soft moan from the sofa brought his attention to where he supposed it ought to have been. Now that Mildred was regaining consciousness, he would need to be wary. He had been warned that she and her mother were not beyond capturing a viscount by trickery.

Until ten minutes ago, there would have been no need to. He would have taken the occasion of her revival to propose. But Anna Liese was here and he had every intention of proposing to her. This time with a declaration of love. Not only love—undying, unconditional, for better or for worse—but a true love match was what he would offer.

If she turned him down after that—then he would do what he must, as distasteful as it was.

His gaze shifted to Mildred, who blinked her eyes open. Funny how they did not appear disorientated as one would expect after a faint. If it came down to it, would he really be able to spend his life with a woman like her? How could he possibly?

No, it would be a grave mistake for more than the obvious. If he married Mildred, it would mean Anna Liese would be often in his life. He could not possibly live so closely to the woman he loved and remain faithful to the one he did not.

What he needed to do was get out of the library, find Anna Liese and admit his love for her. As soon as

Mildred sat up and looked the slightest bit recovered that was what he was going to do. In a moment he was going to dash out if this room and into the arms of the woman he loved.

If she would have him. He must face the fact that she might not believe him since it had only been days since he indicated he did not love her. Dash it. While he stood here waiting for Mildred to 'recover', how many gentlemen were vying for Anna Liese's attention?

'Mildred!' he said a bit more sharply than he ought to, impatience winning out over playing his part as the gracious host. Although a proper host would not be alone with a guest. He desperately wished another woman were in the room.

She blinked again, clawed at the bodice of her gown as if the low cut somehow interfered with her breathing. 'Help—air—can't breathe', yet her bosom was heaving as if it was full of air. He suspected her lungs were working rather well.

'I must go.' He stood away from the hearth, took a step towards the door. 'Just lay still for a while. You will regain your breath. I shall send your mother to you.'

Suddenly she sat up, leapt off the sofa and snagged his coat sleeve. In a move so swift and smooth it could only have been practised, she yanked her bodice down. He heard fabric rip. And then Mildred cried out.

He backed away from her, but she advanced. When one more step would have him pressed against the bookcase, the library door crashed open.

Before the Baroness could gasp in outrage, five women rushed past her.

'Oh, you poor dear,' Aunt Adelia cooed. 'How dreadful that you ripped your gown in the faint.'

'It did not rip when I fainted. He—' She wagged a finger at Peter.

'But of course it did, my dear. I saw it happen. But being unconscious as you were, you could not have known. My nephew was quite the hero of the moment, dragging you out of the ballroom as soon as he did. We can only hope his back is not strained for dancing later.'

'The rip in your bodice would have been a horrid embarrassment had he not managed!' Cornelia, the eldest of his cousins, observed.

'Such things will happen when one's bodice is stressed,' added Felicia sweetly. 'It is not uncommon.'

'This is an outrage!' The tip of the Baroness's nose pulsed red.

'Oh, I agree.' Aunt Adelia said, her smile as bright as bubbles in champagne. 'Whoever produced such inferior fabric should be held to account.'

'It is awful when a lady is not safe in a viscount's ballroom,' Mildred whimpered.

Ginny gave her a compassionate-looking smile. 'Do not worry, Miss Hooper. I carry a repair kit at all times. One never knows when one might encounter an unfortunate event.'

She did? Apparently so since she happily plucked a pouch out of a hidden pocket in her gown. From it she withdrew a needle and thread, dangling them in the air.

'We shall have you repaired in no time at all,' Felicia said.

'And do not worry.' This encouragement came from Cornelia. 'Only someone staring intently will notice that we are forced to use red thread for your green gown.'

'But it does look Christmassy, don't you agree?' Felicia clapped her hands and perhaps she meant it. Felicia adored anything that smacked of Christmas.

Apparently, Mildred began to feel a chill on her exposed bosom. She splayed her fingers over what she had intentionally exposed. One could only hope she felt some shame for what she had done. More than likely she was mortified rather than remorseful.

'Now that help has come, you may go back to your ball, Peter. And do take Anna Liese with you so that no one will think you spent undue time alone with Miss Barlow. It would not do to have her reputation soiled.' Aunt Adelia was smiling brightly at the Baroness while she spoke. 'How relieved you must be to have everything resolved so neatly.'

He did not stay long enough to hear a response. Snatching Anna Liese's hand he fled, like his dancing shoes were afire.

As Anna Liese entered the ballroom beside Peter, the only thing she wished was for a private place to speak with him. He needed to understand the grave danger he had been in and that he must be cautious. With that said, she would tell him she understood his desire to protect her, even if it meant wedding where he did not wish to.

She did not pretend to imagine that marrying either her or Mildred was his first choice. Glancing about the ballroom, seeing so many elegant ladies hoping to win his hand, she found it hard to imagine he would be happy settling for a lower-ranked lady. And yet he was determined to sacrifice himself for her.

Very well, she was determined to do no less for him. Once a private moment presented, she was going to ask him to marry her and not Mildred. She would need to be bolder than she had ever been since such a thing was not done—it was the man who proposed.

Which he had done and she had soundly rejected. There was every chance he would not wish to ask for her hand a third time. She had been firm in her refusal and a gentleman did have his pride.

But at the least she hoped to have a quiet conversation in order to convince him what a great mistake it would be to marry Mildred, in the event he was still set on making such a wretched mistake.

Having a quiet conversation did not appear to be possible. People seemed anxious to meet her. More than likely it was because she was a new face among them—clearly a bumpkin from the country. Hopefully, they would soon satisfy their curiosity about her and she would get her moment alone with Peter.

She hugged his arm, feeling awkward among the titled. Not that she, herself, was not titled, but having grown up as free as a woodland spirit, she did not feel like it.

Peter introduced her to earls and marquesses, to countesses and marchionesses. She was half dizzy with meeting aristocrats. What a lucky thing she was weighted down by heavy walking boots. Boots which had been in plain view when she made her grand decent into society. At the time it had not mattered. Finding Peter in time had been far more urgent than proper footwear was.

After seeing several ladies glancing at the hem of her gown, she decided it mattered after all.

'Peter,' she went up on her toes to whisper. 'I need to get my shoes.'

'But you look charming. Honestly, Anna Liese, the contrast between your gown and your boots is irresistible.'

'Perhaps to you, my friend. To the others I look odd.'

'Are we so stuffy as all that? Look around you. Half the gentlemen in attendance are smitten with you. Perhaps one of them will be your true love match.' He was grimacing when he said so and she hardly knew what to make of it.

'As lovely as that might be.' And it was not at all lovely. There was only one man she wished to be smitten with her and he, apparently, still was not. She stood there, putting on a smile, her heart weeping. 'I am being judged by ladies who know fashion better than you do. I need my ball slippers.'

And her hair done up properly, but no matter that.

'Take my arm before I get snatched away by a marriage hunter,' he said.

She did and unashamedly enjoyed feeling the flex of his muscles under his coat. 'You were lucky to escape the one you did, if you want to know what I think. Had your aunt and all those ladies not burst in, you would be facing a priest.'

The thought of Peter and Mildred together made her stomach churn unpleasantly.

'Which, I realise, is what you intend to do. It's only

that I do not wish for you to do it because you were tricked. You are far too honourable to have your reputation soiled in that way.'

'Is that why you came? To rescue me?'

My word, but she had missed his grin in the two days since she had seen him. Rescuing him was part of the reason she had come. But not all.

'Why else?' she said. She would find a time to ask him to marry her. But this was not it. 'When one overhears a plot to trick one's friend into making a huge mistake, one does what one can to prevent it.'

Please, oh, please let him say she had prevented it, that he had not already proposed. Before he could, the attendant in the cloakroom handed out her shoe bag.

'The ladies...the ones who rescued me,' he said while escorting her towards the women's retiring room. 'They are my cousins and my aunt. Do you remember them from their visits to Woodlore Glen?'

'I wish I did. They were quite wonderful. I admired how they made it known to my relatives that their scheme was exposed and yet did it without making open accusation.'

'I hope in time you will get to know them well.'

Because she would be related to them through Mildred?

'Go back to your party, Peter.' She shooed her hand at him before she went inside the retiring room. 'I shall find you when I am finished here.'

'I'll wait.'

'You have only just avoided a scandal with my stepsister. Surely you do not wish to cause another by showing me undue favour.'

He shrugged, shot her that grin, then turned and strode towards the ballroom. He had not gone more than a dozen steps before an eager lady rushed to take Anna Liese's place on his arm.

Given that he was so set on protecting her, it was unlikely that Peter would abandon his plan to wed Mildred and choose one of the ladies attending his ball. She should not feel relieved at that, but one felt what one did.

Finding a sofa in an alcove with the curtains drawn for privacy, she sat down upon it. While she changed her shoes, she let out a long, relieved sigh. She had overcome more than a few obstacles getting here— acted boldly in taking the train in a ball gown, hired a carriage and then abandoned it to run a street with no escort. Finding the audacity to enter the mansion alone in her walking boots had been something!

For all that she might like to sit here and regather her courage, she did not dare. Now was not the time to give up on her goal. She could not carry on much longer without speaking plainly to Peter about her feelings. After taking a moment to gather her emotions, she would leave the shelter of the retiring room and, properly attired, she would look for him among his peers, find a way to get him alone and speak about her feelings.

A pair of rustling skirts passed by her alcove.

'I look ridiculous, Mother! The red stitches are so large anyone will know my bodice is ripped.'

'Were you more skilled at seduction, you would not have needed to tear your gown. The Viscount would have peeled it from you.'

'It is Anna Liese's fault, you know. She was not supposed to come. She said she would not! And where did she get that gown?'

'Somebody will be held accountable.' No one could make her voice sound as snarly as Stepmama could. 'But do not give up. There is yet time to try again.'

If there was any hope of Mildred being successful, she must not snort as she had just done.

Taking a breath, Anna Liese listened to their footsteps going out of the room. She pressed her fingers to her heart, willing courage into it. Her success was far from guaranteed. She had rebuffed Peter's proposal. There was every chance he would not wish to offer another.

Lady Someone-or-Another was speaking earnestly to him about something, but he had no idea what it was. His attention was latched on the hallway where the retiring room was located. Where, he wondered, would he take Anna Liese once she emerged? It must be a private spot where no one would find them.

He must convince her that he was in love with her although he had so recently denied it. No one would blame her for believing his change of heart was insincere. The truth was far from it—he was completely in love with his childhood friend.

The kitchen would be bustling with activity, his bedroom was out of the question. The garden? Not unless he wished for them both to become icicles. Not the library either. That space had become tainted for declarations of true love.

The Barlow women emerged from the hallway and

entered the ballroom. Suddenly he was grateful for the lady chatting merrily beside him.

Three minutes into listening to a dissertation on feathered hats, he spotted Anna Liese entering the ballroom. As if they had been watching and somehow knew he needed escape, Aunt Adelia and Felicia hurried towards him.

'Lady Lindsey!' Felicia exclaimed. 'We are about to begin carolling. You will not wish to miss it.' It would not matter if she had, his relatives were neatly drawing her away.

Hurrying towards Anna Liese, he deliberately ignored guests trying to snag his attention.

A gentleman blocked his view of Anna Liese. When he stepped around the fellow, he spotted her again. She was frowning and glancing about. She vanished from his sight yet again when a group of laughing guests got between them. Then Anna Liese turned in a half-circle, spotted him and smiled.

He had the oddest sensation of coming home—even though he was home. In that instant, he fell even more in love with her. How could he have ever doubted it?

'I've missed you, dear friend.' He held out both hands to her and she took them. A few people stared, but no matter. 'Take a carriage ride with me?'

She nodded, so he led her towards the ballroom steps, but then caught sight of Lady Barlow and Mildred rushing towards them. Changing directions, he drew Anna Liese towards the kitchens where it would be a short run from there to the stable.

The staff would be stunned to see him in their domain. Especially since he was towing an angel in blue behind him. Even so, they went about their tasks with barely a glance. The pathway to the stable was covered, but that did not prevent the snow from blowing in sideways.

While icy, it also dusted Anna Liese's face and shoulders in flakes which glittered in the lamplight illuminating the way. She looked ethereal, a snow queen. And he, a mere man, was about to try to convince her that he was in love with her.

Once inside the stable he requested the carriage to be warmed and made ready for travel.

'Come, Anna Liese. We will wait by the stove.' The spot was somewhat warmer, but not enough to keep her from visibly shivering. He wished for nothing more than to draw her to himself, warm her thoroughly. Several images of how to go about it presented in his mind, but until he had pleaded his case, he would not act upon them.

'I have something to say, Peter.' She whisked her gloved hands over her arms, chasing away the chill which he anticipated banishing in a few moments.

In the meantime, he took off his formal coat and lay it across her shoulders, tugging it under her chin.

'You look nervous. You know you can tell me anything.'

'Yes, well, I am nervous because I feel I must confess a great mistake.'

'It cannot be as bad as that frown makes it seem.'

She took a deep breath which lifted her bosom, snatched the heart out of his chest and floated it up among the rafters. 'I wish to retract my refusal of your proposal.'

'At the cost of giving up your true love match?'

Knowing she was willing to do this for him touched his soul. How, he wondered, was it possible to love another person as much as he loved her? It did seem a miracle that love could grow so quickly—but then again, it had not been quickly. It had been a lifetime growing. He had always loved her in some form or another.

'I was wrong to refuse. You must not marry Mildred.'

She shook her head, causing a curl to spring loose from her hair and tumble against the fair column of her neck. While he had always noticed how pretty her neck was, at that moment it drew him as if his lips and her skin were magnetised.

He resisted the draw—for now. But with a bit of luck and a heartfelt prayer, in a few moments she would become his lover while remaining his friend. He would be free to express his desire for her.

Please let it be so! Forced to wed Mildred, he would have neither love nor friendship.

'Honestly, Peter, you are not the only one who can give up one's dreams of a perfect future in the name of friendship.'

The last thing he wanted was for her to give up her dream. He wanted to satisfy it. He heard the creak of wheels bringing the carriage around.

'If you are willing to marry Mildred in order to keep me safe, I am willing to marry you in order for you to not ruin your life in a miserable match.'

'That is selfless of you,' he said trying not to smile at how earnest she looked. 'I appreciate your sacrifice.'

He knew what the supposed sacrifice meant to her. To him, it meant she loved him. One would not do such a thing unless it was done in the name of love. For as late as he had come to the realisation, he did now understand that his offer to marry Mildred had not been simply an obligation to protect a friend—although protecting her had been first in his mind.

It was love for Anna Liese which had spurred him to be willing to give up his happiness for hers, as she was now doing for him. Having found his true love match, he was impatient to admit it to her. If only he had recognised his true feelings earlier, they could be well on the way to being wed by now.

The carriage driver opened the door. Peter instructed the fellow to drive slowly about Hyde Park. He helped Anna Lise inside and then climbed up after her.

Only after having sat down in the seat across from her did he wonder what the driver must think of this. Taking a lady for a carriage ride at night with no chaperon was exceptionally inappropriate.

Well, let the fellow imagine what he would. Hopefully, when they emerged from the carriage, the driver would be the first to hear the news that Anna Liese would become Viscountess Cliverton. Peter would be crowing over the news to the first person he encountered. But before he could, he had some convincing to do.

The interior of the cab was dimly lit, the curtains drawn—romantic in a way he had never noticed before. Plush, warm and, with any luck, the small space was about to get heated.

'You cannot know how glad I am to have time alone

with you,' he said once the carriage began to move. 'Having an important conversation back in a house full of guests is futile.'

'And are we about to have one?' She slipped his coat off her shoulders. 'It is nice in here, warm, too. I rented a hackney carriage to get here and it was not nearly as elegant—but it did nearly get me here.'

'Only nearly?'

'It got stuck in the snow, so I had to run the last little bit to Cliverton.'

'I do not believe anyone has ever run to my rescue before—but wait!' He slid out of his seat, moved across and sat down next to her. 'You did it once before—when I was sick to death and you sang to me.'

'I remember it. But your uncle and I were not sure you could hear.'

'But I did and you saved my life then, too.'

He touched the curl at her neck, sifting the strands in his fingers. Ah, good, her smile indicated he was not overstepping. Not yet, anyway.

'All I did was sing, I do not see how—'

'I meant to die. I tried to, but Uncle would not let me. And then you came and sang to me. I decided to live after all.'

'And here we are,' she said softly. 'I will save your life again if you will offer the same proposal you did in the stable.'

She really had no idea how much he loved her.

'No, Anna Liese, I will not offer that proposal.'

'And I will not allow you to wed my stepsister for my sake!'

She looked heartsick, the blue sparkle of her eyes

dimmed, the happy animation that typically radiated from her soul turning sad.

He must clear things up immediately. 'I will not offer that proposal.' He took her hand, felt her fingers trembling. 'It was wrong and so I offer you another.'

'I will not become your mistress, either, if that is what you have in mind.'

The outrage on her face made him laugh aloud because it was sincere and so pretty. Keeping hold of her hand, he slipped off the bench.

On bended knee, he said, 'Anna Liese Barlow, I love you with all my heart. Will you marry me?'

'You do not need to make up affection in order to appease me, Peter.' A tear glistened in her eye, rolled down her cheek. 'I will marry you without it.'

On his knees, he leaned forward, kissing the dampness away. He stroked the wet trail from her eye to her chin. 'You are mistaken. I love you deeply.'

'All of a sudden, Peter?' She shook her head, her frown dipping her fair brows. 'How can that be? You do not need to say those words.'

'No? I suppose that leaves me with no choice but to illustrate how I feel about you, the same as you did to me.'

Chapter Fifteen

'I... Well...' The last thing she was going to do was refuse a kiss from the man she loved. Even though, in the end, what would it prove? One's heart did not change in a matter of days. 'You do not need to prove anything.'

'Not prove...' He touched her shoulders, held them gently in his hands, gently caressed her bare skin with his fingertips. 'Express.'

'Express...prove that it is all—' Any man could woo a lady with kisses.

'I love you, Anna Liese.' His breath felt warm on her face...more, it felt a miracle. *Please, oh, please, please, please let this not be impossible.* 'Do not doubt, trust me.'

'I want to—' She was simply too dizzy to reason anything through rationally.

'Anna Liese.'

He whispered her name in the half-instant before his lips settled upon hers. His large hand cupped the back of her neck, urging her to a deeper kiss.

Oh, my, she had intended to teach him what was lacking when she kissed him in the stable—right now, Peter's kiss taught her something different. Not a lesson, but a declaration.

She was beginning to believe him—that perhaps by some Christmas miracle he was pledging himself to her. No wonder he had not reacted to her in the stable. The kiss she had given had not been an expression of love, but rather a challenge to face it.

He nibbled her bottom lip, then trailed his mouth downwards to kiss her neck. It was nearly the same kiss as in the stable, but oh, so vastly different. For as impossible as it seemed, all at once she nearly believed him, that by some great wonder of love—he was in love with her.

He pulled away from her from kissing her. Covering his heart with splayed fingers, he murmured, 'Will you marry me, Anna Liese? For love only, and no other reason. Let me be your true love match, for you are mine.'

'Truly? I only ask because—' Because her heart was turning and she scarcely knew what to say. 'Only days ago you said you did not require one.'

'I have said many foolish things. You have known me long enough to know it. But this is not one of them. Anna Liese Barlow, you are my true love match and I can only pray that I am yours.'

'You have always been that to me. Peter, why do you think I never married? I loved you as a boy, but I love you more deeply as a man. The love I feel for you now was built upon the one from our childhood.'

'Yes...' He gave her a half-lidded gaze, a seductive smile that young Peter would not have known existed. 'But I wonder if we need further proof of our affections.'

'We do not need proof, but I will happily express how I feel about you.'

Rising, he sat beside her, then lifted her in a manoeuvre which had her sitting on his lap.

For the next five minutes, she kissed him, expressing her love, making sure he would never doubt it.

'May I take this as a yes to my proposal?'

No one would ever be able to convince her that miracles did not happen. Only hours ago, she had been in fear and despair, now her heart sang Christmas carols, one after another, even with no music at hand. Peter's love was her music.

'You may consider us engaged.'

'Good, I shall act accordingly—like a man smitten, for it is what I am.'

She did not know how long they kissed, touched and vowed to love one another for ever. Eventually, Peter tapped the ceiling of the carriage, which she imagined was a signal for the driver to return to Cliverton. He drew the window curtain open. Snow drifted past the glass. The cab had begun to cool, but this was the first time she noticed it.

'We shall announce our betrothal as soon as we step inside the ballroom. People will have missed us by now, so they might as well know our intentions.'

Her hair was in worse disarray than when she had come down the ballroom steps the first time—but, oh, well, what did it matter really? Her love for Lord Cliverton was going to show no matter the condition of her coiffure. People might as well know that the reason she looked flushed and happy was something to be winked at rather than condemned.

'And we shall be wed at once,' he announced, sounding lordly and in charge.

As far as she was concerned the sooner it happened, the happier she would be. Although—

'We will need a licence and I will want a proper wedding gown. There are things to be considered.'

'Do not fear, I have cousins who have experience at quick weddings. They will be thrilled to point the way.'

'Good. Then we will be wed without delay.'

The weight of the carriage shifted when the driver stepped down.

'There is one thing I wish for, my Anna Liese.'

She kissed him quickly. 'What is it you wish?'

'For you to sing to me at our wedding. I want to hear it, knowing this time we will not be saying goodbye.'

If that was not the most touching thing she had ever heard, she did not know what was.

The driver opened the door. Peter stepped out, then helped her down.

'Simons,' Peter said, his grin wide and handsome. 'I would like to introduce Anna Liese Barlow, soon to be Viscountess Cliverton.'

'May I say how delighted I am, miss? May you and my lord be blessed for ever.'

She took his greeting to her heart, cherishing those words against the moment they made their betrothal known to everyone in the ballroom. There were some present who would not think it so wonderful.

* * *

Peter had intended to make an announcement tonight. He just had not expected to be happy about it.

Now, standing at the head of the ballroom stairs with Anna Liese beside him, he felt like singing—like tapping his toes in a happy dance and swirling his fiancée about to express his joy. He refrained from doing so because he was aware that not everyone here would be delighted. Indeed, he spotted two of them, Mildred and the Baroness, elbowing their way through the crowd.

Anna Liese's stepsister already had one foot on the stairway as if to rush to him. He had better make his announcement quickly before she somehow latched herself on to his arm.

'Friends!' he called, just in the event that someone in the room was not already looking at them. 'I would like to tell you the most excellent news. I have proposed marriage to Miss Anna Liese Barlow. She has made me the happiest man in the world by accepting.'

Applause and huzzahs erupted. The sounds of congratulations did not entirely cover a screech.

Mildred tore at her hair, then neatly fainted backwards into the stout arms of Lord Moore. Lord Moore did not appear to be dismayed. On the contrary, he was grinning.

'Oh, dear,' Anna Liese whispered. 'I think she truly has fainted this time. The poor man must be—'

'Delighted.' He caught her hand. They hurried down the grand staircase. 'He is stronger than his round stature accounts for and I suspect this is the closest he has ever come to holding a lady. Women rarely give the poor fellow a second glance even though he is titled.'

They reached the stricken Mildred at the same time Aunt Adelia and his cousins did.

The Baroness cast Anna Liese a scathing glare which his fiancée ignored. Perhaps she was used to such looks, but he was not. As soon as there was a moment he would have a word with her.

'My goodness, Felicia,' Ginny said. 'You might have done a sturdier job on that stitching. It has come apart.'

'Such things will happen.' Aunt Adelia gave the blushing young man a smile. 'Perry, do be a dear and take Miss Mildred to the library.'

'It will be my honour, of course.'

The Baroness muttered something under her breath.

'Do not fret, Lord Moore has the matter—in hand, shall we say?' Aunt Adelia smiled after him proudly carrying his burden, which Peter imagined was not burden at all to the lonely young man.

'Lord Moore?' The Baroness's brow arched, watching her daughter being carried away. Peter had to give Perry credit for strength. All Peter had managed was to half drag her.

'You have not met our dear Perry? But perhaps Mildred overlooked the Marquess, as ladies tend to do. I promise he is a pleasant fellow, despite his rather round bearing.'

'A marquess, you say?'

'Yes, for a year now. But are you not anxious to hurry after them, just to avoid the appearance of scandal?'

'But of course.'

As expected, the Baroness took her time 'hurrying' away. She paused to wish him and Anna Liese well.

Perhaps she meant it, given that the Marquess who had just left the ballroom with her daughter held a higher rank than he did.

By the time the Baroness had meandered her way through the guests and went into the hallway leading to the library, quarter of an hour had passed.

'Lord Moore will have had time to revive her by now,' Cornelia said.

'People will be watching to see how long it takes for her mother to bring her back to the festivities,' Felicia said.

'I have heard that Perry—' Aunt Adelia said.

'You have heard something untoward about Perry?' Peter asked. He would rather not have a scandal attached to his engagement ball.

'Why would I have? But he is in need of a wife and no other opportunity might present.'

'One might not present for Mildred either,' Anna Liese said, her gaze soft, thoughtful. 'And I know he is bound to be a better match than the banker.'

'I cannot speak for the banker, but dear Perry has the best of hearts.' Ginny said. 'He is terribly shy because some of the ladies on the society market are rather unkind in what they say about him.'

'I only hope that he does not regret being with my stepsister.'

'He seemed more than pleased to me.' Aunt Adelia's laugh sounded like bubbles floating on the air. 'We have one engagement to celebrate and one can only guess about another.'

He did not care about the other, only his own.

He was suddenly grateful that his staff had placed

so many sprigs of mistletoe about. He fully intended to take advantage of every one of them. Catching Anna Liese's hand, he hurried her towards the nearest unoccupied sprig. Not that he needed the festive excuse. He meant to kiss her fervently, with a full and grateful heart, every day for the rest of his life.

To Anna Liese's way of thinking, a Christmas miracle was happening. It was her wedding day and it was happening only three days after she had been proposed to.

She stood in the small drawing room, wearing a gown borrowed from Ginny. It could not have been a more perfect fit, or more lovely had she spent months picking it out. What a lucky thing that she and her soon-to-be cousin were the same size.

'Here you are, Cousin,' Felicia declared, handing her a beautiful bouquet of holly and berries wrapped in red and green ribbons.

Aunt Adelia sat in a chair beside the window, stitching silk flowers on the veil which the modiste had sewn in a hurry. 'Oh, look!' she exclaimed. 'It is snowing. That is such good luck, is it not?'

'I thought it was rain which was good luck,' Mildred said, coming into the drawing room. 'May I have a private word, Sister?'

'I will not listen,' Aunt Adelia declared, remaining where she was.

'Nor will we,' Cornelia agreed while Ginny nodded.

'Well, I just want to say—you were correct when you warned me about Mr Grant. I have come to see that a handsome smile can cover many flaws. And a plain face can hide many virtues.'

'Lord Moore, you mean?' Aunt Adelia asked.

'You said you were not listening.'

'Well, my dear, we are to be family and you must get used to such things.'

Mildred leaned close to whisper, 'I'm sorry I nearly cut your hair. Please forgive me.'

That said, Mildred kissed her cheek, then said to everyone, 'It will take me some time to become accustomed to the idea of family, but I do want to.'

She did not ask, nor did anyone else, what Lady Barlow thought of Anna Liese wedding the man she had picked for her daughter, but she could only imagine she had turned her attention to capturing a marquess.

Aunt Adelia stood up, then secured the veil on Anna Liese's hair. 'It is time to become a Cliverton, my dear.'

Just at that moment the carriages Peter had hired to carry them to Woodlore Glen's intimate and charming church pulled up in front of Maplewood. One by one the cousins went out ahead of her, taking their places in the first carriage.

Last of all, Stepmama went out, but first she paused for a second, giving Anna Liese an appraising glance. 'Well played, Anna Liese.' With something resembling a smile, she walked ahead of her towards the waiting carriage.

The second carriage was decorated with red garlands and flowers. She could not imagine where Peter had come by them this time of year. Aunt Adelia, whom she had quickly come to love, went with her into this one.

It was a short but beautiful ride to the village church, with snow drifting past the windows. My word, but villagers stood on street corners merrily waving good wishes. It was not every day that one of their own wed a viscount, after all. Their greetings touched her quite deeply.

The first carriage came to a stop at the church steps. The cousins, Mildred, and Stepmama hurried inside.

Peter came outside, a great grin on his handsome face.

'I cannot believe this is happening,' she said to Aunt Adelia.

'Dreams do come true, my dear. The Penneyjons are blessed with them. Let's go and make yours come true.'

Peter escorted them inside and then went to take his place beside the minister at the front of the church. There were flowers in the church as well, white ones which looked pretty against the snow drifting past the windows.

Standing at the back of the pews, she caught her groom's eye, felt love wash over and through her. *'By yon bonnie banks and by yon bonnie braies...'* she sang while she walked towards him. *'Where the sun shines bright on Loch Lomond...'*

The sun shone bright on her even though she was inside and there was no sunshine. She and her true love were meeting at the altar and, the Good Lord willing, they would never be parted again.

Peter would never forget his wedding day. If he lived to be a hundred years old and forgot everything else, he would not forget this day. Listening to his bride singing in her clear, sweet and utterly beautiful voice, Peter was not dying, but he might have had one foot in heaven.

If he could have seen with other eyes than the ones in his head, he felt certain he would spot his family who had gone before him standing by: Mama and Papa, his aunt and uncle. Unless he was wrong, Anna Liese must have felt her parents' presence there to bless the wedding as well.

They had been bound by the minister's words, of course. Bound by sacred vows and the love behind them, but it had been her song to him that bound him as much as anything else. Her voice had brought him back from death once. Now it was a promise of a life, filled with blessed days and long, loving nights of a more intimate type of blessing.

The first of which was about to begin in his childhood bedroom. His wife awaited him there, in his small bed next to the window.

Standing outside the door, he tightened the belt of his robe, thought again, then loosened it and let it hang. His hand felt slick, turning the knob. Why was he so nervous? He was the man, the one in charge of the direction this first night would take. Catching his runaway heart, he opened the door.

Anna Liese was already in bed. Sitting up and smiling at him, she wore some sort of sheer fabric which covered her from her chin to where the blanket pooled at her hips.

But that was not right. While the magic fabric covered her, it hid nothing. It might as well be made of water or wishes.

'Anna Liese...' Seeing her so left him breathless, lost for words.

'Pirate!' She opened her arms.

'Yo-ho, yo-ho!'

Laughing, he pounced upon the bed and sailed away with her to an enchanted place.

Epilogue

One Christmas later—Cliverton Cottage

'This time last year I was lonely,' Peter said. 'Now look. I can scarcely find a moment to be alone with my wife.'

Standing on the bridge between the cottage and Maplewood Manor, Anna Liese nestled under his arm, laughing quietly. Life in London was busier than it was here and yet Peter never failed to find time to be alone with her.

'We did intend a family gathering,' she pointed out.

'There are a lot of people gathered. How many, I wonder?'

'More than you know,' she said, wondering if he picked up on her clue.

'And a dog!' He hugged her tighter, kissing the top of her head. 'It is a lucky thing the weather is mild and not snowy like last year. So much energy cannot be contained inside.'

'Fannie will be glad when it goes home. I believe she is weary of being nipped on the tail.'

'Abigail's cat will be glad to go back home.' Peter pointed to a second-storey window. 'I do not believe the creature will come down from the upstairs window until they do.'

A second later Abigail, Felicia's young sister-in-law, appeared, plucked the protesting cat off the sill and carried it away.

'Will she offer it as a plaything for the children, do you think?'

'Ginny and William's twin boys are quick, but still too short to reach it if it jumps on a table.'

'You know how it has been my dream to restore the cottage for the family, but with so many of them I'm glad they are at staying at Maplewood and we have the cottage to ourselves.'

'I have a feeling that the nights are busy with all the infants waking up.'

'How many are there, anyway?'

'At last count…' She let the statement hang for a moment to see if he would react to the vague answer. No, all he did was blink at her while waiting for her to tell him what he surely already knew. 'There are Ginny and William's boys—toddlers do wake often, I'm told— then, of course, their twin girls are only a few months old, so they wake every couple of hours. Cornelia's son is nearly a year old and has a very loud cry.'

'And that is all of them—for now?'

'For now.' She swatted his arm in playful exasperation. 'Peter Penneyjons, I cannot believe you do not know how many children your cousins have.'

'The number keeps changing.' The changing number was the reason she had brought him to the bridge this afternoon. He seemed rather dense when it came to the hints she was giving. 'It can't be long before Felicia and Isiah are parents.' He winked at her.

Mildred and Perry came out of the manor. They waved, then strolled very slowly alongside the stream path.

'With Mildred so close to her time, I am surprised the Baroness is not here. It is quite likely our baby count will have gone up by one before this visit is finished.'

'According to my sister—' Mildred was that by now. Over the past year they had become so close that one would never guess they had been at such odds growing up '—you and I are still a sore spot with her, but she is beginning to speak of us without a scowl. Perhaps next year she will leave London and join us.'

'So, after Mildred and Perry have their child, how many babies?'

'More than you can guess.'

'I suppose we cannot guess since there might be twins.' She could not imagine she would ever get tired of seeing her husband's mischievous smile. Whenever he looked at her in this way, she felt like they were carefree children again.

'And if Felicia's family, the Penfields, join us we have no idea how many there will be. They may have adopted another child by the time they arrive.'

'People do enjoy adding children to the family.'

If he had an answer to her blatant clue, he did not express it because Aunt Adelia and William's mother, Violet Townsend, came out of the house.

'May we borrow your bicycles?' Aunt Adelia asked. 'You know, my husband purchased one in the village two days ago.'

'They appear to be great fun,' Violet remarked, although she was frowning.

Anna Liese laughed. 'We would be delighted to let you use them. But be careful.'

'It cannot be all that difficult. More people are doing it every day.'

'Not people as old as we are, Adelia,' they heard Violet announce as they walked away to get the bicycles.

'Do you think they will manage without instruction?' Peter asked, watching them go.

It was a fair question, she decided, watching while they pedalled over the path. They wobbled about, wheels going every which way. Once or twice they nearly collided with each other.

'I think you should refrain from riding for a time.'

'Whatever are you talking about? You know I am an accomplished rider.'

'I am speaking of numbers, of infants to be precise. There are six of them at present and I wish for number seven to arrive safely into our arms.'

'You guessed your Christmas gift!' At long last and after many hints.

'I have been paying attention, Anna Liese.'

'To what? How could you know?'

'To you. There have been changes of late.' He drew his finger from her chin, down her neck and across her bosom.

'Now that you have finally guessed your gift, perhaps you would care to unwrap it?'

'Indeed I would, Lady Cliverton.'

He scooped her into his arms, kissed her thoroughly and she gave the love back to him.

'You know I can walk?'

'I would not wish to risk harm coming to my Christmas gift.'

'I love you, Peter.'

'Show me how much, although you have already,' he said with an enraptured glance at her belly. 'But you know…the other way. Sing to me about how the road leads home.'

And so she did, singing softly in his ear while he carried her from the bridge to the cottage.

* * * * *

If you enjoyed this book, why not check out these other great reads by Carol Arens